Edgefield Press

LEONARD BUTMAN
ILIA BUTMAN

LIFE
WITHOUT
PAROLE

THE TRUTH ABOUT SOCIALISM

Edgefield Press
Chicago
2020

Leonard Butman
Ilia Butman
LIFE WITHOUT PAROLE:
The Truth about Socialism

ISBN: 978-1-7355736-2-5

Library of Congress Control Number: 2020945924

Edited by Tatiana Demakova
Book design and layout by Yulia Tymoshenko
Cover design by Larisa Studinskaya
Pictures by Igor Uzkov
IT consultant: Gene Deriy

Special thanks to Juana Luisa Fonarov and Eugene Noujine.

Illustrations—*Wikimedia.org*

Edgefield Press
Chicago, USA

Printed in the United States of America

CONTENT

For our parents.

FROM THE AUTHORS

This year, we have a significant anniversary. Our combined age is 150 years now.

Wow! About 100 of them we lived in the USSR—a socialist country. So, we know a thing or two about socialism, and we don't wish for anybody to live in a such society. We wrote a lot of books in the Russian language, but this is our first book in English.

We were amazed to find out that more than 50 % of American youth have a positive view of socialism. That is why we decided to pen this book about the life in socialist country. Probably, young Americans are thinking that socialism as a nice society, where people socialize with each other, and without terrible student loans (education is FREE!!!) and NO medical bills (FREE healthcare!!!). Everything is free!!!

But one little catch, comrades—you lose your freedom. To put it briefly, you will become a slave! An American has a real treasury from the birth which includes but not limited to: freedom of speech, freedom of assembly, freedom of religion, right to conduct private enterprise, right to unlimited travel, etc. Citizens of the USSR in opposite HAD NO such freedoms and no such rights.

Sounds like a life in prison, isn't it? That is why we called our book about living in the USSR: "Life Without Parole."

Ben Franklin once said, "Those who would give up essential Liberty, to purchase a little temporary Safety, deserve neither Liberty nor safety." And in addition, after you had a free education, you have to work, practically, for free too. A medical doctor, for example, had almost the same money (or less!) as a factory worker.

The authors used to live in such a rigid society, and we knew if any slave disobeyed the strict rules, severe punishment to follow. Everybody in our country had relatives who had become victims of malicious persecution. There were millions and millions of victims.

Nowadays, every person, including millennials, knows about the Holocaust, which was the World War II genocide of Jewish people committed by Germany under the direction of Adolf Hitler. About 6 million people perished. But this was not the only murderous country in the last century. Many more people were killed in socialist countries. This amount dwarfs the Holocaust's numbers.

In Stalin's time in the Soviet Union, about 20 million people were killed. Among other crimes Stalin conducted genocide against peasants (about 5 million victims) and even against World War II disabled warriors, who dared to protest against inhuman treatment of them (about 2 million died). All those stories you find in our book.

In socialist China, under Mao's direction, about 45 million were slaughtered.

Teaching about the atrocities of the Holocaust is now mandatory in American schools. It is also necessary to make mandatory education about absence of freedom and the mass murders in socialist countries.

If this were the case, the number of young people who sympathize with socialism would shrink from 50 % to ZERO!!

Leonard & Ilia Butman

LIFE
WITHOUT
PAROLE

VOICE OF AMERICA

Listening to Voice of America (VOA) is the best memory of my childhood. I became a regular listener of the "voice of the enemy," which is how they referred to VOA in the Soviet media, when I was seven. It was always a special event in my family. My father and some friends would gather around a type of radio receiver they called "Record." Their gathering would have the appearance of conspirators looking warily around. And they had good reason—every third person at this time was a "siksot" or secret agent, i. e. informant. We lived in a communal apartment shared by eight families, two of which were siksots, we knew for sure. It was obviously tough to go to the bathroom in such an overpopulated place. Somebody usually knocked on the door and asked when you are going to finish. We had no bathtub or shower at that time. For bathing needs, we used a "bania," a public Turkish bath located two bus stops away. Of course, over there, we would again have to queue and wait about one hour.

People would say that simply listening to VOA would be punishable by three or four years in prison. It was 1950, and almost every family had one person in Stalin's jail already. No wonder my father was overly cautious. First, my father would put the regular radio on full blast. Regular radio was a special slave-oriented radio with a single band wired from the government distribution center. It was possible to regulate the volume, but not the government-defined frequency, so the slaves would not stray away from the government broadcast to dangerous capitalistic waves. Every family had one such radio receiver. The official broadcast started at 6:00 am with an anthem of the Soviet Union and finished at midnight with the same anthem. The program never changed.

At 7:20 am, physical exercises with a radio instructor were broadcasted. At 7:40 am was my favorite program for children. At 9:00 am, it was writers' and poets' hour.

At 3:00 pm, there was a sports program. At 7:00 pm, there was news from collective farms, and my father and friends usually gathered at that time to listen to broadcasts of VOA in Russian.

The multiband radio receivers "Records" were in scarce supply and required special registration, and new owners were also told not to use it for the enemy's broadcast.

VOA was available on short radio waves of 16, 25 and 42 meters. And there always was huge interference, like the rumble of a thunderstorm. But sometimes we got lucky and the radio thunder stopped for 5–10 minutes. A usual question when two friends from different cities would meet is how VOA was heard in the friend's city.

I remember in 1953, I suddenly found a very unlikely place where VOA was heard as clear as an official government broadcast. Ironically, it was a place surrounded by GULAG concentration camps.

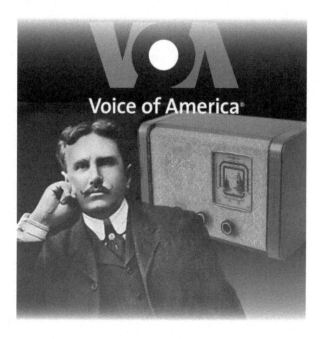

I traveled with my mother for three days and three nights during my school winter break to the city of Kniazpogost in the Republic of Komi, where my brother was an oil storage manager. The Republic of Komi had the biggest concentration of GULAG camps in the Soviet Union. And Kniazpogost was a small city surrounded by several camps. My brother met us at the railroad station and a horse-drawn cart was made ready for us. It was about 6–7 miles away from his home. Of course, it was a nice novelty for us big-city dwellers to ride horses, but the road was strange. The road was actually a corridor and on both sides of it were barbed wire fences with huge dogs roaming behind the barbed wire.

Behind the fence were hundreds of small single-story wooden barracks—two windows on one side and four windows on another side, with a stove stuck in the middle of the roof. Later, I found out that there were about 500 "free" habitants and about 50,000 prisoners living in the town.

Almost all the workers in my brother's oil storage facility were prisoners who went back to prison after 10 hours of work each day.

Of course, the prisoners lived in a very harsh environment, so working in a regular place was a great reward for them. Some of these poor people were university professors, managers of big factories or Communist party executives in their previous lives. But now, they were just humiliated and abused human beings.

But talking about VOA, it was heard crystal clear in that city, like a government radio broadcast. There was another surprise for me in that city—the local bookstore. There were "mucho" books, which would be impossible to find in a big city. I bought such a rarity. It was a book of short stories of O. Henry, who instantly became my favorite author. His story "The Gift of the Magi," I still remember by heart. It is a beautiful tale about a simple working young couple who barely survived on a meager salary and dreamed of making great Christmas gifts for each other.

Her biggest treasure was magnificent long hair while he had a precious gold watch, but without a bracelet. To make a Christmas gift, she sold her beautiful hair and bought a bracelet for him, while he sold his watch to buy a great set of combs for her. The great unexpected twist in the story just knocked my socks off and I decided to become a writer myself.

Recently, I visited the city of Ashville and I found a memory plaque embedded into a pavement downtown area, saying that a great author who wrote his famous story "The Gift of the Magi" was buried at the Ashville Riverside cemetery. I visited the cemetery and was amazed that this world-famous author had an amazingly simple gravestone, something like working class personages of his stories would have.

And in my own life, a great twist would happen, just like in a story of O. Henry.

In 1976, I suddenly received permission to legally immigrate to the blessed country of O. Henry and Mark Twain, my two favorite writers.

Since then, my American dream has come true—my two sons became doctors. I am writing this book to tell the young generation to keep away from the evils of Socialism and to dedicate their lives to protect and preserve this exceptional country, which is a beacon for the hopes and dreams of people all over the world.

BACK TO SLAVERY

In 1861, Russia abolished serfdom, which was nothing less than slavery. Serfs gained the right to own private property, open businesses, and travel abroad. Regrettably, in 1917, slavery returned to Russia. Citizens lost the right to own property and open businesses. Travelling abroad became an exclusive privilege. This was a result of the Great October Revolution, which was ostensibly meant to bring happiness to the Russian people.

According to Karl Marx, Socialist revolutions would first take place in heavily industrialized countries with many proletarians, such as Germany, France, and England. Because of its underdeveloped capitalist system and unsophisticated agriculture, Marx did not view Russia as a potentially Socialist country.

Vladimir Lenin, however, would seek to change the course of Russian history. Lenin, who had rejected democracy, was a Marxist theoretician, an ardent revolutionary, and a born conspirer. His life's ambition was to begin a Socialist revolution, and he succeeded in 1917.

Before Lenin took power, the first and only attempt to carry out a Socialist revolution and create a new society had taken place in France. In 1871, the radical Paris Commune ruled France for 72 days, from 18 March to 28 May. Lenin was later thrilled that his new regime lasted longer than 72 days. The Soviet Union would eventually remain in place for 74 years, until 1991.

Alexander, Vladimir's older brother, was a revolutionary and a terrorist. He was also a promising scientist who studied at the University of St Petersburg. During his third year at the University, Alexander was awarded a gold medal for his zoological research.

He then sold the medal and bought materials to make a bomb in a plot to assassinate Emperor Alexander III. However, the plot was uncovered, and Alexander was arrested along with his co-conspirators on 1 March 1887. They were executed a short time later.

Vladimir was devastated by Alexander's death and wanted to avenge him. He idolized his brother and would see him as a role model for the rest of his life. According to Bolshevik lore, Lenin told his mother that he would "go a different way". He meant that he would orchestrate a revolution, gain power, and then take revenge for his brother's death.

Russia experienced social unrest since the beginning of the 20th century, with widespread protests and strikes. Serfs were granted freedom, but the government did not make much-needed agrarian reforms. Former serfs were in dire need of land and often went hungry. To draw the people's attention away from these problems, the Tsar encouraged brutal mob violence against the Jews. These attacks were known as pogroms. The police never made serious attempts to prevent pogroms, which caused millions of Jews to flee Russia.

The Russo-Japanese war began in 1904 as a dispute over territories that, for the most part, currently belong to China. Surprisingly, Russia suffered a humiliating defeat—this was the first time an Asian country had prevailed over a European nation. American President Theodore Roosevelt was awarded the Nobel Peace Prize for helping to negotiate a peace treaty.

An attempted revolution in 1905 was soon crushed by the Tsar. Hundreds of thousands were executed, exiled or imprisoned. Despite these measures, social unrest continued. Hundreds of people, including the British ambassador to Russia, begged the Tsar to implement democratic reforms and improve workers' and peasants' conditions to ease the tensions. Alexander II refused to yield to their requests. During these crises, Lenin was patiently waiting for the right time to instigate his long-planned revolution.

Grigori Rasputin, a famous mystic, claimed that he could help Russia overcome its challenges. Alexei, the Tsar's only son and the heir to the throne, was born with haemophilia. Rasputin supposed-

ly treated the boy's condition and thus gained the imperial family's trust, even going as far as burning Alexei's medication and keeping his physicians away. Even though he was illiterate, Rasputin became the imperial family's closest advisor. Soon after that, World War I broke out, and when the Tsar went to the front in 1916, Rasputin began to rule over Russia with his wife, Alexandra.

The entire country viewed Rasputin's rule with horror and distrust. On 30 December 1916, wealthy Prince Felix Yussupov invited Rasputin to his palace in St Petersburg and served his guest wine laced with potassium cyanide. The poison was enough to kill ten people, but Rasputin seemed unaffected. Then, Yussupov shot him several times, but he survived. Finally, Rasputin was thrown into the river Neva. Amazingly, the autopsy results show that he survived for about an hour after being thrown into the river.

During WWI, Russia, Belgium, France, and England were allied against Germany and Austria-Hungary. Later, the US and Turkey joined the fight. Nicholas II hoped that an early victory would ease Russia's social upheaval. He was wrong; the war was a disaster, and more than 5 million Russians were killed. The entire country turned against the Tsar. After the February Revolution began in St Petersburg in 1917, Nicholas II was forced to abdicate.

The new Provisional Government then decreed that citizens had the right to free speech and free press. Women were also granted equal rights, and capital punishment was abolished. For the first time in history, Russia was a free country—but not for long.

In 1903, Lenin created the Social-Democratic Workers' Party of Bolsheviks, a secretive and terrorist organization. A small group of professional revolutionaries made up the party. Its membership was about 500 in 1912 and 20,000 in February of 1917. Lenin planned to use his party to seize power. In April of 1917, he returned to Russia from Switzerland after many years in exile. Russia's governmental power was divided between the Provisional Government and the Council of Workers' Deputies, who were widely known as Soviets.

No political party had attempted to take control of Russia, so the Bolsheviks seized the opportunity. On 7 November 1917, they deposed the Provisional Government and established the first Communist state since the Paris Commune. The Russian people were once again slaves.

Lenin accomplished his goal of avenging his brother's death on 17 July 1918, when he had Tsar Nicholas II, the son of Alexander III, executed. In typical Bolshevik fashion, the execution took place without a trial or a defense attorney for the Tsar's family. They were shot at night in the basement of the Ipatiev House in Yekaterinburg. The family's bodies were taken to a nearby forest and burned.

The right to own private property was abolished, as the Communists claimed that it contributed to social injustice. They also abolished the people's freedom of speech, assembly, and press only eight months after these rights had been granted because of the February Revolution. Capital punishment was reinstated, and it would become a staple of proletarian law enforcement. Notably, none of the Communist leaders was educated in economics, agriculture, business, or engineering. In this sense, they were as ignorant as Rasputin, who refused to use medicine and even burned it. The Communists leaders were politically incompetent. To make matters worse, they were city folk who knew nothing about agriculture.

Lenin's most reprehensible policy was the abolishment of private property; the land is every country's most valuable asset. After the Communists took power, Russia's land lost its value, since it could not be bought, sold, or rented. Russia's territory was made up of approximately 70 million acres. Assuming that each acre cost USD 1000 (at modern values), Russia lost 70 trillion dollars—about 40 times more than Russia's current GDP. The Bolsheviks showed that they only cared about securing as much power as possible.

Usually, people who own private property are independent-minded and do not like to rely on the government. Such people are not slaves. The Communists viewed these traits as undesirable. Therefore, the Russian nobility was robbed of its lands, palaces, and mansions. Businessmen were robbed of their private and industrial property. The banks were stolen, and private safe deposit boxes were seized by the government. All of Russia's foreign debts were repudiated.

After the revolution, robbery became one of the government's hallmarks. They aimed to "expropriate the expropriators." When the Bolsheviks needed warm clothes for the Red Army, they simply confiscated them from families' homes. When the Red Army needed food, they robbed nearby peasants. This state-sanctioned robbery was called War Communism (also known as Military Communism). Unsurprisingly, a Civil War broke out, and 10.5 million people died.

About 2.5 million people managed to flee Russia until 1922. After that, anyone who tried to cross the border was jailed. In 1935, a new law decreed that anyone who wanted to escape could be executed. Russia's colossal border patrol was ready to brutally punish anyone who tried to escape slavery.

An internal passport was introduced in 1932. This measure severely restricted citizens' freedom to travel inside of Russia. The most important part of the new passport was the propiska—the residential address. If someone visited another city, even for a few days, they had to register with their passport, and citizens always had to carry their passports with them. Subsequently, a new profession became common in Russia: the passportistka, or passport lady. These workers, who had excellent calligraphy, were all KGB informants.

Ironically, only 20 % of the population was able to get new passports. Therefore, peasants and other citizens could not even move from their native village or city. Young peasants could only obtain passports by serving in the military. Instead of avoiding the draft, young kolhozniks (members of collective farms) were now eager to serve in the military.

In 1921 the Civil War, along with War Communism, had brought Russia to the brink of collapse. Its GDP had decreased by about 80 %. Furthermore, the typhus pandemic contributed to widespread hunger. Clearly, socialism could not survive much longer. Only capitalism could save the Bolshevik government.

In 1985, General Secretary Gorbachev would introduce perestroika, a restructuring program. However, this was not the first time such a program was implemented in Russia. An earlier perestroika took place in 1921 and was known as the New Economic Policy, or NEP.

Lenin had no choice but to temporarily abolish slavery. During the 10th Congress of the Russian Communist Party, he introduced the NEP, which partly reinstated private property and the right to open businesses. Of course, Lenin did not grant freedom of speech or press.

Almost immediately, the dying country seemed to resurrect. Hunger and food shortages reduced drastically. Suddenly, Russia was practically a healthy nation with a vibrant urban life. In 1926, the country regained its pre-war GDP. With free competition, this limited form of capitalism unquestionably beat socialism. The Communists, however, suspected that they would lose power if capitalism continued. In 1927, the NEP was abolished, and Russia was enslaved once more.

The history of the USSR shows that socialism is irrevocably linked with slavery.

GENOCIDE OF DISABLED WAR HEROES

In 1949, the Soviet Union was making preparations for an anniversary—Stalin's seventieth birthday. The whole world was to watch the Soviet people unite in their zealous adoration of the person known as "the great helmsman," "the architect of communism," "the locomotive of the revolution," etc.

But how could one possibly talk about unity when in the summer of 1949 disabled war veterans, unhappy about the deprivation of their rights, held a demonstration on Red Square, in front of the Kremlin, right before the revered Comrade Stalin's eyes! Some were "bouncing" on their crutches, others were hobbling along or moving about in homemade carts. The "father of the nation" was furious. He ordered that Moscow be cleared of that "trash" immediately. Stalin's command marked the beginning of the years-long persecution of those who had sacrificed their health for their native land.

Law enforcement agencies rushed to execute the order—and not just in Moscow. Veterans who had lost legs and arms, fighting for the fatherland, were kicked out of the cities. Security officials seized unwanted citizens and delivered them to railway stations, where they were put on special trains waiting to carry them to the final destination mostly located in abandoned monasteries. There were exceptions, however—some mutilated veterans from Moscow, for example, were brought to a former camp for German prisoners of war in the city of Noginsk. One could imagine how comfortable the place was! The crippled veterans were also relieved of their passports and military records and pay books.

The fight against the penniless war-maimed veterans was long. In 1951, the USSR Council of Ministers issued a secret resolution

"On Measures to Eradicate Poverty and Intensify the Battle against Anti-Social Parasitic Elements."

Many "parasitic elements" remained at large. Here is an official police report: "In the second half of 1951, 107,766 people were detained, in 1952—156,817 people, in 1953—182,342 people. Disabled war veterans make up 70 % of beggars detained."

Crippled warriors rejected by their families also joined the ranks of homeless war veterans. In 1951, the Presidium of the Supreme Council of the USSR made an update related to the "Measures to Combat Anti-Social Parasitic Elements." It was proposed that "parasites"—the unemployed and the homeless—be exiled to remote areas of the country by force. The network of homes for crippled veterans continued to expand.

In 1954 and 1955, thirteen prisons were converted to institutions for crippled veterans. The fact that many of them escaped to return to their beggar's lifestyle would hardly suggest excellent living conditions in the institutions. The outflow was so massive that it was decided to transform a number of homes for invalids into special closed-type regime homes. Prison buildings suited that purpose well enough. Bars reappeared on windows, security was strengthened, and penalties tightened. The term "special regime" is telling in itself—its implications are well known to everyone familiar with the concept of Stalinist camps. And what their "closed type" status indicated was as follows: guards can do anything to the inmates, no one will ever come and check.

Obviously, there were a great number of disabled war veterans in post-World War II USSR. It would seem reasonable that people would be proud of those who had sacrificed their health in combat against the fascists. Nothing of the kind. Apparently, the government believed the mutilated front-line soldiers to be a bunch of worthless nobodies. No one considered improving the war heroes' living conditions or showing any concern whatsoever.

According to the post-war statistics, there were 2,650,000 invalids in the Soviet Union. While the average monthly wage was 515 rubles, the pensions they were allocated ranged between 70 and 150 rubles.

With that amount of money, it was extremely hard to make ends meet; it was barely enough to buy very cheap food. Buying new clothes was impossible.

Starving, sick and disabled veterans would seek alms outside churches, ask passers-by for charity, sometimes ring doorbells begging for help. Even worse, their hopeless existence led many former war heroes to ceaseless heavy drinking.

Normally, the war disabled—laden with war medals but also nervous, dirty, restless and drunk—irritated others, causing squeamishness among the population.

While the country's infinite gratitude to its heroes was discussed on the radio, in newspapers and magazines, the reality was drastically different.

It is shameful that guards gave some of the most derogatory nicknames to the disabled veterans. One-legged invalids were known as "kangaroos," the armless ones were "the wingless," people who had lost both legs and moved on homemade roller carts were "scooters," those wounded in the pelvic area were "the lopsided," those with damaged spines, "paralytics," and those with mutilated faces, "Quasimodo."

In 1945, the People's Commissariat for Internal Affairs suddenly ruled that all photographs of invalids, whose wretched appearance apparently undermined the image of the USSR in the eyes of the world, be confiscated. The authorities somehow believed that foreign intelligence agents were after the pictures. The disabled war veterans were strictly forbidden to send their photos by mail.

The island of Valaam was among the most well-known places of confinement for the disabled war heroes; their transfer to the island began in 1950.

Crippled war heroes were housed in former monastery buildings, some of which did not even have roofs. For two years, there was no electricity either. Many of the veterans died in their first few months in the monasteries.

People with neither arms nor legs, the so-called "Stalin samovars," made up a large proportion of the local invalids.

Working on Valaam as a tour guide for forty years, historian and art expert Evgeny Kuznetsov saw what was happening there with his own eyes; his Valaam Notebook (Valaamskaya Tetrad') is the story of what he witnessed. Kuznetsov wrote that doctors barely tended to the disabled—several months would pass before they changed the patients' underwear. War veterans were fed very poorly, and the food prescribed to them was regularly stolen.

A large apple garden by the monastery served as a "walking" area for the "samovars." The crippled heroes were brought there on carts and then transferred into baskets, which were hung on the tree branches. The staff would occasionally forget to bring them inside for the night. And the nights outside were pretty cold.

Many writers and journalists have portrayed the horrors of war heroes' lives on Valaam, and historians have created records of the events.

The Soviet country punished its disabled victors for their injuries, the loss of their families, of shelter, of family nests wasted by the war. It punished them with poverty, loneliness, hopelessness.

Everyone who found himself on Valaam realized at once: This is it! It was a dead end. What followed was silence in an unmarked grave in an abandoned monastery graveyard.

In 1974, the artist Gennady Dobrov came to Valaam to paint portraits of a few surviving veterans. There was a former military pilot among them who had been awarded the gold medal of the Hero of the Soviet Union; his name was Grigory Voloshin. The man had lost his arms and legs and could neither speak nor hear. Voloshin spent almost 30 years on Valaam. In 1994, Voloshin's son spotted the portrait of his father at exhibition of Dobrov's work. He went to Valaam, but his father had already died. The son erected a headstone with a touching inscription on his father's grave.

The other graves of crippled war veterans, very plain, have long been overgrown with weeds. They are now falling apart.

This genocide against disabled war heroes is by far the biggest crime committed by the USSR—Socialist country.

THE MAN WHO REFUSED TO BE A SLAVE

In March of 1945, while the Soviet children were celebrating the future victory of the Allies over Hitler, they presented the US ambassador with a beautiful gift. It was a replica of the Great Seal carved in wood. The ambassador proudly hung it in his office. Only seven years later, however, it was discovered that a strange small electronic device was hidden inside. It took the CIA several years to successfully replicate this eavesdropping device. Today, this technology is known as Radio Frequency Identification, or RFID for short. Basically, this is made of passive transmitters which are now in our keyless remotes and credit card chips.

Lev Termen, the Russian inventor of that eavesdropping device, which was much ahead of its time, was awarded with the Stalin Prize for the invention. The tragi-comical part here is that the genius inventor was, at that time, a prisoner of the most dreaded prison in the world: Stalin's GULAG.

Termen was a world-class scientist, an astronomer, a successful businessman, a classically trained cellist, and the founding father of electronic music. This incredible man was a prisoner of the GULAG and a Soviet spy—all in one person! His friends and well-wishers were some of the most famous people on the planet: Vladimir Lenin, Charlie Chaplin, Albert Einstein, George Gershwin, Maurice Ravel, John Rockefeller, and Dwight Eisenhower, the future US president.

Termen, also known as Leon Theremin, was born in 1896 in St. Petersburg, Russia. He was from a well-established family with French noble roots. At the age of fifteen, the young astronomer discovered a new star. He was also an outstanding physicist and well-trained cellist. In 1916, he graduated from the St. Petersburg Music

Conservatory, receiving a degree in cello. Simultaneously, he was a student of the Physics and Mathematics Faculty of St. Petersburg University. At the age of twenty-four, this unique combination of education allowed him to invent the first electronic musical instrument, which he named etherophone or termenvox. He noticed that the generator of electrical oscillations produced a musical sound when he waved his hand near it. He played on it like touching invisible strings.

In 1922, Termen showed a new electronic musical instrument to the founder of the Soviet state, Vladimir Lenin, who admired the device and even tried to play the song "The Lark" of the Russian composer Glinka. Meanwhile, Termen also arranged a presentation of a security alarm system based on the same principle as the termenvox, which Lenin approved and recognized as well. This meeting with Lenin had opened all doors for the young inventor. Later, this security system was implemented to guard the Kremlin and the Hermitage Museum in St. Petersburg. Unfortunately for Termen, Vladimir Lenin died in 1924, and nobody in the highest echelon of power was interested in his inventions.

In 1926, Termen invented the "distant movable photo", which was actually a projector set with a huge screen measuring 5ft by 5ft. All existing televisions at that time were much smaller, with dimensions like that of a match box. In 1927, he presented this invention to the top Soviet leaders. It was an honor for him, but it did not work in his favor. When Termen turned the device on, the Kremlin grounds showed up on the screen, with dictator Joseph Stalin striding across the courtyard.

"Good grief!" Voroshilov, a Stalin henchman, sprung from his seat, fright-stricken. "What is all this? Are we spying on the comrade Stalin now?!"

By 1927, Stalin had managed to amass great personal power. With equal fervor, he would dispose of opponents and adherents alike. Stalin was fiercely suspicious and mistrustful. Voroshilov's alarmed response, therefore, came as no wonder.

Termen's invention was immediately classified and "shelved" in the archives.

Termen continued to contrive another musical instrument, which came to be known as the theremin. Actually, "Theremin" was the name of his French noble family, whose history dates back centuries and originated from medieval France. This instrument was played by changing the distance between the performer's hands and the highly sensitive antennae of the musical device. These movements shaped the frequency of the sound it produced. One antenna controlled the pitch, and the other controlled the volume.

In 1927, Termen was invited to an international music show in Germany to demonstrate his inventions. It was a great success. Laudatory reviews made him famous. His new compositions were "The Music from Space", "The Music of Air Waves", and even "The Celestial Music".

In 1928, Termen went to the USA, which was "close to a miracle" at that time. Only few people could penetrate the "Iron Curtain" of the Soviet Union and travel abroad, especially to America. Obviously, the final permission to travel came with the approval of Stalin himself and the OGPU (the Joint State Political Directorate), the predecessor of the KGB. To make the story short, Termen was obligated to provide "the relevant" information about American secrets in exchange for unprecedented permission to move to America.

Upon arrival to the States, Termen patented his musical instrument, the theremin, and his security alarm system. He sold the rights to manufacture his theremin to the Radio Corporation of America (RCA). Then, he transferred the money to the OGPU.

Termen also established the companies "Teletouch Inc" and "Theremin Studio", and he rented a six-story building in New York, where he allowed USSR trade representatives to work. These representatives happened to be undercover agents, and this was a great help to the Russian Secret Service.

In the US, the musician and inventor was given the best concert halls, and his shows were unfailingly drawing a full house.

One day, Termen received a call from a stranger.

"Good afternoon, Mr. Termen! I am terribly sorry to bother you, but the thing is, you see, they say I make a fine violin player. I would so love to collaborate on a violin-theremin duet."

"Well, who the hell are you?!" Termen snapped at him, exhausted.

"My apologies. I didn't introduce myself. My name is Albert Einstein."

The great Einstein turned out to be a skillful violinist. He once confided to Termen that it was his dream to unite the enchanting sounds of music with spatial imagery. Einstein found himself unable to make it, whereas Termen succeeded. He invented a light-and-sound machine called Rhythmicon.

Americans were completely enthralled by the theremin. Its inventor and performer became an A-list celebrity.

One day, Yehudi Menuhin, a sublime genius and outstanding musician, paid Termen a visit. Soon after, two other eminent composers, George Gershwin and Maurice Ravel, wished to make his acquaintance. He then met with Charlie Chaplin, which left a truly indelible impression on him. John Rockefeller and Dwight Eisenhower considered themselves privileged to have made friends with Termen. His most cherished acquaintances, however, were high-ranking American servicemen and politicians. After all, Termen was expected to make good on the promise he had given to provide relevant information to the Russians.

In August 1929, an economic crisis erupted in the USA, followed by the stock market crash in October. The situation was deteriorating dramatically. The industries stalled. Unemployed citizens became aggrieved and desperate.

Luckily, Termen himself weathered the financial crunch virtually unscathed. Reports on bank robberies, shop break-ins, and house burglaries overflowed the newspapers, and Termen's alarm systems were sold like hotcakes. The alarm was even commissioned by the nation's financial sanctuary, Fort Knox, which houses America's gold reserves.

The Soviet authorities had never furnished money for Termen; on the contrary, they forced him to give them as much money as possible. He earned his own living and sponsored his own espionage activities. Unfortunately, the factory that manufactured Termen's musical instruments curtailed their production. Some people found themselves unable to afford a ticket to his performances. Many of the popular musician's well-heeled friends had gone bankrupt.

Termen's name might no longer ring a bell with anyone today, but back in 1934, it made the list of 25 most famous people worldwide. Some people lost fortunes; others gained theirs. Termen had joined the club of the rich and famous. One day, Termen met the beautiful dancer Lavinia Williams, who was one of the first African-American ballet dancers. The young woman swept him off his feet at first sight, and soon enough, they got married. Sometime after the wedding, Termen paid a habitual visit to the Duponts, but the servants would not let him in. Many of Termen's former acquaintances broke all ties with him as well due to his decision to marry an African-American woman.

Up to that point, the authorities back in the USSR had been pleased with the way Termen carried on with his affairs. However, his marriage with the African-American girl led to the consequent loss of informers, who used to feed him with classified data. This resulted in Termen's rush return to his homeland in 1938. When they came for him, Lavinia happened to be at home, and she was sure that he was forcibly taken away. The OGPU reminded him that though in America he was amongst the 25 most famous, in his homeland he was still a slave.

From then until the end of the 1960s, Termen was considered dead in America. Upon returning to Leningrad, Termen, a world class scientist, could not find any job! Obviously, the OGPU was playing a "cat and mouse" game with him, and in March of 1939, he was arrested. The long interrogation sessions were often interrupted by severe beatings.

It turned out that Termen had been recruited by nearly half of the world's foreign intelligence agencies and held membership in a number of Jewish terrorist organizations. His secret mission, which was further revealed, was to eliminate every single Soviet leader. After this, he was supposed to annihilate the Stalin Car Factory, ZIS, disguised as a naval lieutenant-captain.

While signing interrogation reports, Termen thought of inquiring as to why he needed the uniform of a lieutenant-captain, out of all others, but was too exhausted to ask.

Termen was lucky—he was spared the firing squad and sent to a Kolyma GULAG camp. There, sick and tired of hauling heavy loaded wagons, he invented a motorized cart running on a monorail. The management got it and quickly reassigned Termen to Tupolev's sharashka, the scientific center located in the GULAG and staffed with the most gifted scientist prisoners. In the sharashka, one of his helpers was Sergei Korolev, the future main figure of the Soviet Space Program. He was responsible for launching the world's first satellite, Sputnik, in 1957 and sending the first man to space, Yuri Gagarin, on April 12, 1961.

In the sharashka, Termen distinguished himself by producing a few outstanding research designs. He invented an eavesdropping system code called "Buran", the same "trojan horse" device gifted to the US embassy in 1945 inside the wood-carved Great Seal.

The Kremlin was exultant over the occasion. Although a victim of Stalinist repressions, he was awarded the Stalin Prize right there in prison, and he was released shortly after. He was a "free" man but continued to work for about another 15 years in the secret labs that belonged to the NKVD (a new name for the OGPU).

From 1964 to 1967, Termen worked in the acoustic laboratory at the Tchaikovsky Moscow State Conservatory. In 1967, an American music critic, Harold Schonberg, interviewed the conservatory's director and found out about the legendary Termen, whom Americans had believed dead since 1938. The reporter trumpeted the news all over the world. It was published in the New York Times. The lab was deluged with letters and invitations to various countries. The management, terrified, promptly dismissed Termen and destroyed all his designs, just in case. Termen's new brainchild was a prototype of the future synthesizer, invented by the Japanese shortly after.

Sadly, the inventor and genius had to work as a simple mechanic.

In 1991, Termen, together with his daughter Natalia, traveled to the USA at the invitation of Stanford University. He visited his former studio and received a prize for his inventions. Upon returning to Moscow, he continued to live in his communal apartment, which he had also made into his laboratory.

One day, walking into his communal apartment, Termen discovered that all his chattels and records had been thrown out and that his room was occupied by neighbors. He had no other choice but to move into his daughter's apartment, where he died at the age of 97, in squalor and obscurity, in 1993—one of the greatest men of the 20th century, who refused to be a slave.

GENOCIDE AGAINST PEASANTS

After the Bolsheviks' October revolution of 1917, Lenin declared:

LAND TO THE PEASANTS,
PEACE TO THE PEOPLE,
FACTORIES TO THE WORKERS!

It was lie, lie and lie! No land was given to peasants. No factories were given to workers, and no peace was given to people—more than 10 million were killed over the next five years during the Civil War.

World War I was raging. In 1917, as part of the Entente (France, Russia, Great Britain, as well as the US and other countries that joined later), Russia was making a significant contribution to the fight against the triple alliance (Germany, Austria-Hungary and the Ottoman Empire). The Russian army held the front line of more than 1,500 kilometers long, fending off 120 of the 262 enemy divisions fighting in Europe. In Asia, Russia engaged 29 of the 54 Turkish divisions.

But much earlier, in 1914, Lenin had declared, "Let's turn the imperialist war into a civil war."

So it was much more important for the Bolsheviks to kill their fellow citizens in order to achieve a socialist utopia than it was to fight the enemies of their country. In 1917, Lenin was in Switzerland. He dreamed about reaching Russia to start a revolution, but had to travel through Germany.

So he entered into a secret agreement with the German government, which allowed him to travel in the famous "sealed train" through Germany to subvert Russian participation in the war on the side of the Entente. It was actually treason, punishable by firing squad.

Karl Marx—father of all socialist revolutions, predicted that a proletarian revolution would happen in a developed country like Germany, France or England, not in Russia with its small proletariat and large, awkward peasant population. Socialist agitators, "narodniks," spent a lot of time with the peasants, but without any success. Very often these agitators were injured or killed. Peasants were very religious and hated the Bolsheviks, who were atheists.

But even though they despised the peasants, the Bolsheviks realized nonetheless that it was quite impossible to do without them, since rural residents in pre-revolutionary Russia amounted to nearly 78 % of the population. Besides, they were also the core of the army, whose help the revolutionaries wanted to secure.

Through agitators, the soldiers learned that Lenin, chief of the Bolsheviks, had proclaimed, "Land belongs to peasants and factories belong to workers." The slogan was brilliant—it was brief and clear and people wished to believe it.

Bolshevik agitators intervened at that stage, suggesting favorably that the Russian peasant soldiers should stop rotting in trenches and risking their lives so everyone could go home and plow their land.

In spite of the Russian provisional government's determination to bring the war to a victorious end, which by all odds was about to occur, there was a powerful outpouring of soldiers from the front lines. (Abandoned by Russia, the Entente won anyway; the war was over on November 11, 1918.)

Individual deserters could be stopped, but entire regiments leaving the front would have had to be fought by military means. Lenin said that soldiers voted against war with their feet.

Soldiers returned home and broke into their landlords' mansions, rifles at the ready. Landowners were informed that they owned the land no longer; it would be divided among those who worked it. An angry man with a rifle was a persuasive force. In addition, that force was totally self-propelled and stuffed with Bolshevik propaganda.

Landlords' houses were robbed along the way, all the valuables expropriated. If the owners dared to protest, they were informed that all their property had been acquired through the exploitation of the working class and was now being legally reclaimed. Should the owners become bold and try to protect what they thought was theirs, there were always bullets in rifles for them.

On February 19, 1918, Lenin craftily modified the first Decree on Land. Apart from everything else, it now contained the following, "All ownership of land, subsoil, water, forests and living forces of nature within the Russian Federation Soviet Republic is permanently abolished."

As a result, peasants found themselves in a situation far worse than it had been under Czarism. This amendment deprived even those who had acquired land upon the abolition of serfdom in 1861. From now on, land belonged to the state, and former landowners became tenants.

Both World War I and the Civil War distracted the peasants from their work. The country was feeling the growing lack of grain. Where could one get any? From the very same peasants, of course. Yes, it was pretended that robbing them was legal, since bread was taken in exchange for money. It was just that that money had completely depreciated, so no one cared about it. The peasants needed nails, agricultural equipment and tools, leather, manufactured products and industrial goods. The state did not provide all those.

Those who, according to the authorities, had surplus bread and did not turn it in within a week could be sentenced to at least ten years in prison. Neighbors who volunteered to report on the "concealers of grain reserves" were rewarded with half the value of the seized crops. Volunteer rats multiplied across villages.

Workers, sailors, and soldiers were organized into special food detachments, whose task was to destroy peasants' barns and get rid of the owners. Seventy-five armed men or more, with two or three extra machine guns, were listed in each detachment.

A lot of peasant blood was shed in the first years after the revolution, but this turned out to be just the beginning. The real Bolshevik terror against hardworking peasants with higher income ("kulaks") started in 1928, with the beginning of collectivization. Lenin wrote that a private economy gives birth to kulaks every hour, every day. Accordingly, the kulaks did not fit the socialist form of agriculture and needed to be eliminated.

The collectivization meant that all agricultural land was given to collective farms and controlled by the Communist state. Peasants became like factory workers without any private property and were 100 % dependent on the state.

In the first two months of 1928, about 2,000 peasants were exiled to Siberia; 3,500 farmers were arrested in the North Caucasus, with another 5,500 people throughout the country in April alone.

That triggered around 1,500 peasant riots in 1928, drowned in blood by the OGPU (Joint State Political Directorate).

50,000 more villagers were arrested in 1929. In 1930, tens of thousands of peasants were exterminated. Oddly, the most savage executioners were young people—rural Komsomol activists (Young Communist League members), who outperformed their elders in brutalizing wealthy fellow villagers. They would beat kulaks and change into their clothes before their very eyes, grabbing valuable objects and money and shoving them into their pockets. They were intoxicated by impunity. Komsomol members craved blood and demanded that their better-off neighbors be destroyed "to the last baby." At a meeting in the village of Kirsanovka, Komsomol members decided to shoot thirty of their wealthiest neighbors.

Komsomol activists were absolutely convinced that justice was on their side, since they followed their older comrades' communist wisdom which claimed that all the rich were criminals, so their property must belong to the common people. That was thought to be the foundational principle of socialism.

Komsomol members targeted everyone and would torment not only the living "exploiters," but also the dead ones. For instance, some Komsomol youngsters, wild with hatred, once dug up the coffin of their former rich neighbor and threw his corpse onto the road. The young Communist followers' message was clearly conveyed: "No place for the rich on this earth or below, we'll come for them anywhere!"

During the years 1930–1931, two and a half million people who resisted collectivization were exiled from the villages, and many peasants were shot or sent to concentration camps.

Every village had a committee of "bednoty" (committee of the poor people). This committee had the authority to sentence their rich neighbors to exile. It was genocide sponsored by the socialist state. Even a person who had two cows could be considered rich and consequently end up in Siberia. All arrests were made at night and prisoners were immediately forced to march to Siberia. Family members were deliberately sent to different parts of the country. Anyone who objected was shot on the spot.

There were no trains or other types of transportation. The march to Siberia took six to eight months, and typically 80 % of the people died on the way.

As soon as navigation opened on the Ob River in Siberia in the spring of 1933, the exiled peasants who had survived the march were brought to the city of Tomsk. Several caravans of ships took them further to an island in the middle of the river, near the village of Nazino.

Not a single house, hut or barrack had been prepared for them. They had to build their own dwellings from felled trees or dig dugouts for shelter.

Hunger was so severe that some parents killed and dismembered their own children.

Residents of Nazino called this settlement Cannibal Island.

Cases of cannibalism among the exiles dying of starvation were also recorded in other areas of the Soviet Union.

Let me ask this question: Who is the real cannibal—the person who lost their mind from starvation and endless torture, or the person who directed the killing of millions and millions?

So the REAL CANNIBALS are the comrades Lenin, Stalin, Mao, Pol Pot and their henchmen.

More than five million peasants were victims of this genocide.

THE POET THAT NEVER WAS

This is the story of the Russian poet Joseph Brodsky, who won the Nobel prize for literature in 1987. In Russia a poet is much more than just a poet. The most respected persons in Russian history are not generals, politicians, or Czars, but poets and writers. And the number one of them is Alexander Pushkin, who died in 1837 at a pretty young age of 37 years. He is the founder of our modern Russian language; he is a Russian icon and hero. Every Russian poet, including Joseph Brodsky, considered Pushkin to be a teacher.

There is an interesting detail about Pushkin. He actually is an Afro-Russian poet. His great-grandfather by the name of Abram Hannibal was a black man from Africa. As a young boy he was somehow spirited to Russia and became a page and servant of the Czar Peter the Great. Peter loved this smart and talented boy and sent him to the French military engineering academy.

With years Abram became a top Russian general and was granted a Russian nobility. But his biggest legacy in Russian history, lies not with his military achievements, but being an ancestor of the greatest ever Russian poet, Alexander Pushkin.

Pushkin was a fierce critic of the Monarchy and was exiled for several years. Since the times of Pushkin, every Russian poet was in opposition to the Monarchy and their existing regimes. But it all changed during the Soviet years. Poets were forced to glorify the Communist state, those who refused faced concentration camps. Those who complied were rewarded with many perks and privileges, like freedom to travel abroad or receive a free suburban house ("dacha").

Joseph Brodsky was a talented man, but he refused to join the chorus, and that decided his fate. He was persecuted and finally exiled from the country.

Joseph's childhood was far from peaceful. He was born in 1940. One year later Germany invaded the Soviet Union and his father went to war. His mother and he remained in Leningrad (now St. Petersburg) which was 900 days under siege. There were almost no food supplies in the blockaded city, and they lived in hunger. Like others, they received one quarter of a pound of bread per day. About one million of people perished in the city, but Joseph and his mother survived.

Joseph went to school in 1947. He was a mediocre student, not particularly fond of learning, so he only completed seventh grade. In 1954, he applied to a naval school but was not admitted. His performance at school got even worse. That prompted Brodsky to drop out and go to work as an apprentice milling machine operator at a factory. Not quite happy with the job, he attempted to enter a school for submariners but failed again. Thinking about his future he real-

ized he would love to be a doctor and took action right away. Leaving the factory, he became assistant at a morgue. He was entrusted with cutting corpses, and that was how he lost interest in medicine. Hearing that hands were wanted for some forthcoming geological expeditions, Joseph headed to the Arctic Geology Research Institute. He was extremely worried about getting the job. But he got it. The young man was so glad: there it was, the chance to travel. He worked in the White Sea region in 1957 and 1958, and in Siberia and Yakutia in 1959 and 1961.

Bored as he was with formal schooling, Joseph had a passion for self-educating. He started learning English by himself. Once he read poetry of the Polish writer Adam Mickiewicz, and he was deeply fascinated and decided to read them in the original. He started teaching himself Polish as well. He was an avid reader, primarily of poetry collections and volumes on philosophy and religion. He would carry books with him on the expeditions and spend almost all his free time reading, despite loads of exhausting physical work there.

In addition, Joseph Brodsky started writing his own poems. At nineteen, he met the remarkable Russian poet Evgeny Rein, who introduced him to other remarkable authors Sergei Dovlatov and Bulat Okudzhava.

In 1960, Brodsky made his debut as poet at the Gorky Hall of Culture. He shared the stage with the true giants of Soviet poetry.

From then on, Brodsky's name was on everyone's lips. Some praised him high enough to recognize the twenty-year-old man as a well-established literary talent.

However, Brodsky's publication record was at odds with his status of a gifted poet. Nobody was willing to print his poems. That was natural enough: Brodsky did not write about hard-working farmers, machine workers' callused hands, the leading role of the Communist Party and monstrosities of capitalist society.

Not until late 1962 did Brodsky's poem "The Ballad of a Small Tugboat," in abridged form, appeared in the kid's magazine Kostyor ("The Built Fire"). Some of his verses for adults—very few indeed—were published after that. But they sufficed for the newspaper Vecherniy Leningrad ("The Evening Leningrad") to publish the article titled "Paraliterary Drone" in November 1963. It related to Brodsky's "parasitic lifestyle." Another newspaper also exposed Brodsky as a sponger living off his parents' charity. Besides, some of his lines were deemed anti-Soviet. The attackers were outraged by the title line of "Lyubi proezdom rodinu druzey" ("Adore your friend's land when you're passing by"). In their interpretation, the main idea of the poem was, "I love a foreign motherland." However, the Soviets citizens were programmed to be true patriots who not only loved their homeland unconditionally but also despised all other lands.

Persecution of unwanted citizens would normally fall into a certain pattern. The next step would employ fabricated letters from citizens outraged with his portry. Employees of the KGB (Committee for State Security) manufactured the letters, which were then sent to mass media.

One day, the letters of "outraged workers" appeared in newspaper. Joseph Brodsky was stigmatized as a cosmopolitan parasite unwilling to march in perfect unison with the entire Soviet people from the socialism of the bright today towards the even brighter tomorrow—mankind's highest goal, communism. Each letter contained a demand to punish the parasite.

Under Soviet law, only kids, pensioners, and invalids had the right to have no job. Others were either employed or imprisoned. Brodsky knew that he was about to be arrested. Besides, he was going through hard times after splitting up with the woman he loved, Marianna Basmanova. All that resulted in attempted suicide. Luckily, the poet failed to take his own life.

Brodsky was indeed arrested on charges of social parasitism. That happened on January 13, 1964. The day after, the poet fell sick in his cell. It was the first attack of angina, the disease that would become his permanent companion for the rest of his life.

Under Soviet rule, it was not enough to throw the unwanted into jail. It was necessary to abuse them. In February 1964, Brodsky was sent to a psychiatric hospital for three weeks. At night, they would shake him awake, drag him to the bathroom and plunge him in ice-cold water. They would then wrap him in a wet bedsheet and lay him down by a hot radiator. Drying quickly, the sheet would dig into his body. The pain was excruciating, and Brodsky was unable to move. At first, he would try to resist, but the hefty orderlies would "talk" him out of it easily.

At the next court session, the defense argued that Brodsky was no parasite—on the contrary, he was a very hardworking man. By that time, the poet had been making money by translating English poetry. A number of well-known poets served as witnesses, testifying that Joseph Brodsky was so talented that he was the jewel of Soviet literature. No one took the lawyer's or the witnesses' words into consideration; the court decision had certainly been pre-arranged. According to the judge, unless one was a member of the official Union of Writers, one's poems could not be any good. Everyone knew that the trial was a sheer formality necessary to legalize the primary verdict. The defense's last words were as follows: "Not one of the witnesses for the prosecution either knows Brodsky or has read his poetry; the witnesses for the prosecution testify based on unverified documents received through some unspecified means and merely express their opinions in the form of accusatory speeches."

Brodsky was sentenced to five years of forced labor in a village near the city of Archangelsk. Every day, when his physical toil was over, Joseph would spend several hours working on his English and his poetry.

Brodsky's sentence was commuted in 1965 after protests by prominent Soviet and foreign cultural figures, including Evgeniy Evtushenko, Dmitry Shostakovich, and Jean-Paul Sartre as well as Akhmatova. Brodsky became a cause celebre in the West also, when a secret transcription of trial minutes was smuggled out of the country, making him a symbol of artistic resistance in a totalitarian society, much like his mentor, Akhmatova.

In 1965, Brodsky submitted his poetry manuscript to the publishing house Soviet Writer. Several poets were asked to evaluate his work and wrote rave reviews. Nevertheless, both the party and the Committee for State Security banned its publication.

In 1968, Joseph was invited to participate in an international poetry festival in England. However, the Soviet Ambassador in London declared brazenly that there was no such poet in the USSR. Meanwhile, the no-such-poet's books appeared in the US and in Western Europe one after another. Clearly, they were smuggled by foreigners, diplomats among them, whom even the Soviet authorities dared not search.

In his home country, Brodsky's poems were copied on typewriters and circulated among the numerous admirers of his art. He was not allowed to perform in front of an audience, so the poet would meet his readers in his friends' apartments. The KGB agents kept a wary eye on Brodsky. His activities annoyed them a lot, and for a good reason: there was no such poet, yet here were the readers being introduced to his work, which apparently was there. What is more, from time to time, the no-such-poet was internationally awarded honorary titles. In 1971, Brodsky was inducted as a member of the Bavarian Academy of Fine Arts. That caused a Soviet newspaper article to wonder ironically what kind of institution the Academy was to make a man of seventh-grade education its fellow. A Bavarian newspaper responded, "What kind of poets are most Soviet poets if, despite having college degrees, they are still nowhere near the talent of renowned writer Joseph Brodsky, who only has seven years of school?"

For the Soviet officials, that was the last straw. To simply do away with the poet, who had already gained international acclaim, would mean touching off a storm worldwide. Therefore, it was decided to expel him from the country.

In May 1974, Brodsky was obliged to show up at OVIR (the visa and registration department for foreigners and Soviet citizens arriving in or leaving the Soviet Union). He was advised to either leave the country immediately or undergo "treatment" at a psychiatric hospital. Joseph Brodsky had already been "treated" in that way twice in 1964 and knew all too well what unbearable torture he would experience unless he accepted the former option. That sort of torture came to be known as "punitive medicine" among the Soviets. Later, Brodsky would say that, to him, such "treatment" was much more terrifying than prison or exile. Brodsky was given no other alternative; with his weak heart, he would not survive another series of torture.

Moreover, Brodsky had experienced all the "charms" of the socialist regime back when he was twenty years old. Together with his friend, the ex-pilot Oleg Shakhmatov, he had tried to design a hijacking plan aimed at crossing the border of the Soviet Union. They could not make it on their own though, nor could they find any trustworthy partners.

Joseph agreed to leave his unwelcoming motherland. The poet was deprived of Soviet citizenship and flew to Vienna on June 4, 1972. Professor Karl Proffer met him at the airport. He offered Brodsky a poetry lecturer position at the University of Michigan. Joseph accepted the offer with open arms.

Once again, Brodsky was invited to take part in the Poetry International festival in London. This time, no one said that there was no such poet, so Joseph left for Great Britain.

Returning to the US, he went on with his teaching career. He was offered professorships at other universities as well. Within a twenty-four-year period, he taught at six American and British universities.

In 1987, Brodsky was awarded the Nobel Prize in Literature.

All those years, the poet's parents had been dreaming of seeing their son. Twelve times they asked for permission to take at least a short trip abroad, not necessarily to the USA—their son was willing to fly anywhere to see them. They were denied a trip even after their son had a major heart surgery. They were deprived of their dream to hug their son again. Brodsky's mother passed away in 1983. A year later, his father died. Both times, Brodsky's request to attend the funeral was vindictively turned down.

Only after the collapse of the Soviet Union would the poet's writings be extensively printed in his home country. Meanwhile, the poet himself would never go back.

Joseph Alexandrovich Brodsky died of a heart attack at his home in January 1996. The poet was just fifty-five years old.

SOLZHENITSYN

One of the greatest fighters against Communist tyranny and Communist slavery was Russian writer, Nobel Prize winner and former GULAG prisoner Alexander Isayevich Solzhenitsyn—a towering figure of the last century.

He was a war hero, wounded several times but continued to battle the German army during World War II. But even though a hero, he was still a slave in the Soviet Union. Between battles, he sometimes wrote letters to his friends, wherein he criticized the government. The KGB had a special censorship department. Even during the war, all letters were opened and examined. In February 1945, Captain Solzhenitsyn was captured, stripped of his military rank and taken to Moscow's Lubyanka jail, which was notorious for its particularly brutal treatment of political prisoners. Alexander Isayevich was sentenced to eight years in the GULAG (Main Administration of Corrective Labor Camps). The GULAG system was established in 1919, and by 1921, it had 84 camps. But it wasn't until Joseph Stalin that the GULAG became the world's largest prison system, stretching on 11 time zones.

Solzhenitsyn was the first man to tell the world about The GULAG. He went through many camps. He was beaten many times and was living in horrendous inhuman conditions. But he told himself that he needed to survive all this to tell mankind about the GULAG. In 1952, he was diagnosed with cancer. His chances of survival were none. But again, he told himself that mankind is waiting for his book, and a miracle happened—he survived.

One of his favorite authors was Dante Alighieri, a 14th century Italian poet who wrote the famous Divine Comedy, where he described how the ancient Roman poet Virgil is guided him on a journey through the nine circles of hell. One of the Solzhenitsyn's books is entitled In the First Circle. The hell according to Dante Alighieri has nine circles. Hell by the name of GULAG has thousands of circles, spreading throughout the largest country in the world—the Soviet Union.

The mother of the Soviet concentration empire was the Solovki camp. The camp was located in the White Sea, in a 300-year-old monastery with the same name. Communists loved to use churches and monasteries for prisons and camps.

First of all, communists hate any other religion, except their own. An order to rob churches was issued in the first week after the October Revolution. Church was declared as the main enemy of the people. A favorite saying of Communists is: Religion is the opium of the people. Hundreds of thousands priests and monks were murdered. Everything that has any value was stolen from churches and monasteries.

Solovki, which was in a secluded location with strong 4—to 5-foot thick walls, was an ideal place to imprison enemies of the Socialist revolution.

Many monks were murdered (probably those who show some kind of displeasure with atheist thugs) and the remaining monks were sent to other concentration camps.

For Communists, the only way to combat political opposition was to murder opponents or imprison them. The first prisoners of Solovki besides priests and monks were members of the Socialist Revolutionary Party (ESERS). At first, Communists shared power with them, but after the October Revolution, Lenin started to wrestle them away from governing positions and ship them to Solovki. In 1923, there were about 3,000 slaves inside the mother of all Soviet camps.

At first, the camp had no economic significance. The only objective was to "educate" the convicts, which equaled maltreatment. So they were "educated." The guards, for example, made the convicts count seagulls. A most vital task, you see. Another task was to carry heavy stones away and then carry them back to the same spot. If a person failed to lift the weight, dropped the stone or just halted, they were killed straightaway. In winter, the prisoners were forced to pour water from one ice hole to another. Scholars, doctors, educators and priests were often arranged in a row and made to yell slogans praising the Communist party and the guards or sing International. Someone who sounded insufficiently enthusiastic would be beaten at best and, at times, shot down. The guards were free to do whatever they wanted to the inmates. What those young men wanted most often were women. Women, obviously, were not strong enough to perform all the camp labor. To ease the workload, many of them had no other choice but give themselves to the watchmen. If they refused, it was no problem to rape them.

At a certain point, it was decided that the Solovki camp had to "feed itself." New prisoners were delivered, with most of them workers and peasants this time. No one was forced to count seagulls anymore. There were other things to worry about. A local law was introduced—the "performance-based bread ration." The more work you did, the more bread you got. Work quotas were to be met in local railroad construction, deforestation and other kinds of hard labor. As a result, death rates rose among the weakest and the oldest.

Obviously enough, some inmates tried to flee. While there was a small chance to pass the ever-drunken negligent guards, escaping from the hungry locals, who were perfectly familiar with the terrain, posed a much more difficult problem. Camp administration would give up 200 pounds of wheat flour for each captured escapee. Peasants preferred to turn in the prisoners alive, since corpses only cost 70 pounds of rye wheat, which was cheaper. A Polish citizen named Billas wrote about this in his article "Terrors of Solovki's Drudgery" for the newspaper Kurier Poranny (Morning Courier). He miraculously survived, having spent five years in that hell.

But Solovki was a paradise compared with the Butugychag camp in the Far East Magadan region, which was called the valley of death, and for a reason. The slaves' task was to mine uranium with bare hands and with zero protection. Slaves died from radiation within two weeks, but new ones were brought in their place. About 380,000 people died in the Butugychag.

Another circle of hell was the Akmolalag, which was designed for the wives of "traitors to the Motherland." They were sent there

following their husbands' arrest. Captured and driven to the camp, they were not even allowed to change their clothes. Some women arrived in nightgowns and slippers, others wearing evening dresses. Mothers had to bring their small children with them. In the camp, babies were taken away. They were detained until they were three years old and then sent to orphanages. Their last names would often be changed to prevent reunions with their mothers, should the latter manage to survive. However, not all of those little ones left the camp territory. Some died of hunger and cold within its walls.

Upon arrival, all women were escorted to shower rooms, which they had to exit naked. The camp authorities would meet them outside and select personal concubines. Some officers held entire harems. Women were informed in advance. If they refused, they would be given to their guards for fun, and if still alive after the fun, they were crippled.

While the guards dared not touch the women picked by their bosses, they raped all the others with impunity.

As soon as World War II was over, prisoners of war and former captives of fascist concentration camps came back home. Most of them would wind up in camps again—this time the Soviet ones. They had no right, Stalin believed, to have yielded themselves prisoners.

According to historian Pavel Polyan, who had thoroughly examined the available documents, most of the Red Army soldiers were taken prisoner within the first year of the war, which the Army was totally unprepared for. By Stalin's order, a great number of senior military ranks, primarily those who were most experienced and proactive, had been eliminated before the war. Generals and marshals faced false accusations, and most were shot after continual tortures, some sent to camps and jails. Occasionally, lower-rank officers also ended up in camps.

Other crimes were committed as well under Stalin's rule, which enabled Germans to wipe out entire army troops and advance at full speed in the early months of the war. This explains why entire Red Army divisions, surrounded by the fascists, yielded themselves prisoners.

Like Cronus devouring his own children, Stalin dealt away with the Comintern (Communist International). The organization was aimed at waging a worldwide Bolshevik revolution. Since the Comintern had its own management, it did not fall under Stalin's absolute power. Besides, it so happened that certain Communist parties belonging to the organization did not express their complete agreement with the leader. That lay an obstacle on his way toward total dictatorship. The Kremlin autocrat was not used to such demeanor because he did not tolerate it in his own country. At first, foreign Communists residing in the USSR were captured. There were many of them since they had fled genocide and escaped to the Soviet Union from the territories occupied by the Nazi. Their further path was trodden. Those people were tortured, forced to confess to nonexistent crimes ascribed to them by the executioners, and then shot or taken to death camps. Some German Communists were sent to their homeland by Soviet authorities, where they were placed, naturally, in Nazi concentration camps or killed. Needless to say, Stalin knew perfectly well what awaited them in Germany.

The claims voiced by Russian "patriots" that Stalin had no idea about the mayhem happening in the USSR do not stand up to scrutiny, since those repressions were sanctioned and further managed by the Kremlin despot himself. As people who recognized that would say at the time, "A bird dared not poop without Stalin's order." The bird part, to my mind, might be an exaggeration, but the state security apparatus obeyed the leader unquestionably.

NKVD (People's Commissariat of Internal Affairs) agents had to extort confessions from "enemies of the people," since what was filed against them was forged with false evidence. In January 1939, Stalin sent an encoded telegram to party leaders and the NKVD reminding them that applying physical force in interrogations had been authorized in 1937. To meet the target figures for supplying slaves for the camps, security officials were free to go after common people, while Stalin himself dealt with arresting high-ranked public officials and cultural celebrities. He also calibrated what appeared to him as the "adequate" number of mass shootings.

The surviving protocols of interrogations for "unyielding" prisoners transmitted to Stalin by NKVD head Yezhov have the former's directives on them. His note "Beat!" is written there in a bold hand.

"Stalin's falcons" had grown so accustomed to torturing that they would beat convicted prisoners brutally in the cars while transferring them to places of execution. There is evidence that some of those people died on the way, before the execution. The beatings made no sense at all because all the "confessions" had long been received. But faithful servants of the regime, having tasted blood, could stop no longer.

The GULAG has over 30,000 places of incarceration. Perhaps between 20 and 40 million slaves went through the GULAG system, among which between 2 to 2.5 million died.

Of course, not all camp prisoners praised Stalin. Alexander Isayevich Solzhenitsyn was one of those who loathed him.

Alexander was born to a very religious family of a Russian peasant and a Cossack woman. Both peasants and Cossacks experienced the "charms" of the Soviet rule to the full. The boy inherited his parents' attitude to the regime.

In primary school, he had a very hard time. Learning that Sasha, as he was known, wore a cross, his classmates would not leave him be, mocking him continually. Once the boy was seen entering a church. The problem was that Communists were battling religion, denouncing it as "opium of the people." Solzhenitsyn was warned: if that happened again, he would not be accepted into the Young Pioneers organization (the Soviet youth Communist scout group). The boy replied that he had not intended to join it anyway. As time passed, however, under the sway of state propaganda, the young man acquired Communist ideology.

In 1936, Solzhenitsyn joined the Communist Youth Union, without which it was extremely hard to enter the faculty of physics and mathematics at the university. He was so carried away by Marxism-Leninism that university lectures on that subject were no longer enough for him. Alexander began to study the books of communism propagators by himself. At the same time (starting in the seventh grade), he wrote poetry and essays.

During World War II, disregarding the ban, Alexander Isayevich kept a diary, which would later lay the foundation for many of his works. At the front, he generally wrote a lot, sending his manuscripts to various periodicals.

Captain Solzhenitsyn's battle route took him from the Soviet city of Oryol to East Prussia. He would have reached Berlin very soon. However, Alexander Isayevich Solzhenitsyn had already learned that charges pressed against many Soviet citizens were ridiculous, that people were doomed to torture and death for no reason, and that the Kremlin autocrat had something to do with the weakening of the Soviet army. Alexander Isayevich shared his attitude toward the supreme ruler in his letters to a friend. Military censorship took measures. In February 1945, Solzhenitsyn was captured, stripped of his military rank and taken to Moscow's Lubyanka jail, notorious for its particularly brutal treatment of political prisoners. Alexander Isayevich was sentenced to eight years in Stalinist camps, which was to be followed by lifelong exile.

The great hero of our time, Solzhenitsyn, was released from prison in 1956. He started to work as a math and physics teacher in a provincial school, but really, his workday was 18 hours long.

Publishers refused to print Alexander Isayevich's first works. It was only in 1962 that his short story "One Day in the Life of Ivan Denisovich" was published in the magazine New World. The piece was later printed as a stand-alone book and translated into many languages. He instantly became a celebrity. Suddenly he was on the level of Tolstoy, Dostoyevsky and Chekhov. In 1963, the Soviet leader Nikita Khrushchev banned the publication of Solzhenitsyn's novel In the First Circle. When Leonid Brezhnev came to power, Alexander Isayevich was totally banned from publishing.

In 1965, KGB officials seized the writer's manuscripts and archives. In 1967, Alexander Isayevich completed his famous The GULAG Archipelago, in secrecy.

In 1968, Solzhenitsyn's novels In the First Circle and Cancer Ward were published abroad. By 1970, the works of the writer had been printed in twenty-eight countries. Sixteen separate books and the collected works in six volumes were published abroad, in Russian. In the same year, Alexander Isayevich became a Nobel Prize winner in literature "for the ethical force with which he has pursued the indispensable traditions of Russian literature."

As early as in the late 1960s, the KGB tailored a special division to spy on Solzhenitsyn. The writer's views on the Soviet rule, expressed more and more overtly, led to the authorities' attempt to assassinate him. In 1971, during his trip to Novocherkassk, he was injected with poison without knowing it. Solzhenitsyn survived, but it took him long to recover.

Had it not been for the numerous protests voiced by various international organizations and public figures, the KGB would have certainly seen its plan through. Now the state authorities had little choice but to order the writer out of the country. In 1974, Nobel laureate Alexander Isayevich Solzhenitsyn was arrested, deprived of Soviet citizenship and expelled from the Soviet Union. He spent most of the next 19 years in Vermont, USA. In 1994, he returned to Russia and received a hero's welcome.

The man and the writer who helped destroy the Empire of Evil died in August 2008 in Russia.

IDENTITY HANDS

"**P**ublix—where shopping is a pleasure!" read the sign at my favorite supermarket. It was 44 years ago, and I had just come from the Soviet Union, where shopping was never a pleasure. It was rather chasing and hunting for desirable items.

I remember vividly the tense faces of Leningrad citizens and visitors who formed lines to wait for the stores to open. Those faces were more suitable for attacking an enemy with bayonets than pushing through crowds to buy German lingerie, Hungarian shoes, or Yugoslavian purses. They called those hard-to-get items "deficit."

There were lines that would last for years. That was true for furniture, carpets and many more. My aunt, for instance, spent five years regularly confirming her fridge waitlist number. Some people could sign up to a car waitlist at work. But they had to be efficient employees and preferably drink less than others, especially at work. Membership in the Communist party helped a lot as well. But membership in that one political party only, for there were no other parties.

I remember a typical skirmish that happened not long before my departure. I was walking to work in the early morning, along Moskovsky Avenue in Leningrad. Having spent the day before at my friend's birthday party, I had gone to bed late and woken up early, as I always did on workdays, so now I was dozing off as I walked. When I approached the Frunzensky department store, I suddenly heard some women yelling. I looked up—a woman had knocked down another woman and was banging the latter's head against the ground. Another two women were pulling each other's hair. An elderly lady in a torn blouse, her naked breasts swaying as she ran, knocked someone off their feet but was immediately taken down herself by another woman.

I joined a small group of men who rushed to pull apart the female folks. Making use of their huge numerical advantage, and overwhelmed with rage, they fought us off with ease. One of the viragoes managed to scratch my face. The arrival of the police prevented a second attack.

Later, I learned what had sparked the battle. Word had leaked out that knee high Italian boots for women would be available in the store. Many days before the event, people started signing up. The waitlists were arranged by female volunteers, whose feverish activity bought them the right to get first crack at the shoes. Each potential buyer was assigned a line number which, for some reason, was written on their hand. To simply have a line number was not enough though; it had to be constantly confirmed. Occasionally, there would be a roll call. If a person was late or failed to show up for confirmation, their name would be ruthlessly crossed out

with perverse delight. It was no use demonstrating the numbered hand later. Doing so would only receive a sarcastic response that a hand which missed a roll call was not an "identity" hand anymore.

Among the women were some who realized that the list was so long that they had no chance whatsoever to get the boots, so some of these activists came forward and declared, "This registration is totally illegal; we'll come to the store early in the morning to be the first in line." As it turned out, the women from the list had shown up the night before. That triggered the previously mentioned combat.

But for the fierce fight, the line would have hardly attracted anyone's attention. Back then, the entire country was constantly lining up for something. The phenomenon was as habitual as rain, or as the endless radio talk of how the capitalists were all bastards, while we were the real good guys.

There was a popular joke circulating in those days. An American tourist is passing by a department store, accompanied by a Soviet interpreter, and spots a giant line. He wonders what this is about and makes his way to the shop counter. The translator explains that some locally manufactured shoes have been "dumped." The American, who had been squeamishly examining them in the meantime, replies, "That's fair enough, in the US we dump such stuff too."

Back then, "to dump" meant "to deliver goods to shops for common people to buy."

Those who signed up to a waitlist in advance knew that on a certain strictly designated day, they had at least a small chance of buying something. Then there were lines where nobody had any idea of what they were waiting for. At the opening hour, shoving each other, people would rush to the counters, even if there was nothing there—who knows, maybe something would be "dumped" suddenly? If nothing was dumped, they would wait for the rest of the day and come home empty-handed. If something was "dumped," they would buy whatever it was. Later, they could exchange it for what they actually needed with someone who had managed to procure that thing elsewhere. People would phone each other and discuss their catch:

"What did you buy, a kid's fur coat? What size? Ah, that sounds just perfect for my Mashenka. I snatched an overcoat yesterday, a great fit for your Vasya."

So they would meet, and if both parties were satisfied with what they saw, they would perform the exchange.

In times when there was enough meat for sale in Leningrad, the freshly chopped slabs were brought to the display cases from the back of the store. Customers would snatch up the best slabs and leave those that looked less attractive, waiting for another fresh batch. Meanwhile, visitors from outside the city would take the worst parts. They would often call the locals "fussy fat snobs"; as for themselves, they added, any piece of meat was bliss.

Leningrad citizens did not like visitors, especially in lines. Comments about "clogging up the city" circulated all the time. The "cloggers," in turn, explained that they, too, had children, who were also hungry. Occasionally, the visitors had to explain to the locals that it was they who raised those cows and pigs for the meat they never saw in their own village grocery stores.

Line members kept a wary eye on the intruders who tried to break their more or less orderly rows. Great Patriotic War veterans, who were all but carried in people's arms on Victory Day, were loathed deeply in lines for their legal right to be served first.

It was quite common for someone to approach a person at the end of the sufferers' line, saying that their number was close and offering to buy it. If the price was reasonable, people would agree. The money made in that way was usually spent on vodka.

Of course, those endless lines to buy a "deficit" created a huge black market. Black market operators were called "spekuliants"— they could get 2–3 years of hard labor for their illegal activities. They would resell goods for 2–3 times more than the nominal price. Store managers became a kind of elite because they had first access to "deficits." They also had an obligation to keep a "deficit" ready in the back of the store in case local party bosses needed one (although party bosses had their own secret stores full of "deficits"). At that time the country had "dollar stores" called "Berezka" where "deficits" were sold for dollars or other capitalistic currency.

The "spekuliant" profession has not died in Russia. A couple of years ago I visited St. Petersburg and there was a huge line to get into the Catherine the Great palace and museum.

Using my non-forgotten skills, I promptly found "nice guys" who sold me a ticket for a desirable entry time with a 300% mark-up. So, if you go to Russia don't be afraid of long lines for museums or theaters—just look for the right guys to help!

UNCLE GRISHA AND COMRADE STALIN

Joseph Stalin was the omnipotent dictator of the Soviet Union, and my uncle Grisha was a humble tailor living in the northern city of Leningrad. They never met each other, but their destinies crossed on the day of March 5, 1953.

In the Soviet Union, communism was a main religion, and the tyrant Stalin was a god.

My teacher in school often said that one god existed in the sky and another on earth, and his name was Stalin. And on March 5, the god on earth suddenly died. This shook the country as much as if there had been an earthquake of 20 or more on the Richter scale. People were crying on the streets and at home. Many frantically asked to die themselves, just to keep Stalin alive, but he did not accept their generous offer of exchange, and continued to rest in peace.

The health of the dictator was the biggest state secret. He had obviously had some health problems before, considering he was 74 years old, was a heavy drinker and had an unhealthy schedule: he was sleeping in the daytime and working at night. He kept all Soviet bigshots in heart-wrenching suspense as they watched the secret red phones in their offices, because he could call on those phones at any moment during the night. Anybody who failed to answer this government phone call from the Communist god risked losing his high position.

The news of Stalin's expiration were only announced the next day, March 6, by the state's official announcer, Yuri Levitan, who was the most famous radio broadcaster of the country. Everybody knew his voice, but nobody saw him in real life or even saw his image.

In actuality, he was a pretty small man with a huge, thunderous voice, exactly suited to announcing Stalin's great triumphs to the world during World War II and especially on Victory Day, May 9, 1945. On March 6, 1953, exactly at 6 o'clock in the morning, he read a medical report, signed by the biggest names in the Soviet medical world, confirming that Joseph Stalin had died on March 5 from collapse of brain functions. Nobody had died from such an illness before, and nobody would die from it after. The whole disease was specifically invented by brightest medical minds for the god of the Communist world.

If my uncle Grisha had not come to work that day, March 6, this story would never have happened. And everybody would have understood that great sorrow had kept him at home. But unfortunately, he came one hour before his shift, as always, and later uttered those several words which forever changed his life and finally killed him.

My uncle Grisha was a humble man, but a great tailor. In the Soviet Union in the Fifties, "prêt-a-porter" (ready-to-wear) clothing was practically unknown. Everybody who wanted to get a more or less decent suit needed to make it from scratch or order it from one of the government-run tailor shops. At that time, a tailor was not only a tailor, he was a fashion designer, a fashion consultant and a sewing person as well. And Grisha was one of the best. He had a special, unparalleled technique. Young tailors love to watch how he handled fabric. He never humiliated himself by drawing lines with chalk on material before cutting it, like other tailors would do. Instead, he fearlessly cut through rolls of fabric with his big scissors, producing pieces ready to sew and giving them to the seamstresses who worked with him. He would say that his job was very simple. He just cut away the extra that did not belong to the suit and left only the necessary parts.

He echoed one sculptor who said that to create a sculpture, he just chiseled away some pieces to free a statue that was hiding inside of a rock. Uncle Grisha was very fast. He worked with a team of three seamstresses: Nadia, Luba and Vera. He cut pieces with lightning speed, and the girls had a hard time keeping up with him. But if they were too slow for him, he would put away his scissors and measuring stick, take a needle and do the sewing with girls. And of course, his sewing was exceptionally fast and efficient and precise.

He started tailoring when he was only 9 years old, watching his older sister Fannie as she sat behind the old Zinger sewing machine. He learned fast, without anybody explaining anything to him. He was very short, and worked on the sewing machine standing up because he could not reach the pedal from a chair, but this did not discourage him from sewing and tailoring. He joined Fannie in the trade, and together they provided clothing for all their family—father, mother and five brothers. Fannie was the oldest child and only girl in the family. She was happy to see success of her young brother. He really was a young genius of tailoring. At the age of 11, he invented the recycling of clothes—he would turn an article of clothing inside out and make it new again this way. He was very proud to be the official tailor of the family at that age.

The family lived in the tiny Jewish village ("shtetl") by the name of Berezka, which was actually a ghetto, like other places where Jewish people lived at that time in Russia. Their father was a small-time merchant, who provided the peasants in neighboring villages with necessary goods and delivered them to their door on his own horse-drawn cart, while the mother had a small store, located right in their house. Grisha loved his sister Fannie very much. She was a fearless girl. Everybody in the shtetl was afraid of a bull by the name of Lesh. When Lesh was walking on the single street of the village, all the inhabitants hid. Only Fannie was not afraid, talking to the animal and even stroking his hard fur.

In 1913, when she was only 19 years of age, she went to America. One Brooklyn businessman heard about her unmatched beauty and sent her a bridal visa. The parents were reluctant to allow her to go because of her young age. They went to the rabbi to ask for advice. He looked at them carefully and said if Fannie could take him in her suitcase, he would go with her too! And he added that if she was not afraid of the terrible Lesh, immigration would be nothing for her.

Soon after her arrival, Fannie wrote that she was happy in her new country. She landed at Ellis island, like other immigrants. The immigration authorities were very nice, but they cut her last name Finkelstein, which they considered too long, so now she was Fannie Stein. Her future bridegroom, who had invited her, happened to be a very nice man, although a little bit fat.

She found job right away, it was small alteration shop. Her duties were to shorten pants or dresses and she was very good at this, so the owners were very happy with her. She was making 10 dollars per week, which was very good money, especially in Berezka. There, 20 dollars could buy a good cow or bull like Lesh. So Fannie could buy a cow or bull every two weeks. It very much impressed everybody in Berezka, where they had to work for one year to make the same amount of money. Her letters were read aloud.

Many villagers, including young Grisha, were dreaming about immigrating to America, but in 1914, World War I began and all immigration plans came to a screeching halt. Grisha belonged to the Russian generation that went through horrible times—

wars, revolutions, famine, civil war, and the Red Terror, just to name a few.

In 1925, the situation stabilized and Joseph Stalin became a sole dictator with unlimited power. Any immigration or travel outside of the country was prohibited by Stalin. If anyone tried to flee the country, they would face a firing squad.

Every two weeks, Grisha received a letter from Fannie. She was crying about the life of her little brother, and hoping that one day, when the terrible bull Lesh die, they would reunite. "Lesh" was of course a code name for comrade Stalin.

And on March 6, 1953, it happened. Lesh was dead and everybody was crying, but not Grisha. He was mostly interested in his trade. Events beyond his tailoring world did not bother him, even such a national disaster as a death of Stalin himself.

As always, he came before anybody else to the shop. A large portrait of Stalin was hung in the most visible place in the vestibule. To the right of Stalin was a board of honor, where photographs of best workers, including Grisha, were pinned. To the left of Stalin was a small poster reading, "TIPS INSULT WORKERS," which reminded workers that taking tips was illegal. But all fashion industry workers, including Grisha, were dependent on tips, because it was impossible to survive on the miserable official state salary of about 60 dollars a month.

My uncle was only one who was working that morning. Everybody in the shop was weeping, especially the three girls of his own staff, who sounded like they were in some kind of crying competition, with each one trying to outdo the others.

Grisha honestly could not understand them. He eagerly started to work. He was to finish two suits for his high-ranking communist clients, and was patiently waiting for girls to stop crying and start to work.

He brought them water and asked paternally, "Why are you crying? It is not your father who died!"

The girls stopped crying right away. "Not your father?" But Stalin was much more important to them than their own fathers. They immediately ran to the secretary of tailor shop's Communist cell and reported the impossible heresy they had just heard. In one hour, a KGB team came and took my poor uncle to the Big House, as people called the KGB headquarters at that time.

After two days of non-stop beatings, an investigator came and offered to my uncle to confess that he was an American spy.

"I don't even speak English," protested Grisha.

Instead of answering, the investigator hit him several times. After that, he opened a folder and took out papers—copies of letters from Grisha's American sister. "You received coded instructions from the USA every two weeks, you son of a bitch! We are going to interrogate you until you give us a full confession."

"Interrogation" meant beatings, beatings and more beatings, realized my uncle, and so he signed all the papers, confirming that he was an American spy.

After two weeks, there was a parody of a trial. The judge gave him a lenient term— "only" 10 years of hard labor.

"They beat me day and night," my uncle complained to the judge, rolling up his shirt to show his wounds.

"They beat people in America, not in our free country," retorted the judge, and added five years to the sentence for slander, making it a total of 15 years of hard labor.

Three years later, the cult of personality of Stalin was unmasked by Khrushchev at the 20th Congress of Communist Party. Victims of the cult of personality, as they called millions of sufferers, were rehabilitated, and my uncle, like others, returned home.

The next day, he reported to his tailor's shop. Everything had changed. The portrait of Stalin had disappeared and been replaced with a portrait of Lenin. The photo of the uncle was gone from the board of honor, but the sign that tips were illegal still remained. The three girls—young Communists—who had reported him to the KGB were also gone. They went to develop virgin and fallow lands in Kazakhstan, at the call of Khrushchev and the Communist Party.

Grisha wrote a letter to his sister and explained, without giving much details, that for three years he had not been able write letters, but that now he was OK.

But he was not OK. He was limping and he was walking with the cane. He was so weak that he could not even hold tailor's scissors in his hands. They took him to the hospital. The doctor made X-ray and was amazed that uncle was still alive: almost all internal organs were damaged during endless beating in prison. The doctor gave my uncle one month and he was right—in the month poor uncle died.

THE LONG AWOL

OF

PRIVATE

ABRAMOVICH

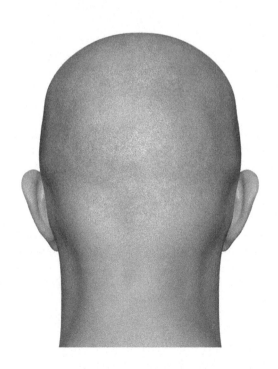

Chapter 1

YASHA AND YOUNG LENIN

Yasha was late to the folk theater rehearsal. The bus in which he was riding in was old and shaking as if they were diving through an earthquake. It sneezed and coughed at every turn of the wheels as if it had the bus flu. Exhaust gases penetrated inside, causing the passengers to sneeze and cough in unison with the bus.

Yasha paid no attention to the bus or its ailments. He was lost in a state of creative enthusiasm. The day before he had been awarded the main role in a classic play at the community theater. Yasha was dreaming madly. To him, the bus platform he was standing on was a stage, and the passenger compartment was the theater auditorium.

When he delivers his line: "To be, or not to be!?" the audience jumps up and the applause causes the chandelier to swing. They are calling him back a dozen times for an encore. The newspapers write accolades about his wonderful acting at the community theater. Everybody insists that he enroll at the Theater School and become a professional actor.

During the entrance exam, he takes the proper political steps and plays a young Lenin. There hasn't been such a young Lenin yet. Besides, Yasha already has a small bald spot and he artistically burrs, like Lenin. When he says: "No, mom, we will go a diffeg-gent way!" and raises his hand, showing the way forward, the members of the examination board are delighted. They are eager to applaud him, but not allowed to.

He is accepted unanimously at the Theater School. By his fourth year in school, he will be nominated for the highest title, as an Honored Artist of the Soviet Union.

Undoubtedly, he will have to create himself an alias. This is due to the fact that his name, Yasha Abramovich, sounded far too Jewish. So Yasha Abramovich will disappear, and newly minted, but already famous actor Yan Abramov will appear in his place. One of the passengers on the bus, a man in an old army hat with earflaps with muddy eyes, was shaking his head thoughtfully. A five-pointed indentation from a star remained on the fur visor of the cap. Did he know about Yasha's creative impulse? He seems to be delighted. Maybe he would even like an autograph?

"What are you looking at, kike face?" The passenger suddenly said with a drunken slur. Yasha's world immediately collapsed. Yasha felt like a skydiver whose parachute failed to open. Or maybe not. He felt like he was hit with a pillow, and instead of feathers, it was filled with lead. Any other time, he would have kept silent as customary for a Jewish man, accustomed to anti-Semitic street slurs. But not this time. He felt young Lenin stirring inside him, coming to the rescue. Unexpectedly to even himself, Yasha clearly ordered:

"Stop the tg-g-ganspog-gt immediately, my deagg!"

To Yasha's surprise, the driver stopped. The phrase "my dear" impressed the passengers. They respectfully looked at Yasha and kept quiet. Yasha saw their reaction and suddenly felt powerful like Incredible Hulk.

Lightly, like a bag of hay, Yasha hoisted the drunk on his shoulder and got off the bus. There was a militia station nearby. Yasha remembered it well. Four years ago, he ended up there for jumping off a moving trolley before it came to a complete stop. There was a reception desk covered with leatherette and a group of old Vienna chairs in poor condition. His brother, a medical student, took him back home last time, after an exhausting lecture from the militia officer.

With his drunken burden on his shoulder, Yasha carefully opened the door. The old reception desk was in the same old place. A sergeant in an unzipped overcoat was sitting on one of the Viennese chairs, turned backward, and examining a picture of a flying gymnast in the magazine Soviet Circus.

She was wearing sparkling panties and a tunic. For half an hour the sergeant had been trying to understand what was under her panties. He scraped the page with his fingernail, he tried checking it from all angles in the light, but that didn't help.

Yasha threw his drunken load down on a chair and announced: "He called me a kike face."

"How did he call you?" the militiaman regretfully put the magazine aside, without having been able to solve the problem of panties on the gymnast.

"Kike face."

"So, kike face..." Yasha heard a slight enjoyment in the sergeant's voice. "Kike face," he repeated and started writing something. Then he pressed the intercom button and informed his boss over the speaker.

"Comrade Lieutenant, it seems that somebody called somebody else a kike face," and now an entire orchestra sounded in his voice.

"A kike face, Sergeant?" the distant Lieutenant repeated tastefully.

"Yes, yes, a kike face, comrade Lieutenant."

Yasha realized that he'd better leave. "I'm late for rehearsal!" he interrupted the duet of the two uniformed anti-Semites.

"Thanks for bringing it to our attention," the Sergeant said. "We'll try to get to the bottom of this."

The Sergeant turned off speaker, picked up the magazine with the gymnast, and once again began viewing the picture in the light.

Chapter 2
CONSCRIPT ABRAMOVICH

The month of June started very unpleasantly. Several times a week, he began to receive the summons, notes about the size of postcards, from the Military Registration and Enlistment Office demanding that he be summoned before Commander Pregarok.

Yasha had other plans. Studying at the Theater Institute, and then, after graduation, appearing at the best theaters. Maybe even the Soviet version of Hollywood, the movie studio MosFilm would invite him, and he will become very famous.

The Major, with all of these summons papers, simply did not fit into Yasha's creative plans. There was just no place for him there. Yasha had been carefully pinning the accumulating summons cards to a board on the bathroom wall and was not in any hurry to meet with Commander Pregarok.

From the experiences of his young life, Yasha learned that if something hurts, its better just wait until the pain would stop. He thought the same way of the summons from the military draft board. But they were not stopping, Commander Pregarok was eager to meet him. He was ready to crush Yasha's creative dreams with his chrome knee-high boots. But then one day the summons stopped arriving. They went away like a toothache.

The world seemed amazing and beautiful once again. Yasha appreciated his life much more than he did before the start of the attacks from the military enlistment office. He would walk past big theaters and he sees huge billboards shouting about the wonderful artist Yan Abramov, a creative pseudonym for Yasha. His headshot, retouched by the best artists, was up there to be seen by all.

The famous Yan Abramov was welcome everywhere. He is constantly surrounded by people who love him. He visited collective farms, huge factories, mountain villages. He would not refuse any of his fans. One day, an elderly General from a military unit asks for his autograph.

"What's your name?" he asks affectionately the General.

"Pregarok." the General answers, stands at attention and salutes him.

"At Ease!" Yasha smiled. "Where did I hear that ridiculous surname Pregarok?" He thought to himself but could not remember.

"The main thing is to get to the Theater Institute," Yasha thought, returning to an unpleasant reality. "Just to get inside, and then all the best and famous artists will stand up for him to defend all his talents against all the Pregaroks and Overgaroks."

On TV, Yasha saw African Americans fight for their rights. They heroically rode on the front of the bus, even though racists of all stripes, as well as Governor Wallace, were attempting to prevent this and force them to ride in the back. This was called civil disobedience, and in the end, the African Americans won.

Yasha himself started to think about civil disobedience. Or about young Lenin, how he always used the rear exit, and always done so brilliantly. That is how he escaped the bloodhounds of the Provisional Government. They would chase after him, but Ilyich, with a cap or ill-fitting wig over his head, would run through the rear exit to Shpalernaya or to Moika Street.

If this bastard Pregarok were to appear in his communal apartment, Yasha will trick him, running away through the Leninist rear exit. Although Pregarok never showed up at Yasha's apartment, the red-faced janitor Uncle Kolya did. It happened when Yasha had just finished his gymnastics exercises, under command from a radio instructor.

An unusually early knock rang at the door, and Yasha immediately realized they had come for him. He managed to get dressed as in the army, in only 40 seconds, while his mother has opened the door.

"Who is it?" he asked his mother.

"Janitor Uncle Kolya," the mother said with a frightened voice. She knew about the situation with the summons.

"Mom, we'll go another way," he dropped famous Lenin line, pulled his hat over his ears, and tried to evaporate through the back exit. But it would not work.

There, the block militia man Uncle Misha lay in waiting for him. So, from his own experience, Yasha was convinced that it is much harder for him to deceive janitor Uncle Kolya and the block militiamen than it was for Lenin to deceive the bloodhounds of the Provisional Government.

At the Military Registration and Enlistment Office, uncles Kolya and Misha surrendered their prize to Commander Pregarok and set off home with a sense of accomplishment. That week they had already caught several wayward conscripts, including Kostya Sheikin, Yasha's best buddy.

There were ongoing renovations at Pregarok's office. The files of conscripts' information were removed from their shelves, and piles of files were lying on the Military Commissar's desk. The file with the case of Yasha Abramovich was at the very top.

Wherever Pregarok went around the office, the unfortunate folder was always in front of his face, like the eyes of Giaconda by Leonardo Da Vinci. And now Yasha completely understood the secret of the endless summons from the Military Registration and Enlistment Office. He had always been under the eye of Commander Pregarok.

Yasha had not realized that the vindictive military commissar had reserved for him the worst duty station. He was going to be sent to a place where after a year of service, radiation sickness afflicted a quarter of the personnel.

In late September Yasha, Kostya Sheikin, and other conscripts said their goodbyes to civilian life. Per tradition, the farewell was in the Lenin Room of the House Management Office. The red-faced janitor Uncle Kolya was the representative of the House Management this evening. Before the celebration, at the insistence of Uncle Kolya, Lenin's bust was transferred from the Lenin Room to the reception area. This was done as a precaution.

Two years ago, one of the conscripts, having consumed a large number of alcoholic beverages, could not withstand the stress and vomited right on the leader's face. They hurriedly wiped the bust with a towel, but the janitor Uncle Kolya informed the authorities about this unpleasant situation. After that, the KGB investigated whether the act of vomiting on the bust was the tantamount to ideological sabotage or terrorism.

Before the farewell evening began, a solemn event took place. First, the block militia man Uncle Misha spoke, and on behalf of the Soviet law enforcement, congratulated everyone on the onset of the happiest time of their life, their service in the Soviet Army. Then, on behalf of the janitorial team, Uncle Kolya spoke. He, too, congratulated the conscripts on the happiness that fell upon them, military service in the ranks of the Soviet Army.

To conclude he said "When you return from the service, I invite you to join the ranks of the Soviet janitors. We need smart and educated janitors. The Soviet government, as never before, is concerned about the urgent aspirations of janitors. We are tirelessly equipped with crowbars, shovels, ice scrapers, and other equipment, and recently special bonuses have been introduced for the apprehension of evading conscripts, for 3 rubles per conscript. And remember, when Lenin said that in Communist society every cook and cleaning persons would rule the state, he meant, of course, the janitors as well."

The solemn part of the ceremony ended with that. Conscripts politely applauded, and all eyes turned towards the case of vodka in the corner of the room. With true military speed, tables and chairs were set up, newspapers instead of tablecloths were laid down, and aluminum forks were laid out. It seems bottles of vodka themselves jumped out of the box onto the tables for the waiting draftees. Yasha celebrated with everyone, clearly unaware of the radiation sickness that Major Pregarok had in stock for him.

In the middle of the celebration, Kostya Sheikin suddenly did something unexpected. He climbed on a chair and announced to everyone "I can't join the Army, I'm still a virgin!"

"Don't f... ng lie!" the table responded amicably.

"But I had these women, ooh," said Uncle Kolya. "Especially after the war."

"I'm not lying!" Kostya burst into tears and nearly fell off his chair.

"We need to deflower this kid," Uncle Kolya shook his head. "Otherwise the army service will not work."

"You should have told me earlier," Uncle Misha lamented. "I keep dispersing these whores all the time."

After all the vodka was done, the line between the authorities and the conscripts became blurry. Uncle Misha and Uncle Kolya had recently caught conscripts, but that was only their duty, and the conscripts were understanding of this. And now, together again, were formulating a plan to deflower Conscript Sheikin.

After a short debate, the Committee for the Loss of Virginity of Conscript Sheikin, consisting of Yasha and two more conscripts, was formed. The committee, headed by Uncle Misha, immediately went towards the railroad station, where one could normally meet female consultants about resolving this pressing issue.

On their way, the committee members spoke with the passing men, confidentially told them of Kostya Sheikin's situation, and asked for help. They sympathized with Kostya, shook their heads, and pointed in the direction of the railroad station.

As it sometimes happens, you hear of a place where the fish bite nonstop, but when you get there with fishing rods and bait, not see a single fish bites during the whole day. A similar situation happened with the members of the Committee. There was nobody there when they approached the station.

That is, certainly, there were passengers, there were greeters, and there were the station bums and drunkards. But those female consultants whom Sheikin wanted to see were nowhere to be found. Either all the consultants left for an intercity seminar, or they were on strike, or they had the night off. They did not leave a note. The Committee members and Sheikin circled the station several times, looked in all the hidden places, to no avail.

Discouraged, they boarded a city trolley and headed home. This was the last ride and the car was empty. Sociable Yasha talked with the blonde conductress and for some reason told her about Sheikin and the unsuccessful raid to the station.

"How many of you?" the conductress asked.

"Four people," Yasha said. "But the boy is only one."

"And the cop... he is with you, too?"

Yasha looked around and realized why the station option failed. Uncle Misha was in full law enforcement uniform.

"Yeah," Yasha nodded. "But the cop is with us."

"Wow, gosh! Four boys," the conductress sighed dreamily, and her eyes clouded over. "You all go!" she decided.

"Where are we going?" Yasha did not understand.

"You will see, dear, do not be afraid," the conductress sang softly.

"Yeah, let's all go," Sheikin smiled happily. The issue of bringing him to full military readiness was about to be resolved.

Three days later, conscripts gathered with all their belongings at the Military Enlistment Office. As they stood calmly and waited their turn, the Committee members and Sheikin showed extraordinary activity and anxiety, constantly running to the restroom and wincing in pain. The experienced Pregarok immediately diagnosed them. While the rest of the conscripts went marching and singing songs, and the Committee members and Sheikin got five days of punishment for immoral behavior and sent for treatment at the garrison hospital.

From the Canadian newspaper Daily Dollar, August 18, 1978:

According to sources, a prominent member of the Soviet Secret Service, also known as the KGB, Colonel Ivan Zimukhin, has appealed to the Canadian government for political asylum. He served as Deputy Head of the Heritage Department, one of the KGB's most secretive units, of which almost nothing is known in the West. The Heritage Department was created at the initiative of Soviet dictator Joseph Stalin to finance the so-called Great Communist Construction Projects. Its tasks included working with Soviet citizens who received inheritances from Western relatives. Those who had received a foreign inheritance, according to Zimukhin, were called "sources" by the department.

Thanks to thoughtful and thorough work with the "sources", the KGB, according to Colonel Zimukhin, managed to acquire many millions of dollars, which went towards the construction of the huge Dnipro Hydroelectric Power Plant, the Volga-Don Shipping Canal, and other large Soviet construction projects. Prior to being transferred to the Heritage Department, Colonel Zimukhin worked in the Letters Department, which dealt with the correspondence which Soviet citizens receive from abroad. Offices of the Letters department were located at each major city post office. If an intercepted letter had any mention of a possible inheritance, the information was transferred to the Heritage Department and the potential heir came under the scrutiny of the KGB. If the potential inheritance exceeded a million dollars, a special task force was to be created.

Chapter 3
THE DISAPPEARANCE OF THE HEIR

Every year Yasha's mother, Galina Solomonovna, would receive Passover packages from America, from her older sister Feiga, who came to America 50 years before. The huge cardboard parcel was full of expensive American gifts in beautiful bright packaging, intended for her numerous relatives in Russia.

Out of their entire family, only Feiga and cousin Zuya managed to escape to America before the Soviets closed all borders in 1917. The rest of the family members were steamrolled by cruel Soviet reality, the Bolshevik revolution, collectivization, and the mass incarceration of half the country.

Fifty years later, Feiga still remembered and still sent gifts to everyone. Relatives, of course, also remembered her, but they did not dare to correspond with her for obvious reasons. Only the tiny Galina Solomonovna, less than five feet tall, fearlessly wrote to her far-away sister, even in the most unbearable years.

In 1948, at the height of the 'Cleansing of Cosmopolitans', a serious threat loomed over Galina Solomonovna. Anti-Semitism had always been a cornerstone of Stalin's internal policies. 'Cosmopolitans' were Jewish actors and writers who changed their Jewish names to Russian ones and who would ostensibly worship to the Western and American culture.

This 'Cleansing of Cosmopolitans' was just a euphemism for the preparation of the planned exile of Soviet Jewish people to Siberia in 1953. Luckily, the dictator died in March of that year and the Jewish people were saved from exile.

At that time as the Soviet Union had very ambitious plans for the development of the steel and oil industries. The KGB officers also received an ambitious plan for the mass incarceration of the Enemies of the People. If there was to be a shortage of enemies, they turned to an inexhaustible source, people with relatives abroad. And if any of these unfortunate people started a correspondence abroad, only a miracle could save them from the concentration camp.

Such a miracle happened to Galina Solomonovna, and the creator of that miracle was Feiga. In one of her letters, she notified sister that their loving cousin Zuya had passed away and willed Galina Solomonovna a sum of $100,000. In the Letters Department, this important message was intercepted and then transferred to the Heritage Department.

The mother of Yasha was removed from the list of Potential Enemies and was transferred to the list of Potential Sources. However, it was subsequently determined that the money was intended for an entirely different person. But by then Stalin was dead, the struggle against cosmopolitans ended, the large-scale incarceration plans for the mass arrests of Enemies of the People were scaled back, and the life of the innocent Galina Solomonovna was miraculously spared.

According to family stories, Feiga was very beautiful. Even the Russian Tsarina recognized this. She recognized this fact in Nevel, before the confluence of the entire population of this glorious city in the Pskov province of the former Russian Empire.

It happened in 1909 or 1910. Feiga came to Nevel with her family and other Jews to see the Empress. And if they would dare not to come, the regional Sergeant (uriadnik) appeared in all Jewish shtetls.

"And if some bastard doesn't come to greet the tsarina," he said. "Then I will arrange for him a second circumcision." It was his favorite joke in relation to the Jewish subjects of the Russian Empire.

The tsarina appeared before the people in an open carriage with her two daughters. The streets were full of greeters. The brass band played "God Save the Tsar" and other patriotic melodies. Roosters and hens, which usually roamed the streets of the provincial Nevel, sat in barns as if also understanding the greatness of the moment.

The mother and the young princesses wore beautiful wide-brimmed hats and long gloves to their elbows. They smiled sweetly at the provincial audience and waved faintly with their gentle monarchical arms.

Suddenly, the royal carriage stopped right in front of the family of Feiga and Gail.

"What a beautiful Jewess," the queen said affectionately, looking at older sister. And the next carriage with the maids of honor of Her Majesty also stopped. And all the maids of honor chimed in after the queen:

"What a beautiful Jewess!"

"What is your name?" the queen asked.

"Feiga-Leah," Fanya said her full name.

"Feiga-Leah," repeated the first lady of all Russia.

"Feiga-Leah," maids of honor sweetly sang and the royal motorcade moved on. The story about the extraordinary beauty of Feiga, noticed by the Russian tsarina herself, swept through cities and towns and reached the glorious borough of Brooklyn, where the mighty scrap driver Izya Pechuk heard about the overseas beauty and quickly fell in love, sight-unseen.

Recently, Izya decided to end his scrap carriage business, sold all of his bullies, and bought four taxi medallions in the borough of Manhattan. The new business went surprisingly well, and Izya suddenly realized that, since he was already thirty-two years old, it was time to start a family.

He sent Feiga a wonderful gift in the form of a ship's card, which at that time meant a ticket for a transatlantic voyage to America. In those days, the word "ship's-card" was on everyone's tongues in the European Jewish villages. The legendary ship's card meant freedom. At the same time, it was an invitation to America, and a visa, as well as what is now known as a green card. It was not necessary to go to the American embassy in those days, but a doctor's examination was mandatory, confirming that the potential immigrant had no signs of trachoma and sexually transmitted diseases.

Izya Pechuk ship's card for Feiga cost a hefty sum of sixty dollars for a Second-class accommodation. But in the future, as it would turn out, the sixty dollars was the best investment he made in his whole life. After several years Izya and Feiga had three children and owned three dozen yellow New York taxis.

In 1928 they successfully sold their fleet of taxis, and when the Great Depression erupted six months later, they successfully purchased property in Brighton Beach. So recent newlyweds became millionaires. Yasha often heard about this story from his mother, but he never expected that this story would ever touch him personally.

Chapter 4
THE HERITAGE DEPARTMENT

The Heritage Department's Major Sergey Andreevich Yanchuk sat in his office and tried to concentrate. He heavily drank the night before and his head was in a miserable condition. Early in the morning he had been called to the General's office and was given an important top-secret assignment. But what the assignment was, Sergey Andreevich couldn't remember.

That is, he could remember how he got to the General's office, and he remembered that the General's secretary Ludochka was rapidly typing on her typewriter, and that he was consciously trying to breathe in another direction, so that the general would not notice anything wrong.

Volobuy, it seems, paid no attention to the grave condition of the Major, shook his hand at the end of their conversation, and gave him two days to familiarize himself with the new case. The thoughts in Yanchuk's murky brain scattered like drops of mercury from a broken thermometer.

"It seems the general mentioned some Jewish name, either Rabinovich or Khaimovich," the Major mused. But as soon as he came closer to unraveling the name, for some reason a machine-gun burst rattled off in his heavy head, and his meditation had to start over from the beginning.

"Gershovich, Movshovich, Zalmanovich," Yanchuk enumerated all conceivable Jewish surnames, but once again a machine-gun burst, and again all was lost. Suddenly, someone scratched at the faux leather upholstery of his office door. It was the secretary of General, Lyudochka Pyreeva, and the same one who rattled on her typewriter in the morning during a meeting with the General. She was the only one in the headquarters who was able to type with the lightning-fast speed of 150 characters per minute. Only then did the Major realize where those damned machine-gun sound came from. It was the sound of her typewriter from the morning meeting echoing in his already sore head.

"Excuse me, Comrade Major."

"Please, ensign," Yanchuk came to life.

"As of today, it's Junior Lieutenant!" the secretary said proudly and glanced up, placing her right hand against her lush mop of blond hair.

The smell of foreign perfume quickly attacked the Major and distracted him from his unpleasant thoughts. Luda liked him. Each time after returning from a business trip, Yanchuk, an attentive man, brought her foreign perfume or some other thoughtful gift.

They had a promising relationship that Sergey Andreevich did not intend to rush. They liked each other. Sometimes, being alone with Luda while checking the materials printed by her, Yanchuk's hand seemed to be thoughtfully placed inside her skirt, penetrating into the area where the nylon stockings ended and the silk panties began. Lyudmila would not push away his hand, but their relationship did not go beyond these visits to her underwear.

"Here is today's assignment," Luda held out a sheet of paper freshly typed on a typewriter.

"What assignment?" the Major did not understand.

"What, what!?" she mimicked. "About a certain Yasha Abramovich, the heir to an American aunt."

"Abramovich!" he finally remembered the surname.

He realized that during that morning's meeting, Luda had secretly transcribed the conversation with the General on her typewriter. She noticed the deplorable state of the Major and decided to help him. Had the General seen what the brave Luda was typing, she would have been expelled from the ranks of the KGB, or maybe even sent to the criminal military tribunal.

"My Savior!" Sergei Andreevich went into ecstasy. "Savior!"

His right hand extended to Lyudmila's round knees and rushed to the coveted strip between the nylon stockings and secretary's panties, and without stopping, went higher and higher.

"I already submitted the request to the draft board and determined that Yakov Abramovich, 1943, had been called up to the ranks of the Soviet Army two months ago," said Lieutenant Pyreeva calmly.

"Write down what you need to do." Lyudmila abruptly pulled the Major's hand out of her panties and deftly put a fountain pen into it.

"You have to hurry. I don't want the general to see me in your office. Write this down."

"I am writing it down," the Major obeyed.

"First. It is necessary to send a request to the personnel department of the Soviet Army and find out where Private Abramovich is serving."

"First, send a request to the Army," Yanchuk repeated, recording.

"Second, find out..." the secretary hesitated halfway. "What do you have in your pants? And what if anyone comes in? Cover yourself immediately."

Yanchuk unquestioningly carried out her command.

"Second," she repeated. "Find out the size of the inheritance. Contact our New York office if necessary. Third. Ensure the safety of Source Yakov Abramovich."

Cautiously, so as not to stain her lipstick, Luda kissed the Major on the forehead, mischievously patted the bulge in his trousers, and slipped out of the office, trying not to click with her sharp heels.

"What a gal!" the Major thought admiringly, looking at her beautiful body.

Following her instructions, Yanchuk sent an urgent request to the Personnel Department of the Army. The reply came two days later, to the surprise of Yanchuk, it said:

"Private Yakov Lvovich Abramovich, born 1943, a Jew, is not among the personnel of the Soviet Army."

Major Yanchuk and General Volobuy were at a complete loss. The heir to the American aunt, Yasha Abramovich, had disappeared.

Chapter 5
YAN ABRAMOV IS BORN

"**F**lash to the right! Dive down! Crawl now, crawl straight! Crawl faster, shit heads! Get up! Stand at attention! Turn around! Flash to the left! Dive down! Crawl now, crawl straight! Crawl faster, faster, even faster!"

Dirt clogged in his mouth, nose, ears, and eyes.

"When will Ensign Dubina come?" thought Yasha. "He promised."

Yasha and other prisoners crawled around the courtyard of the garrison prison, following the commands of Ensign Brytov. A year ago, upon his arrival, Brytov made a great innovative suggestion. Previously the prisoners were only forced to endlessly march the prison grounds on foot, from side to side. Brytov upgraded the punishment system. Now guilty soldiers had to crawl. After an hour of hugging the dirty ground, the prisoners looked like dirty coal miners. Brytov's innovation was called the coal mine, and more often, the Crematorium.

"Flash to the left! Dive down! Crawl faster, faster, even faster, shit heads!" yelled Brytov.

The Flash command meant a nuclear explosion. Upon this command, the soldier was supposed to immediately dive to the ground. Whoever failed to do so fast enough risked earning an extra five days in the so-called crematorium?

"Crawl faster, faster, even faster, shit heads!"

Ahead was a huge puddle with colorful oily streaks. To Yasha, it seemed as wide as the Dnieper River. He paused.

"When will Ensign Dubina finally come?" Yasha thought with great sadness, looking towards the front entrance gate of the military base.

"Crawl faster, faster," rumbled Brytov. "Crawl through the puddle, straight, shit heads!"

"How about you crawl in it yourself?" Yasha thought to himself angrily. "I forgot my swim fins at home" was about to drop off his tongue.

This phrase would have evoked laughter from the soldiers and earned him an additional five days in the crematorium from Brytov. The day was saved by the arrival of Ensign Dubina, who appeared on the horizon. Noticing his colleague, Brytov ordered: "Get up! At ease! Break it up!"

He did not usually like uninvited visitors, however, Dubina was an exception. It was at Dubina's discretion for whether Brytov would be able to take his leave in the cold winter or the warm summer. Of course, everybody loved summer vacations.

"He's finally here," Yasha rejoiced.

He knew that Dubina had come to rescue him from the crematorium. The life trajectories of Warrant Officer Dubina and Private Abramovich intersected just one day prior, and it immediately became clear that they were very necessary to one another.

Dubina was in command of the military bus which took Yasha and other perpetrators to the military hospital and afterward to the location of their five-day detention. The cunning Ensign did not appear in vain before the draft board on behalf of the four arrested. To hang around these kinds of perpetrators was undignified for him.

Dubina held an important position as a clerk in the human resources department, he was in charge of scheduling leaves for the officers and was also in charge of an important supply department. He could send anyone else to retrieve Yasha. But in this case, Dubina decided to go himself. Looking over the report of Major Pregarok, he noticed the name of Yasha. His instincts told him that this particular person, with a Jewish surname, would be able to help him with his shirt question.

Yasha Abramovich had no idea about his role in Dubina's plans. That morning, at the Military Registration and Enlistment Office, Yasha and his friends were being showered with mockery. Their sins came to light, and the conscripts amicably teased and pushed them around. And soon, even though Yasha's other friends were all ethnic Russians, the Jewish nickname "Abramoviches" was applied to all of them.

Most of the new recruits looked homeless. They were wearing ragged clothes that looked like they came out of a dumpster. Some were wearing house slippers, and one even wore shabby rubber galoshes. By morning the recruits were starving and looking forward to a march to the garrison, where they were promised hot food.

For the "Abramoviches" the already bad situation was even worse. The conscripts were pleased to discuss how the "Abramoviches" would be hazed in the garrison prison for the next five days. This feeling of joy had partly drowned out the feeling of hunger and uplifted their moods. Finally, the accompanying Sergeant barked:

"At At-t-t-attention! Turn all head-d-ds to the R-r-right!"

"Com-m-rade Major, conscripts of the district at your disposal!"

Major Pregarok examined the ranks of poor guys and proudly announced, "Comrades conscripts, I congratulate you on the beginning of your military service!"

"Hurrah! Hurray!" the accompanying Sergeant thundered.

"Hurrah, hurray." the hungry conscripts weakly repeated.

"It has been brought to my attention that not everyone has conducted themselves responsibly," the Major continued. "We've got us some lowlifes who have demonstrated improper and immoral behavior. Private Abramovich!"

"Present!"

"Two steps forward! For immoral behavior, you are sentenced for five days in garrison prison, with compulsory treatment!"

With considerable pleasure, the Major announced that the three remaining "Abramoviches" would also be sentenced to five days punishment and afterward retired to his office. The command of the cadets then passed to the accompanying Sergeant, who did not hesitate to march the hungry conscripts straight to the garrison where they were eagerly expecting to get a hot meal. Once there, Dubina quickly signed the necessary papers, spoke with Pregarok, and put the four perpetrators on the army bus.

Despite his surname, Dubina, which meant cudgel in Russian, he was known as a fashionista. Many of the officers' wives would often secretly glance at him. While the rest of the ensigns cut each other's hair by putting clay bowls on their heads and cutting the hair that stuck out, Dubina would go to the city hairdresser, which cost him as much as thirty kopecks. While the other officers smeared their boots with pork lard for shine, Dubina did not skimp on the real shoe polish. He always wore a neatly folded handkerchief behind his bootleg.

Recently Dubina drove a Major from the Moscow General Staff to the rail station. Like all Moscow's staffers, the Moscovite was a dandy, according to Dubina's opinion. Dubina noticed that the Major's uniform shirt was shining in the sunlight as if it was made out of metal.

"Maybe he smears it with a special solution?" Dubina thought to himself, and asked, "Comrade Major, what can I do to make the cotton of my shirt shine like yours?"

"This is not cotton, Ensign," the Major grinned. "This is a new fabric, by name of nylon. It never wrinkles and 20 years from now, when communism becomes reality, our happy people will forget all about cotton and silk, because everything will be replaced with nylon."

"Did you get your nylon shirt for free at the General Staff warehouse?"

"No way! I bought it myself for twenty-two rubles and fifty kopecks at the specialty military shop Voyentorg. They were almost was sold out, I managed to get the last one!"

"Twenty-two, fifty," Dubina repeated and realized that despite the fiercely high price, owning a nylon shirt had become his life's goal.

After receiving his monthly payment, the Ensign hurried to the Voyentorg store to buy the nylon shirts only to be laughed at. Scarce nylon shirts were reserved only for those with the rank of Colonel and above.

"He is my key to getting those nylon shirts." Dubina dreamt back on the bus while looking at the prisoner Abramovich.

At the drafting office, Dubina fiercely shouted at the perpetrators, but as soon as they left, he immediately turned into a diplomat and graciously pulled Yasha aside. He took out a handkerchief from behind his bootleg, wiped his nose, and began a polite conversation.

"What is your name?"

"Abramovich!"

"I'm Dubina."

Yasha clenched his teeth tightly so as not to burst out laughing. Dubina, meaning cudgel in Russian, was also a term for a dimwitted person.

"Have you heard about nylon?"

"About nylon?"

"Well, this type of fabric is brand new, it never creases!" Dubina said with a sense of superiority.

"In 20 years, under communism, everyone will forget about cotton and silk, everything will be made of nylon. Even stockings!" he added and fell silent. He must have dreamt of communism with nylon stockings.

"You need nylon stockings?" a surprised Yasha asked.

"You are a nylon stocking! I need a nylon shirt. Do you know how to obtain a nylon shirt?"

"Of course, I'm from the dynasty!"

"What you mean, what dynasty?"

"Well, there are dynasties of kings but in our country, there are dynasties of great workers, metallurgists, or farmers. We, the Abramoviches, are a dynasty of procurers. We can obtain anything. As you know, in our country always is a shortage of something. Today there's a shortage of ladies' shoes, tomorrow of toothbrushes, and toothpaste. Therefore, we are very important, since everybody could use our help! To obtain a nylon shirt or blast furnace is not a problem for us, comrade Ensign!"

At that moment, the bus passed the rest of the new conscripts, who were marching gloomily towards the garrison. It rained, and the hungry conscripts were soaking wet. The accompanying Sergeant tried to rekindle the patriotic song, but no one paid attention to him. Suddenly, the entire column noticed the Abramoviches riding in a dry and comfortable bus.

"Look, f-ck them!" the column gasped at once. This short exclamation meant the following collective displeasure. "Here we are, the rule-abiding soldiers, soaked to our underwear, treading dirt, while those f-cking perpetrators are riding on the bus and laughing at us. Where is the justice?"

"Tomorrow you will eat dirt from Brytov," said Dubina, looking at the dull column.

"Which Brytov?"

"Head of The Crematorium."

"Cre-ma-torium!?"

"You will see." Dubina grinned mysteriously. "But tomorrow I will come and get you from him."

And now, having come to the crematorium for Yasha, Dubina kept his word. After a short haggle, he took Yasha, having promised to change Brytov's vacation from cold March to warm July.

The dynastic procurer Yasha did not let Dubina down either. He called his uncle Sema, who worked as a procurement officer at the Pravda Newspaper Publishing House. Uncle Sema called Galina Petrovna at Soyuzpechat Printing, who called Fatima at Aeroflot Airlines, whose husband, Ravil, worked in the Ministry of Defense.

Two hours later, two uniform nylon shirts, size 41, were awaiting Warrant Officer Dubina in the pickup booth of the specialty military shop Voyentorg. And it only cost Uncle Sema a pair of ballet tickets and a medical thermometer. Taking the nylon shirts, Dubina noticed a small piece of paper pinned to one of them, it read: "Reserved for General Zhivok."

Dubina made friends with Yasha. They often spoke together. Yasha even told Dubina of his dream to play young Lenin. Dubina had no doubt that a man who could get him nylon shirts intended for General Zhivok himself was able to do anything he wanted, including playing the role of a young Lenin.

Yasha also shared with Dubina his thoughts of Yan Abramov, his future stage name. Now it became Dubina's turn to amaze Yasha, and a week later, just before leaving for his place of permanent service, Yasha was summoned to see Dubina. The Ensign chuckled and asked,

"Why wait until you play young Lenin? I'll make you Yan Abramov now."

"What do you mean?"

"Have a look at what I mean!" Dubina said and handed Yasha a new military identification booklet.

Opening it, Yasha saw his photograph along with his new name, "Yan Lvovich Abramov".

So Yasha Abramovich disappeared. In his place appeared Yan Abramov, the soon to be famous actor. It took God six days to create Man. Ensign Dubina was able to accomplish that feat in twenty minutes.

Chapter 6

THE TOILET OF GOVERNMENTAL IMPORTANCE

The next day, General Volobuy called together an urgent meeting. Present were Major Yanchuk, Junior Lieutenant Pyreeva, and the General Volobuy himself. The topic of discussion at the meeting was the mysterious disappearance of the heir to the American aunt's millions, Yasha Abramovich.

"People don't just disappear like that in our country," Volobuy began. "At least not now, after the 20th Communist Party Congress, which has forever restored Leninist norms of justice. The task ahead is difficult, it will not be easy to search for one man among millions. November holidays, which will celebrate the anniversary of the Bolshevik Revolution, are approaching. This holiday will be celebrated by all Soviet as well as other progressive people worldwide. Of course, there will be celebrations in honor of the Communist Party and the Soviet people, in honor of the Leninist Central Committee. Alcohol will flow like water, but we, the Chekists, must work tirelessly nevertheless. Remember, according to the orders of our leadership, I must report to comrade Alexander Nikolayevich Shelepin within seven days on the search progress of this private Rabinovich."

"Abramovich!" prompted the Junior lieutenant Pyreeva.

"Well, yes! In the case of failure, we can all be demoted in rank. And maybe be brought to justice, as you know, Alexander Nikolayevich does not like to lose millions which are so necessary for the national economy and the construction of the great projects of Communism."

Needless to say, the gathered subordinates of Iron Shurik, formally known as Alexander Nikolayevich Shelepin, the head of the

KGB, were afraid. Sometimes after a meeting with him, generals again became colonels, and Majors turned back into lieutenants.

"So how much time do we have left at this point?" asked Yanchuk, who did not want to turn back into a lieutenant.

"The investigation officially commenced a day ago, therefore we have five days and eleven hours remaining at our disposal," the general said, glancing at his watch. "Does anyone have any proposals?"

"Perhaps we just send a new request to the Military Personnel Department, it's possible there was just some sort of mix-up," Yanchuk suggested.

"What do you think, Junior Lieutenant Pyreeva?"

"I think that repeated requests we will not get us far. There is not enough time left, as you said, Comrade General, only five days and change. We must go there in person, interrogate the personnel from the Military Registration and Enlistment Office. Also, we must look into all the murders in that area over the past three weeks, and identify corpses if necessary."

The general looked at Pyreeva with approval.

"What a gal!" thought Major Yanchuk. "Joan of Arc, Mata Hari."

"Furthermore, we must begin surveillance of Yasha Abramovich's apartment," continued Pyreeva. "It's possible that he simply went AWOL. On the bright side, we already have a very experienced agent close to that location, his codename is Badger. He is the Militia Lieutenant responsible for the city district in which Abramovich resides. He is familiar with the people in that district, the inhabitants affectionately refer to him as Uncle Misha. He will help organize around-the-clock surveillance and coordinate inspection of the mail as well."

"So, what should I do now?" asked Yanchuk, looking not so much at the general as at the junior lieutenant. She was prepared for his question.

"Depart in under two hours. Despite the holidays, I managed to reserve you a ticket. You will receive money and travel authorization from the accounting department. Write down or memorize the passphrase for initiating communication with agent Badger,

AKA Uncle Misha. Question: 'Where can I buy some codfish for my cat?' Answer: 'The codfish ran out, there's only flounder left.'"

The general looked at his watch again.

"Only five days and ten and a half hours remain before we must report back to Comrade Shelepin. Act quickly, Major. Congratulations on the Great October Revolution. The Junior Lieutenant will be in touch with you throughout. If you need anything, contact me anytime, day or night. Do not waste time. Agent Badger / Uncle Misha will meet you at the airport," Pyreeva finished. "In order not to attract attention, the meeting will take place in the public restroom. The second stall on the right. Do not forget the password."

Upon his arrival at the airport, Yanchuk headed straight to the public bathroom, which was on the second floor. This restroom was considered one of the best in the city, perhaps even in the entire country. Each booth was equipped with a payphone and even toilet paper.

At that time modern toilet paper did not yet exist in the Soviet Union. Instead, people would use daily newspapers. Neatly cut pieces of "Pionerskaya Pravda" (Boyscout's Truth) were located in special boxes. "The Boyscout's Truth" was considered the softest toilet paper and graced only the best public restrooms in the country.

The music of famous Soviet composers was constantly playing, and the fancy toilets and urinals were imported from the Czech Republic. Nikita Sergeyevich Khrushchev, who once visited this restroom, although it is not known for what exact purpose, noted that 20 years in the future, all public restrooms would be like this one. Guests of the city were customarily brought here. The bathroom attendants were old Bolshevik revolutionaries, two of whom have personally met Lenin.

Most visitors to the city, of course, had no idea that this public restroom was under constant KGB surveillance. The toilet stalls and urinals were wiretapped, and hidden surveillance cameras were built into the payphones. The old Bolshevik bathroom attendants were veteran KGB agents.

As per Pryeeva's instructions, the Major carefully approached the second stall on the right and lightly knocked on the door. The cabin was locked, so Badger was likely in waiting in a combat position inside.

Yanchuk leaned against the door and whispered distinctly, "Where can I buy some codfish for my cat?"

But instead of the expected answer, he heard an inarticulate and rather impudent sound coming from behind the stall door.

He repeated a little louder, "Where can I buy some codfish for my cat!?"

The impudent answer also resounded louder. At that moment, one of the old restroom attendants, who had once seen Lenin, came up and said,

"The codfish ran out, there's only flounder left."

"So, you are Badger?" an amazed Yanchuk asked.

"Badger left to take care of an emergency, he left a note."

She held out a small folded piece of paper upon which Uncle Misha scribbled "I was urgently called for at the flour distribution center located at High School number 218 on Rubinstein Street. Br."

"B-R?" the Major repeated thoughtfully. "Badger!" he finally realized. "What kind of flour?" he asked the old Bolshevik. "And why at the high school?"

The old Bolshevik, who was a KGB agent codenamed Rhapsody, seemed to be anticipating this question. She was wearing a double-breasted men's jacket with the Order of the Badge of Honor pinned to the lapel. She seemed excited for a chance to relive her old Communist Party exploits.

"The Party deeply cares about the needs of the people. For the upcoming holidays, the Party allocated two kilos of flour per family. However, the train failed to arrive on time, and flour was delivered late, only arriving the day before. During the past holidays, many undesirable incidents occurred during the distribution of flour, so this year, the entire detachment of the Militia was called to supervise, including Senior Lieutenant comrade Badger. Furthermore, I received a message from Headquarters, in light of the situation with Agent Badger, you should head to the Enlistment

Office immediately and report to General Volobuy about the results of your investigation. I have been instructed to take you there."

Five minutes later, they were sitting in the cramped cabin of a small truck. Cakes and pastries were painted on the side of the van for camouflage, and the inscription read "Confectionery".

"So, is it true, you have actually met Lenin?" the Major asked respectfully.

"Several times," said Rhapsody proudly. "Major, I'll tell you a story I rarely tell anyone."

Her chest was agitated, for some reason, her hand lingered on Sergei Andreevich's thigh. Her old Marxist heart was not indifferent towards the handsome Major.

"I was then sixteen years old. We were four sisters; we came to Moscow from the Kursk region to help the revolution. We were poor, and we four sisters, excuse me, we only had one pair of underwear. We took turns, whoever needed them. The party entrusted me with the cleaning of the apartment of Comrade Lenin. I told my sister Nyusha, 'Give me underpants for today, I must clean the apartment of Comrade Lenin.' And she, who later died from the Spanish flu, said to me, 'I have a date with a revolutionary sailor today, I will give you the underpants tomorrow.'

"Well, when I came to the Kremlin, security guards searched me and discovered the absence of underpants. They called Comrade Stalin, and he said to them, 'It's okay, let her come to me later, after she is finished with Comrade Lenin.' Well, when I came to Vladimir Ilyich's apartment, I was bending over occasionally, in order to remove every speck of dust from the leader's floor. Suddenly I felt that great man put a hand up my dress and start to touch me, and it became so pleasant to me as if the whole world proletarian revolution had been victorious. And suddenly I hear his kind voice, 'Why is it that you do not have any underpants, young lady?' Well, I explained to Ilyich that we four sisters only have one pair. And he became so gloomy, and then he said, 'The bourgeois bastards left the whole world without underwear. But now, with us, every cleaning lady will have new panties.' And so now, when I buy underpants, I always remember our leader," agent Rhapsody finished.

With such a remarkable conversation, they quietly drove over to the Draft Office. It was already four in the afternoon. The door to the Draft Office was open. The Major left Rhapsody in the truck and entered the building by himself. The front desk guard was nowhere to be seen.

Vigilance was not there, but the odor of alcohol was. Without waiting for the rest of progressive mankind, Major Pregarok and his subordinates celebrated the October Revolution anniversary ahead of schedule. The celebration took place in the Lenin Room, amongst other places. Drunken staff scattered throughout the many rooms. Next to Lenin's bust was a plate with unfinished herring surrounded by onions and sardines in a tomato sauce and sloppy sliced salami. Empty bottles of vodka were scattered everywhere.

After a brief search, Major Yanchuk discovered a completely drunk Major Pregarok in the utility closet. He was sitting on an overturned bucket while kissing a radio operator from the communications platoon, who was sitting on another bucket. The radio operator was wearing the Major's tunic, and Pregarok had her bra hanging around his neck.

Having wiped his hands on the bra, Pregarok took Yanchuk's documents and attempted to sober up, to no avail. According to existing guidelines, a KGB Major was of equal authority to an Army Colonel or even a General.

"If the KGB Major reports me to his superiors, I am done for" Pregarok realized.

In his confusion, the Military Commissar took his tunic off the radio operator, revealing her large tits. The half-naked radio operator and empty vodka bottles in the room were a clear sign of immoral behavior, which could easily result in demotion and possibly relocation to a distant duty station. His fate was entirely in the hands of Yanchuk. Out of fear, Pregarok came up with an idea.

"Vika, please extend some hospitality to our guest from Moscow," he asked the radio operator.

Vika already liked the prominent metropolitan visitor, in the perfectly tailored suit. With womanly instinct, she realized that it was necessary to save the boss and save herself well as.

The radio operator came up to the guest and slowly ran her hand over his pants. Yanchuk, exhausted by the flight and the stories of Agent Rhapsody, did not seem to mind much. Vicki's hand stopped at his fly; the buttons were being unfastened one by one. What emerged delighted the radio operator. She knelt down to get a closer look.

Pregarok grinned and carefully left the closet. Ten minutes later, the pacified Yanchuk was sitting in his office. Pregarok had removed the bra from his neck, brushed his hair, and looked quite presentable.

"I propose a toast to the anniversary of October Revolution," he suggested.

"A wonderful holiday," Yanchuk confirmed.

They clinked glasses and drank.

"Now then, you recently had a new conscript come through here by name of Abramovich, do you happen to remember him?"

"Abramovich, Abramovich, no, I can't say that I do."

Suddenly the phone rang. "This is for you," said the Commissar respectfully. "It's General Volobuy."

The Major asked Pregarok to wait outside and picked up the phone. "The old man is worried," the Major thought.

"Well, how is Pregarok?" a drunk voice inquired.

"The son of a gun partied since morning. Doesn't remember a thing."

"Yes, it's hard for us Chekists. Everyone parties and gets drunk, yet we must still work tirelessly! The party obligates us so. And the great Lenin taught us this way!"

"That's right, Comrade General," said Yanchuk, as he stood at attention and fastened his fly buttons.

Chapter 7
FINNISH EGGS

The interrogation of Major Pregarok revealed next to nothing. For over an hour, Major Yanchuk attempted to get at him from different angles, all without any success. The half-drunk military commissar would not directly answer questions, instead, he kept bringing up unrelated nonsense and redirected the conversation to the "Spartak" national soccer team, then to Jawaharlal Nehru, the Indian Prime Minister, then to the new method of planting corn, which was endorsed by Premier Khrushchev.

Yanchuk had little doubt that the military commissar was concealing something, but he couldn't determine what it was. By the time he concluded his interrogation and left the Military Registration and Enlistment Office, it was already six o'clock in the afternoon. It was already dark outside when suddenly thousands of loudspeakers around the city activated.

"This is a voice of Moscow! All radio stations of the Soviet Union are on! A ceremonial meeting dedicated to the anniversary of the Great October Revolution is broadcasted directly from the capital!"

The announcer of the radio transmission was the famous Yury Levitan, whose deep voice was beloved by all Soviet people. The speaker started to list attendees of the aforementioned meeting in his powerful voice.

When the announcer called out the name of the faithful Leninist, his boss Comrade Shelepin, the Major involuntarily glanced at his watch. 4 days and 19 hours remained until the head of the KGB expected to hear the results of their operation.

Yanchuk felt uneasy. The success of the operation hung by a thread. He had no doubt that in the event of failure, the cunning

General Volobuy would likely lay all blame on him. He would be demoted and reassigned to some cold remote outpost in Siberia. He looked enviously at carefree passers-by. Most of them firmly hugged their two kilograms packages of flour, which were being rationed out for the holiday. Alcohol bottles were clinking in their bags like xylophones. A festive dinner table awaited them at home, Russian salad, pork, herring with onions, and local vodka.

"Comrade Major, why don't you give me your phone number?"

The Major turned around. It was the little radio operator who had serviced him an hour ago in the closet of the military enlistment office. She was gazing at Yanchuk's face. The little radio operator's romantic encounters included warrant officers, junior and senior lieutenants, but he was her first ever KGB Major, and from the capital, no less.

Her little heart was gushing with love. In her imagination, she had already moved to Moscow with the Major. The Major would go on dangerous spy missions to capitalist countries and return with stunning clothes for her. The famous director of the national movie studio, Pyryev, will see her on Red Square wearing these clothes and will invite her to appear in his films, where she will impress everyone and steal the main role. Or maybe Yanchuk will even take her abroad to spy with him.

Moreover, she is a first-class radio operator with the quickest proficiency of her entire radio platoon. For this unusual speed, she was nicknamed Lerka, the sewing machine. Despite her busyness, she will give her husband love sessions that will make him forget about all other women in the world. Can cold Muscovite women or strange foreigners compare to her? She remembers how Ensign Sereda once remarked, having slept with her: "Well, in general, Lerka, you are simply the best. You're moving your ass as fast as a sewing machine."

Having heard her request, Yanchuk pointed to the loudspeaker and said:

"Don't interrupt, can't you hear, Comrade Shelepin is speaking?"

"After comrade Shelepin concludes?"

"After comrade Shelepin concludes, then we can talk."

Suddenly the first snow began to fall. Flurries of snowflakes spun merrily in the air, creating a festive mood. The little radio operator, who was staring at her wonderful Major, stumbled on the slippery ground, and to her pleasure, the Major quickly grabbed Lerka by her slim waist. She pressed her entire body against his, taking advantage of the moment to check with her hand whether the Major was ready for a second round of love. She saw that he wasn't, and Lerka became slightly upset. Together they went to the Confectionery van.

The undercover van was still parked where Yanchuk left it two hours ago. The fallen snow refreshed the pretty cakes painted on the walls of the van, and they glistened with their sweetness. To the Major's surprise, a long line queued up at the back of the van. Other people crowded around the driver's side, mostly senior citizens. He wanted to get closer, but a hefty disabled pensioner on two crutches blocked his path.

"What are they handing out?" squealed the little radio operator.

"They haven't started." the invalid answered.

"And what will they be handing out?"

"Don't know, there's nobody there."

"Why are you waiting then?"

"Why don't you mind your business?"

"I got word from the Society of Veterans," the one-legged man confidentially leaned toward Yanchuk, "Apparently, there are chicken eggs from Finland in the van! Ten thousand Finnish eggs, enough for everyone!'

"Finnish eggs!" the radio operator repeated dreamily.

"Have you served in the military?" asked the invalid person.

"I served." Sergey Andreevich answered.

"Then you'll help me. Give me your hand."

He pulled out a greasy pencil, grabbed Yanchuk's hand, wrote 82 on it, and asked, "Are you two together?"

"Together, together!" The little radio operator squealed joyfully.

"Then you only get one number."

"I have to find a payphone," Yanchuk asked. "I will be right back."

"Go, number 82, but hurry up, they will start selling the eggs soon."

Radio operator Lerka was certain that the Major had come up with his phone booth idea to be alone with her. She loved intimate moments in phone booths. But when they arrived, the Major entered alone, asking her to wait outside. According to the protocols, he covered the dial with his hand and punched in a secret number. Two minutes later he was on the line with General Volobuy.

"You're late, Major. Its 18:00, According to the plan, by now you should already be at Khaimovich's apartment!" The General said with displeasure.

"Abramovich, Comrade General."

"Well, yes..."

"There are seniors, and they aren't letting the van leave, Comrade General, they are waiting for eggs from Finland."

"Wasn't everybody already given a couple of kilos of flour for the holiday?"

"They were, but now they want eggs to go with their flour."

"Yes, the needs of the Soviet people are growing" the General wisely concluded. "So, what are we to do?"

"We will send Soviet militiamen" Yanchuk suggested. "A pair of sergeants will be enough to disperse those old folks."

"On the eve of the Great October Revolution, this would be a very politically improper thing to do." said the General.

"Regardless, the Militia people are all busy supervising the flour distribution," Junior Lieutenant Pyreeva picked up the phone. "We need you to try something else. Talk to those folks, pretend you're going to get something out of the van, get inside and just leave, understand?"

"Understood."

"What a woman!" the Major thought admiringly. "Mata Hari! Amelia Earhart! Edith Piaf!"

At this moment, far away from her, in a snowy telephone booth, did he realize the strength of his feelings? How lovely it would be to have her here with him now.

A mighty internal wave rose to its highest peak and demanded an immediate release. He looked back at the radio operator. She faithfully waited for him outside, and she was dying a bit of jealousy, curious about the woman the Major was speaking with.

Sergey Andreevich opened the door of the cabin. Radio operator Lerka understood. The act of love in a telephone booth was her specialty. Before the Major had time to close the door, she already working under his coat. "Unzipping the fly is much easier than unzipping a bra," the Major thought philosophically.

"...In the apartment of Abramovich, introduce yourself as a correspondent for the military newspaper Red Banner," continued Pyreeva, "tell them that you are writing an article about cadet Yasha Abramovich. Check out the family photos. Talk to those people. Are we clear? Major, why aren't you responding? Major, you are breathing heavily, are you feeling ill?"

"No," breathed Yanchuk. "Not-at!" He could not speak.

"Make sure that Private Abramovich is not on the run and is not laying low at his apartment. Try to get an article of clothing in case we need to use the hound dogs. Clear?"

"Perform this task, and before going to bed, take an anti-inflammatory," the General picked up the phone, "Chekists have no time to get sick."

At this time, the little radio operator fluttered out from under his coat. The Major finally regained his ability to speak.

"That's right, Comrade General, they haven't!" He confirmed and hung up respectfully.

Lerka deftly fastened his pants and stared through the glass of the booth, as if nothing had happened. "The long-jump is over," Yanchuk, who was once a paratrooper, thought approvingly, "the girl is great." When they returned to the Confectionery van, the line had doubled in size.

"Number 82!" Cried the invalid. "You called home? Everything alright?"

"All good. They are waiting for the Finnish eggs."

"They'll soon have them. Tell me, what did you do in the service?

"I was in the airborne."

"Come on, paratrooper, keep a watch on the driver so the van won't leave."

"Why watch? I'll drive it myself!"

"Good idea! Let this paratrooper inside of the van!" The old-timers approved. Under happy exclamations from the retirees, Yanchuk opened the door. The engine was running, the cab was warm and cozy. To his surprise, Agent Rhapsody slept, curled up on the seat, with her double-breasted jacket under her head as a pillow. She snored calmly in her sleep, unaware of the Finnish eggs and the long line behind them. Gently nudging Rhapsody, the Major got behind the wheel. The chairman of the line looked up into the cab.

"What's going on in there, number 82?

"I'm going to spin the truck around," said number 82 with concern, "to make it easier to sell the eggs."

"Well done, paratrooper, it seems like you really care about this." Approved the chairman. Line activists rushed to take the bricks out from under the wheels. The van slowly sailed forward. Once the distance grew to twenty meters, the activists realized that they've been had. Finnish eggs swam away from them forever. The chairman of the line threw his crutch out of anger. It glanced off a cake painted on a van and fell harmlessly.

Out of everybody, of course, the radio operator Lerka, nick-named "sewing machine," was the most upset. With the van, float-ed away from her dream of a Major, of beautiful spy life, and a meeting with the famous movie director Ivan Pyryev...

The song "The International" started playing from the loud-speakers, which traditionally signified the end of the solemn meet-ing in distant Moscow. Some listeners would try to distinguish the voice of Nikita Khrushchev among the general choir, but it seems that he was always cunning: he was lip-synching as usual. Upon hearing "The International", Rhapsody roused right away.

"A true Bolshevik," the Major thought warmly. "Dozed for hours, but woke up immediately to the sounds of the party anthem." He stopped the van to switch seats with her.

"Well, how was Major Pregarok?" asked Rhapsody, getting be-hind the wheel.

"He doesn't remember a thing."

"A 12-volt battery would help his recollections"

"How's that?"

"Most effective when applied to genitals, he will sing like a bird."

"You know, such methods have not been authorized much lately."

"Yes, we are losing our best traditions," Rhapsody sighed. "I re-member how in 1930 they sent me off to find gold ..."

"...To Siberia?"

"Siberia? All the gold was here in the hands of the capitalists, but they did not want to give it up. I went to comrade Surov, the head of the department, he was later executed by the revolutionary court. I told him 'I got an idea, I need 12-volt batteries.' He said: 'We have no batteries, we gave them all to the scientists.' I then went to Epikhin in Moscow, the head of the department, he was also exe-cuted later by the revolutionary court. Again no. I finally wrote to Comrade Stalin, saying that I have an idea. Comrade Stalin sent me three brand new 12-volt batteries. I took money enough to build a power plant with those batteries. All those damned capitalists kept quiet until you apply the battery to genitals, after that they talk like parrots. Then they shared the results of my experiment with the management."

The car stopped. "Do you have a weapon with you?" asked Rhapsody.

"I do."

"Be careful. We're here. I need to go to another operation. Someone else will come to get you."

Yasha Abramovich's apartment was on the second floor. It was an old communal apartment in which eight families lived. The Major found the name of Abramovich on a long list under the doorbell. There were five long rings to call the Abramovich family. For a long while, no one answered. Suddenly the lock turned, and a disheveled woman appeared at the door dressed in a nightgown.

"I'm here to see the Abramoviches, I'm from the newspaper," introduced Yanchuk.

"Wrong address."

"Yet another mystery, such rubbish," thought Yanchuk.

He glanced at his watch. The meeting with Comrade Shelepin was only 4 days and 16 hours away.

Chapter 8
OPERATION A.S.S.

8hours 40 minutes. Warrant Officer Dubina arrived at his small office, located at the headquarters of the anti-aircraft artillery brigade.

8 hours 42 minutes. Dubina began initial observation of the subject. In order to do this, he bent over and peeped through the keyhole. It had an unobstructed view of the office of brigade commander Colonel Grom. His door was supposed to open at exactly 9:00 AM.

8 hours 52 minutes. Only 8 minutes remain until the Action of Sergeant Sarnov or, as it was abbreviated in the brigade, A.S.S. All 12 divisions of the brigade anxiously await the results. All other worries and concerns become irrelevant.

8 hours 53 minutes. Someone knocked on the door. Dubina looked through the keyhole but couldn't see anything besides the soldier's badge. He opened the door. On his threshold stood Private Abramov, a former stove-maker who, per Dubina's orders, was repairing the statue of Lenin located at the entrance to the building.
This particular monument suffered from some unexplainable and incurable disease, similar to leprosy. One day a hand fell off, then the visor of his famous cap disappeared. Once the leader lost his nose. A team of soldiers searched for several hours, but the nose was nowhere to be found. To make matters worse, a Colonel had arrived from Moscow to conduct an inspection. The noseless Lenin would be a dark mark on the reputation of Colonel Grom. The

inspector could easily reprimand Grom for the weak brigade morale and delay his promotion.

Ensign Dubina saved the day. He remembered that since the end of the cult of personality of Stalin, an old monument to the former leader was sitting in storage at the warehouse. The rest was a matter of technology. Former stove-maker Abramov conducted a successful nose transplant from one leader to another. Stalin's nose was much larger than Lenin's, so Abramov resized it with a file. The inspector did not notice anything amiss. Since then, Dubina's duties included the daily inspection of the capricious monument and the transplantation of stone organs from the leader to the leader, as necessary. Private Abramov put a mitten to his cap and reported,

"Comrade Warrant Officer, the replacement of Lenin's parts has been completed successfully!"

"Everything is in place?"

"Everything."

"Nice and tight? Did you make sure?"

"I did. Nice and tight!"

"Now look, Abramov, if something were to fall off, you'll lose the same part as well. Dismissed!"

"Comrade Warrant Officer, I have a request," the private hesitated.

"Tell me quickly," Dubina glanced at the round electric clock, which showed five to nine.

"Would it be possible to change a couple of letters in my last name?" the private reached inside of his shirt for a piece of ham, wrapped in a white rag, and dropped it out onto the table.

"What have you done?"

"Before I got drafted in the army, two truckloads of bricks accidentally disappeared."

"And now, they accidentally want to give you three years in prison?"

"Five, they already questioned my mother."

"This ham better be good. Go on, I'll think about it."

"The Abramovs get the best ham, enjoy!" the former stove-maker said proudly and left.

8 hours 59 minutes. There were loud steps as two people appeared in the corridor. They stomped past the Dubina's observation point and headed for the commander's door. One of them had an impressive behind. The Ensign knew that the large-caliber rear belonged to Colonel Grom, and another much smaller one, to the Sergeant Sarnov, adjutant of the colonel.

9 hours 00 minutes. The colonel's large-caliber backside stopped in place and the adjutant approached the office door. The Dubina moved closer to the keyhole. The brigade's entire day depended on how well the Sergeant will conduct the door opening. If successful, one could ask the Colonel for any favor. In case of failure, it would wise to stay clear of him for the rest of the day.

9 hours 00 minutes 30 seconds. The right hand of Sergeant Sarnov made a sharp fencing motion forward. In his hand was not a sword, but an ordinary door key. The insertion was inaccurate, and the key did not enter the keyhole on the first try. Worse, it dropped out of Sarnov's hand and loudly landed on the painted cement floor. The Sergeant immediately picked it up, but it was too late, Grom's mood was hopelessly ruined. The superstitious Grom loved it when Sarnov got it right the first time and effortlessly opened the door for him.

9 hours 02 minutes. Dubina began phoning the divisions. He said only three words: A.S.S. has failed. These code words were enough to let everyone know that today, life in the division would be miserable. No one would dare call to the commander over the phone or appear before him in person.

9 hours 05 minutes. Suddenly, a black Volga sedan appeared in front of the headquarters. It drove past the two stop signs without stopping and parked next to the compact Moskvich which belonged to Grom, who was watching everything from his office window.

"Only the Commander of the Army could breeze through two stop signs like that without slowing down," thought Grom, and realized that the base security did not notify him about this visit. "Bastards! I'll have them thrown in the brig for ten days!"

Without wasting a minute, he ran out of his office to greet the Commander, as his adjutant Sarnov ran behind him with a blue notebook in his hands.

"All checkpoint soldiers will be sent to military prison for ten days!" Colonel dictated on the run. "For carelessness, for lack of vigilance! Actually, fifteen days! Make that fifteen! Make a note in your blue notebook! Report back when my orders are executed!"

9 hours 06 minutes. Out of breath, Grom ran up to the black Volga and prepared for the solemn meeting with the Commander of the Army. The car door swung open and out of it, to the Colonel's great indignation, appeared not the General, but the chubby Senior Lieutenant Nikitin. A typical not well put together person. The right shoulder lower than the left, the uniform jacket sticking out like a peasant woman's apron, ready to gather chicken eggs in it, the belt buckle has slid to the side.

"Good morning, Comrade Colonel!"

They could sense that the whole headquarters' personnel detachment was glued to the windows, looking at him and bending over with laughter. Even the loyal Sarnov behind him could hardly restrain himself so as not to burst out laughing. Grom looked furiously at Nikitin.

In his raw fury, he became aware of all his failures recently. The fact that he had not attained the rank of general yet, that he drove a little Moskvich, not a black Volga sedan, and that he wasn't even permitted to purchase a coveted nylon uniform shirt from Voyentorg yesterday, which other colonels and generals flaunted.

"So, how did you manage to get the Volga?" He asked sullenly.

"My mother-in-law bought it, Comrade Colonel."

"Who is she? Famous actress? Artist?"

"She sells flowers."

"So, illicit income? Swap with mine."

"You want my mother-in-law?"

"Mother-in-law? No stupid! The Volga for my Moskvich!"

"I don't think that mother-in-law would like that."

"So you want to do this the hard way, eh?" the colonel was indignant. "Okay, we'll see what happens."

9 hours 09 minutes. An enraged Grom burst into Dubina's office. "Give me the personal file of Senior Lieutenant Nikitin!" He shouted. "Urgently! I'll show this asshole, how to drive a Volga."

Suddenly, the Colonel's became filled with rage again. He stared with hatred at Dubina, or rather, at his nylon shirt, exactly the kind that the Colonel unsuccessfully attempted to buy the day before at the Voyentorg military store.

"Ensign, where did you get the nylon shirt?" he asked suspiciously. "Even General Zhivok couldn't get one at Voyentorg yesterday."

The cunning Dubina hesitated before deciding on his answer. He decided to blame everything on Yasha Abramovich.

"There was one Jewish soldier, Yasha Abramovich or rather Yan Abramov, he said that he could obtain anything. And I didn't know that this shirt was rare anyway."

"Can he get me a Volga" the Colonel asked.

"Sure, he can even get a blast furnace, he said. He comes from a family of procurers with great connections."

"And where is this Yasha now?"

"The day before yesterday he was sent off to a duty station in Kazakhstan, he was only here for five days."

Grom recalled the prediction of his wife, who loved to read tarot cards. Six months ago, the cards foretold that the Jack of Crosses would come and would help him finally become a General and even get the long-awaited black Volga. However, she did not warn him that the Jack of Crosses would be a person of Jewish origin.

"Ok, Dubina, get ready for a business trip. Bring me back this magician Yasha."

"Okay, but wouldn't it arouse suspicion if a soldier were to just disappear."

"No problem, just bring someone else to replace him with. You know how it goes."

20 hours 35 minutes. In the reserved seating car of an express train sat Warrant Officer Dubina and former stove-maker Abramov. Private Abramov is perplexedly inspecting his new identity documents, made by Dubina. The Russian man Yan Abramov has disappeared and a Jew Yasha Abramovich reappeared in his place.

"So, now I'm a Jew?" whined stove-maker. "I can't even speak their language."

"Yes, but now the authorities won't be able to catch you. You can start stealing building materials again. Or do you want them to find you and put you in jail?"

No, I guess I'd rather be a Jew" the former stove-maker finally agreed.

Now there were two teams were simultaneously hunting for unsuspecting Yasha: one led by the General Volobuy, and the second led by the ensign Dubina.

Chapter 9
THE DOOMED RAILWAY CARRIAGE

For the third day in a row, Yasha was rattling around in the crowded railway wagon that was bringing him and other recruits to their place of service in faraway Kazakhstan. There were 52 cabins, and because there were three times as many recruits, they had to sleep in shifts, right on the bare wood shelves, with stuffed duffel bags under their heads for pillows.

Yasha was an exception. The accompanying sergeant, whom Dubina had instructed to take care of him, gave Yasha a cozy upper-level bunk to himself. From up there, Yasha watched the mass of soldiers with pleasure.

A boring everyday soldier's life did not quash his desire to become an actor and play young Lenin.

He even suggested to the accompanying sergeant that they organize a folk theater themselves, right there in the carriage. The sergeant reasonably replied that there were no provisions for folk theaters in the overcrowded train and suggested that Yasha better shut up. Despite the rejection, Yasha was already picking the actors in his head for his future army theater company.

One of the recruits went by the name of Kirpichev. With his small darting evil eyes, he was clearly suited for the role of a detective in the Tsarist secret police. His friend, nicknamed Dandelion for his cropped round blonde head, "pulled" on an unfinished capitalistic pig or revolutionary sailor. It seemed to Yasha that at night someone had been pumping air into Dandelion's head since it was becoming bigger and bigger.

Thinking about the future performance, Yasha began to write down the assignment of the roles. To better take on the role, he squatted down, like Lenin in exile, while preparing the October Revolution, and carefully wrote in his notebook. His efforts did not go unnoticed.

"Why is he squatting and staring at us?" Dandelion was surprised.

"Maybe he wants his nose broken, or maybe he needs to use the bathroom," logically suggested the tipsy Kirpichev, who had been nicknamed Brick on the train.

Despite the strictest ban on alcohol, most recruits managed to regularly get drunk like it their last day on Earth. Maybe they had a premonition of their fate? After all, there's no way they could know that they were being taken to Kazakhstan, to the site of the underground nuclear testing experiments. The soldiers were going to be the guinea pigs.

Like everything else in the army, this operation had a code name. This one was called EXPIC, for Explosion Impact Check. EXPIC Soldiers were forced to march through the aftermath of nuclear explosions to determine the effect of radiation on the human body. Afterward they were "decontaminated". That is, they were sent to the steam room for a couple of hours. According to Soviet military science, a steam room with a birch broom was the best way to clean up nuclear pollution. Something about this theory did not converge, and about a quarter of EXPIC soldiers experienced radiation sickness.

Dandelion kept his vodka, which he traded for pig lard, in an enameled porcelain mug, covered by a piece of bread. He thoughtfully took off the bread, took a sip and, looking at Yasha, said:

"He has a big nose, it looks fragile. He seems to be Jewish."

"I heard that they cut off their things."

"They are the fools!"

"If somebody were to try to cut mine off, I would break that person's head."

"Look, he's staring at me again!"

Dandelion covered his mug of vodka with a piece of bread and went to Yasha's shelf.

"What are you writing?"

"I am assigning the roles for our army theater," Yasha rejoiced at the attention.

"A theater without women?" asked a surprised Dandelion.

Yasha thought for a moment. Really. He did not consider any female participants for his future theater. And why should he need women?"

"He's trimmed his stick to nothing!" a drunk Brick reached for Yasha's fly. "Well, let's see what is left of your dick."

"Here he is, a typical agent of the Tsarist secret police," Yasha thought with hatred. "Rat's eyes, a brick face, a damned racist!"

Suddenly, personified the image of Lenin and felt a fire flare up inside him from a spark. A flame of hatred filled him up to his fingertips, and a fist, forming a shape of a sickle in the air, thrashed like a hammer into the offender's chin.

In this punch was all the hatred from the proletarian towards the Tsarist secret police and the damned capitalists who exploit workers. The force of the hit turned out to be enough for the Brick to fly up to the second shelf like a bird.

"You're right, comrade director," the startled Dandelion said respectfully to Yasha.

"So, what did you want to know?" asked Yasha.

"I already got it, comrade director."

"What is going on here?" the accompanying sergeant appeared at the noise.

"Rehearsal, Comrade Sergeant," said Dandelion, "rehearsal."

"What is Kirpichev doing?"

"He's resting."

"You need to rehearse quietly, please. Otherwise, you won't make it there alive."

After this episode, the entire population of the doomed train was unanimously enrolled in the future army theater under the leadership of Director Yan Abramov.

Chapter 10

THE VIGILANT APARTMENT

"**W**hat a dumbass!" thought Yanchuk. The redhead slammed the door and shouted: "Wrong address" before disappearing without saying anything else.

The Major began to examine the list of tenants under the buzzer button, wondering who else he could call and ask about Abramovich. Suddenly, the door swung open again, and another occupant of the apartment appeared before Yanchuk.

The lady spoke with a very deep masculine voice, "What did that bitch tell you?"

The owner of the deep voice had strong-willed pleats at her mouth, disheveled wet hair and a terry dressing gown that tightly encircled her strong body.

"I was in the bathroom, suddenly I hear four and a half rings. Well, I thought was someone here to see me about the room exchange. I am trying to exchange my room with somebody from another apartment. Are you looking to exchange your room with me?"

"No, no, thank you. I want to see Abramoviches"

"You see, comrade, we have eight rooms in our communal apartment. And each room has a special ring. Mine is four long and one short ring. Five long rings to Abramoviches, but people always get confused. I just threw on my gown, I didn't even have time to put on my underpants, I'm sorry. I heard this bitch has already slammed the door. What did she say?"

"That I'm at the wrong place."

"She's lying, of course, they live here. The thing is, Galina works on her noisy sewing machine and can't hear the buzzer. So she punishes an elderly woman for not opening the door. Bitch!"

"If I'm a bitch, then you're a spy!" the redhead appeared in the hallway.

"Spy, why?"

"You keep spying on me in the bathroom."

"I do not, I'm simply carrying out my duties as the designated apartment supervisor."

"I can't even wash my ass, without a supervisor spying on me!

"And if you just wash yourself, no one would say anything. But you are not doing what you're supposed to."

"We share a common bathroom, comrade," she explained to Yanchuk. "Everybody who uses the bathroom has to pay the fee."

She pointed to the bathroom price sheet attached to the wall:

Head: 20 kopecks.
All body: 30 kopecks.
Men Legs: 15 kopecks.
Women legs: 10 kopecks.

"But some try to cheat, they will wash their head, which costs 20 kopecks, but mark it down as legs, for only 10 kopecks."

"Maybe others have more hair on their legs than I do on my head," the bald tenant stuck his head out the door of his room. "So I have to pay more? This is unfair, and I do not agree!"

"And if I catch your bald head stealing any more of my meat cutlets from the fridge, I'll call the Militia!" The redhead promised the bald man.

"It was an accident, it was dark..."

"You can tell that to the judge!"

Obviously, on the eve of the revolutionary holiday, the squabble in the communal apartment was about to be particularly hot. But then someone shouted:

"Raikin is on TV!"

Raikin was a favorite comedian of Soviet people. The magic words worked, and the residents rushed to the television. Only two people remained in the hallway, Yanchuk, and the supervisor. She turned and knocked on the door to the Abramoviches, and without waiting for permission, entered their room.

Galina Solomonovna was sitting between the Saratov refrigerator and the Znamya TV, where she was still working at her sewing machine without noticing the people who had entered. Unexpectedly for Yanchuk, the supervisor plopped down in a chair and, reaching under a silk orange lampshade, deftly unscrewed the light bulb. Her dressing gown opened slightly and Yanchuk involuntarily noticed that her words about the absence of underpants were pure truth.

"Galina Solomonovna," the supervisor rumbled, poking at the light bulb, "you are permitted a 75-watt bulb, but instead you twisted-in a hundred watts. This is a gross violation of the rules and is wastefulness of apartment electricity."

Hearing the formidable supervisor, Galina Solomonovna regretfully stopped sewing and turned to her visitors.

"Pardon me, Zoya Ivanovna! The old light bulb burned out, and I did not notice the wattage of the new one."

"We will see, in the meanwhile, I allow it to be lit until tomorrow. And here, by the way, the comrade has come to see you."

"I'm from the newspaper," introduced Yanchuk.

"From the newspaper? Nobody warned me." Zoya Ivanovna muttered and slipped out of the room.

"From the newspaper?" Galina Solomonovna rejoiced. "My son Simon is also a journalist, very talented, do you know him?"

"No, I don't. I have been instructed to write about your other son."

"This is probably about Mikhail; he is a medical professor. Or maybe about my oldest, Zakhar? He is a famous inventor, has about a hundred patents."

"I'm from a military newspaper," Yanchuk said sternly. "I have been assigned to write about Private Yakov Abramovich."

"About Yashenka? He wanted to be an economist and supplier, then an artist, but he had to postpone it..."

"I would like, dear mother, to get a look inside his internal world, in order to help me write a better article. Where are his personal belongings, may I have look?"

"Here, in this wardrobe..."

"Galina Solomonovna come here for a minute!" the apartment supervisor appeared in the doorway.

Sergei Andreevich, taking advantage of the temporary absence of the hostess, quickly opened the closet and pulled out one of Yasha's shirts. He clearly remembered Pyryeeva's instructions to get a personal item for the hound dogs.

By then, the whole apartment had gathered in the hallway. The recent quarrel had long been forgotten. Now they again were friends and accomplices in a common cause. Everyone listened to the supervisor's speech:

"I immediately saw that he was a con artist, a specialist of picking pockets. His eyes were wandering around with one mission: what to steal? He said that he is a correspondent, what kind of correspondent have you seen without a tie or jacket or special identification? And the housing management did not notify me. And I'm not the last person in the apartment! Galina Solomonovna, what did he tell you?"

"He wants to write about Yasha. He asked about where he can see some of his personal belongings?"

"So, he's got his eyes on some clothing?"

The bald neighbor clung to the keyhole and reported to the audience, "Exactly, I see the bastard searching the closet and stealing Yasha's shirts."

"Misha! Perhaps he could use a tap from your baseball bat, or maybe from this?" the redhead handed bald Misha her heavy rolling pin.

"Definitely!" Misha approved. "Now we will train him to write better, the damned crook!"

Misha carefully opened the door, crept up behind the Major, and banged him over the head with the rolling pin.

The next day, the Major did not contact headquarters. Only three days remained before the meeting with the chairman of the KGB, Comrade Shelepin. Operation Heir was in jeopardy and Junior Lieutenant Pyreeva immediately flew out to the scene.

Chapter 11
THE DOUBLE OF YASHA ABRAMOVICH

Former stove-maker Abramov, who by the will of Ensign Dubina turned into a double of Yasha Abramovich, was severely displeased. The new Jewish documents issued to him by the Ensign were burning in his pocket.

"Of course," the stove-maker mused, "the new last name, Abramovich, will confuse the law enforcement looking for me for the theft of those trucks with bricks, but what will my friends say?" The brave Ural Cossack Yakov Ivanovich Abramov went to serve in the army, and instead of him, some Jew Yasha Abramovich came back.

Dubina, on the contrary, was in a good mood. He flirted with the neighbors in their carriage, traveled to the restaurant car, and read newspapers.

"Did you see the Pravda newspaper?" he asked. "Meetings are held in each of the military units. The soldiers are eager to help the peace-loving Cuban people fight against American aggressors. Do you want to go?"

"It's way too hot Cuba, I heard, too hot to breathe."

"Too hot to breathe. But they give one paycheck here, another for over there, and a third—in dollars—direct to your savings account."

"So in a year I'll be able to get a motorcycle?" the stove-maker dreamed.

"A motorcycle? You'll have enough for a real car."

"And if I get hurt?"

"Then they immediately give you enough money to buy the motorcycle and the car. Do you want to go to Cuba? Submit an application."

"Will they even let me go? I'm Jewish now."

"No, you are wrong! We are all equal!" Unexpectedly, the Ensign became a defender of the Jews and almost a Zionist.

"Do you know about Karl Marx?"

"Russian?"

"Russian? Jew! And Jesus Christ?"

"Russian?"

"Are you serious? Jew of course."

"Then why did they crucify him?"

"Not them, but the Romans who occupied them, just like the Germans when they occupied us during the war. Are you from the Sverdlovsk region?"

"Yes sir!"

"Yakov Mikhailovich Sverdlov, for your information, is also a person of Jewish nationality. Who is, by the way, your namesake? So, you Jews are a very necessary people for helping create socialism. You can feel proud."

"Yes sir, per your order I am proud!"

Deep in Dubina's heart, he felt sorry for the guy he had assigned such an unsuitable nationality to. But it couldn't be changed, so he protected not so much the Jews, as he did himself and Colonel Grom.

"Now listen, Private Abramovich! Tomorrow you will proceed with the mission. We will arrive at the 451ˢᵗ Kilometer Station, where you will blend in with a group of recruits and begin your service. Do not reveal your real name. Your life depends on you following this order."

"Yes, I will follow the order!" answered the stove maker.

Having finished his impressive speech, Dubina went to converse with the neighbors in the carriage, while the shocked stovemaker took a ballpoint pen from his pocket, asked the conductor for a piece of paper and began to write something thoughtfully. An hour later, when his painstaking work was complete, he handed the sheet to the Ensign.

"What's this?" Dubina was surprised.

"My request to the military command. Please send me as a volunteer. I want to help the peace-loving Israeli people in their struggle for freedom!

"Well, brother, you've gone too far," Dubina grimaced and tore the paper into small pieces.

Chapter 12
THE JUMP INTO ABYSS

"Private Abramovich, 451st Kilometer Station is approaching, come on!"

"Yes, Comrade Ensign!"

"As I already said, we need to perform a very important assignment. Perhaps life-threatening.

Follow my commands without asking stupid questions!"

"Yes, sir! Without stupid questions!"

Dubina picked up his little brown suitcase, fastened his overcoat, and stepped out into the vestibule of the car. The train passed a railroad marker with the number 448 but did not begin to slow down. Without waiting for the 451st kilometer marker, the Ensign opened the heavy car door. Frosty November air burst noisily into the car.

The former stove-maker barely had time to grab the cap off his head and tuck it under the left shoulder strap of his greatcoat. The 449th kilometer marker passed by, but the train did not even think about slowing down. Feeling that something was wrong, Dubina rushed to the car attendant. She was sleeping and loudly snoring. However, she stopped snoring, opened one eye and informed the anxious soldier,

"The train does not stop here anymore!"

"And where is the next stop going to be?"

"At the 521st kilometer marker."

Dubina returned to the vestibule with bad news, "Private Abramovich! The train will not be stopping at 451st Kilometer Station, and the next station is another 70 kilometers away. We will have to jump off the train, like paratroopers, but without a parachute."

"That sounds very dangerous, we might break our heads!"

"Not at all, you just have to know what you are doing! Haven't you ever hopped off the city tram?"

"No, we did not have even buses in my village. We had to walk ten kilometers to the nearest railroad station."

"I've been jumping from the moving tram daily in my hometown of Leningrad. So, the tram is like a train, only a little bit slower. You just push yourself with all your strength, jump out, and your legs will know what to do."

"And what if they don't?" the poor handyman continued to doubt. He was thinking, that maybe he would be better off in jail, then becoming fricking Jew, and now risking his head by jumping from a train at full speed.

"I told you to follow my commands without asking stupid questions, ok?"

"Yes, Sir, ok!" the stove-maker turned pale but had nowhere to retreat to.

A rather small station with the sign '451st Kilometer' flew by. There were many trains on the siding. In one of them was the real

Yasha Abramovich, the goal of the secret mission of Ensign Dubina. However, this was no time to procrastinate. Dubina threw his briefcase out. Flashing with nickel-plated corners, it rolled downhill. The stove-maker was next, but he cowardly hesitated.

"Jump, comrade paratrooper!" ordered Dubina.

The private held onto the carriage handle even tighter.

"Jump, false Abramovich!" Dubina was losing patience. The discarded suitcase disappeared into the distance. The operation failed.

"Jump, you f-cking Jew" cried Dubina. From surprise, the hands of the false Abramovich unclenched and he flew into the abyss, with the Ensign after him.

Chapter 13

YASHA AND MOONSHINE

The daily mail was brought from the central carriage. One letter was for the accompanying Sergeant Khrolov from his native village of Alushkovo, of the Pskov region. He usually received letters from his mother, but this time it was someone else's handwriting.

The Sergeant opened the envelope with mistrust. Inside was a small election campaign flyer with the inscription "Vote for the candidate of the indestructible bloc of Communists and non-party people, milkmaid Yermykhina."

The flyer depicted the milkmaid Yermykhina herself, an elderly woman in a white apron with two Orders of the Red Banner of Labor on her large chest. The Sergeant turned the paper over and found the slanting lines on the back. Obviously, due to a lack of writing paper, the author used the back of the flyer to write the letter.

"Hello, dear Lesha!" read the lines. "Your aunt Varvara Simonovna Khrolova is writing. You, I heard, you have already gone far in the service and gained the rank of Sergeant. Congratulations. I can only imagine how many important people you know by now, Captains, and even Majors.

Help me, dear Lesha! Do you remember, I had a little shed outside of the village, in which I sometimes brewed wine if people asked for it. And now this hornless serpent, Serega Lastochkin, a district Militiaman, I hate his guts, tracked me down and opened a criminal case against me. Now they want to put me behind bars for a long time. I went to his wife Lyubka. I brought her a chicken and a dozen eggs as a gift and asked, 'Love, help me, since your dad and I are close relatives' and she says to me, 'It is good that we are relatives, but if you can get me some tiles for my slate roof, then my husband would forgive you.' All the huts in the village have straw roofs, and the Militia officer, you see, needs a slated tile roof. I myself had never seen these slated roofs in my life.

They say that some rich people have them in the district center in the city of Pustoshka. Do you remember when you were little, how I always brought you sweets, when I visited? So please help your old aunt and save me from prison."

"Dear Aunt," mused the Sergeant. "How many times did daddy tell you to stop running your moonshine? That it would be better if you raised pigs or goats."

But she knew how to protect her little business. If some Militia man ever appeared in her secret hut for an investigation, Varya would pull down his pants and it would no longer be a criminal case. The whole village would gossip about it. But now, apparently, the aunt got old and these types of favors wouldn't work anymore.

"Dear Aunt Varya, how do you expect me to get fricking roof slates in the army?" thought the Sergeant as he looked around. His eyes stopped on the inhabitant of the third shelf, Private Abramov, who had been writing something in his notebook. The Sergeant recalled now, that before they left, Ensign Dubina invited him into his office. A soldier was sitting there. Dubina pointed to his uniform shirt and boastfully remarked,

"See this fabric?"

"I see it, Comrade Ensign."

"You don't see a damn thing, it's nylon. Feel it!"

Lesha touched without interest. The material was slippery and naughty.

"This is the new material, nylon. It is intended only for generals and astronauts."

"How did you get it?" Lesha was surprised.

"Thanks to him, Private Abramovich. Sorry, Private Abramov," Dubina nodded to the soldier. "He can even get you a blast furnace if you needed one. Take care of him, don't let anyone bother him."

For Lesha, a blast furnace was useless at the moment, but he treated the new recruit well and even assigned him the most desirable top third shelf compartment at his full disposal. True, when this Abramov began to mumble about some theater, Alex quickly cut him off. But now came a moment where the soldier could really be of help.

"Private Abramov, come here!" he commanded.

"Private Abramov has arrived at your order!" Yasha deftly descended from his Olympus and stood at attention before the Sergeant.

"Come with me to the central carriage, we need to pick up dry rations."

"Yes, Sir!"

To accompany the Sergeant to the central carriage was an honor. You could walk along the neighboring cars, meet friends, and hear the news. It was a kind of freedom and entertainment.

"How's it going with your theater?" asked the Sergeant kindly, although just recently, he did not approve of it.

"All the roles are assigned, now I'm writing a director's script!"

"That's nice. Do you know anything about slate roofs?" the Sergeant asked suddenly.

"Do you need it to be straight or wavy?" Yasha was not confused with the sudden question.

"Not me, it's for my aunt, she needs the accordion-type."

"So, wavy. Will she need special nails and special slates for the corners?"

"How do we make this happen?"

"Very simple. I will give her an address, she will go there. They will help her."

"Thanks, you saved my aunt. And very cool you knocked Kirpichev down the other day, even though he is a foot taller than you are."

"I thought you didn't see that..."

"Sergeant Khrolov sees everything, and as for your art, you may rehearse as much as you like. If anything goes wrong, come to me, I will help."

"Comrade Sergeant, can we get some fresh air, I am tired of this stale carriage."

"Why not?" the Sergeant said as he opened the car door with a special key, and they strode along the railroad sleepers to the central carriage. It was getting dark and the air was permeated with the wondrous smell of an autumn forest.

"Look, comrade Sergeant, there are soldiers below, looks like they get lost?" Yasha pointed at two soldiers who were washing themselves in a stream. Their overcoats lay nearby.

"Got lost? They are AWOL! They ran away from the train! They are probably looking for vodka. Now they will find out who Sergeant Khrolov is, and why he has a black belt in Karate."

Sergeant Khrolov quietly, so as not to frighten the absconders, went down the slope, crept behind, then deftly grabbed one and sharply twisted his hand. The perpetrator cried out and fell on the grass. The Sergeant was amazed to recognize that it was his friend and boss, Ensign Dubina.

Chapter 14

THE MISTAKE OF COLONEL GROM

"**I** will break his ass!" Colonel Grom sat at the kitchen table and ate fried eggs. It was early morning. In front of him was the personal file of Senior Lieutenant Nikitin.

"Don't get nervous, Vasek," his wife said. "So what if he bought a black Volga?"

"His mother-in-law got it for him! She is speculating with flowers. That is illegal!"

"Nikita Khrushchev promised to imprison all speculators."

"It's about time. Look at what's going on, lieutenants drive Volgas, and I, a military colonel and war veteran, and I am driving a little Moskvich. This is not fair."

"Be patient, Vasek! General Secretary Krushchev is still busy with exposing Cult of Personality of Stalin, but soon he will take on all speculators."

"I will kick this officer out of the Armed Forces, along with his Volga! By the way, do you remember, Nadia, didn't they cards say that a black Volga was coming for me?" suddenly recalled the Colonel.

"Correct, dear."

"And yet, this SOB is driving a Volga, and I am not!"

"And you will. Cards don't lie, Vasek!" Nadezhda took out a deck of cards, which she always kept with her and laid them out on the empty side of the kitchen table.

"You've predicted a rank of the General in the cards as well."

"Yes, Vasek! The Jack of Crosses had appeared for you. Newspapers lie, but the cards don't."

"Which newspapers are lying?" choked the Colonel. "What are you muttering, old woman?"

Nadezhda frantically gathered her cards into a deck and turned pale from her criminal utterance. "American newspapers lie, Vasek, American, our Soviet newspapers never lie!" She finally found the right words.

"Yes, yes," agreed the Colonel, "American newspapers are real liars! I've never read one, but Khrushchev said that they only lie, lie, and lie."

There was another twenty minutes before the beginning of the workday. The Colonel was sitting at the table almost ready to go. He was wearing a cap and military jacket, underpants, and footcloths. All that was left was to put on pants, his boots, and he was ready to command his brigade.

"Be patient Vasek, the Jack of Crosses will appear. What is his name? Abramovich? The Volga and the general's uniform will come."

"You are superstitious, Nadia. What is the connection between the rank of general and some Jewish boy?"

"Vasek, Vasek," Nadezhda suddenly burst into tears. "You never believe me!"

"Calm down," the Colonel grimaced. "I already sent Ensign Dubina to get your Jack of Crosses, and both of them got lost."

"You will find them! And your dreams will come true!"

Once again, the scoundrel Nikitin appeared in his black Volga. The Colonel looked out of the window with anger. "He ran the stop sign, and another one without stopping! He will kill somebody one day. Terrible driver. I'll give him two weeks in garrison jail!"

The black Volga stopped in front of the headquarters. After a pause, instead of the chubby Senior Lieutenant, the Army Commander himself stepped out.

"Bastards! They did not warn me again. I will show them hell!"

The Colonel shook with rage as he tightened his footcloths, thrust his feet into his boots, and rushed to the exit, forgetting about the last piece of his uniform.

The dismayed wife looked after her fleeing husband and shouted, "Vasek, Vasek, you forgot your trousers!"

But it was too late, Grom had already slammed the door.

Chapter 15
THE SECRET EXCHANGE

Former stove-maker closed his eyes and leaped out of the carriage in horror. Somewhere far below there was a railway slope.

"I'm an idiot," he thought to himself before jumping. "Why did I get involved with this crazy Dubina? I would have been quietly imprisoned for three years, maybe even released earlier for good behavior. With unbroken arms and legs."

The slope of the railway met his body harshly and with all its might hit his side. Then his other side, the blows were no longer counted and the private rolled downhill like a log. At the beginning of the fall, he still dreamed of a quiet prison, where he would have spent calmly three years, but his thoughts soon subsided. Then there was silence. "This is how people get themselves killed," was the last thought that occurred to him.

"Get up!" a voice came from above.

Stove maker opened his eyes, but instead of the Apostle Peter with the keys, he saw Ensign Dubina with a suitcase.

"Well, how was your landing?" asked Dubina.

"I seem to have broken my left arm... and my leg," the cowardly Private said uncertainly.

"Let's see," Dubina suddenly grabbed his 'broken' arm and pulled him up. "Well, it has healed, now march forward with your broken leg," Dubina commanded.

They went on the top of the slope and moved along the railway sleepers. It was getting dark. At the 451st Kilometer Station, there were several military detachments. In one of them, under the auspices of Sergeant Khrolov, was Yasha Abramovich.

"How am I going to find him?" thought the Ensign.

Only now did he realize the difficulty of his task. I have to buy some time, evaluate the situation, and in the meanwhile, get ourselves in order.

"Broken leg, stop! One, two! Let's commence with the water activities!" he said in the voice of a radio announcer.

A small river flowed below. Dubina threw off his greatcoat and began to splash in the water with pleasure. The private followed his lead. He was very glad that the ominous water activities turned out to be a simple wash of their hands and face.

Suddenly, someone crept up behind, grabbed Dubina by the shoulder, wrung his arm, and threw him to the ground. The Ensign turned his head and was surprised to recognize Sergeant Khrolov, commander of Yasha Abramovich.

"Comrade Warrant Officer!?" in turn, Khrolov was surprised too, letting go of his iron grip. "What are you doing here?"

Dubina did not answer immediately. He could not admit that he came for Yasha.

"A special assignment from the Ministry of Defense and the Academy of Sciences," he said with aplomb. "To study the survival of the human organism during conditions of land combat while surrounded by the enemy. We have already spent several days in a dense forest, conducting a scientific experiment."

"And I thought you were just some AWOL guys. They also said that someone had recently escaped from a local prison." Khrolov was embarrassed to have interfered with the important government experiment.

"Also, not everyone can endure the conditions of this experiment. Private Abramov, or rather, Abramovich, my assistant, could not stand it and asked for a substitute... Yes, it is not easy for us experimental people. According to the assignment, one can only eat nettles and tree bark, as well as drink rainwater from puddles, these are the harsh conditions of a government experiment"

"Great!" admired Khrolov. "And how do you stay in contact with command?"

"Through this suitcase," Dubina said for some reason in a whisper. "Satellite communications. The latest technology."

"Here, private, look, satellite communications in a suitcase!" the sergeant called Yasha, who accompanied him and respectfully stood nearby.

"I wish you good health, Comrade Ensign!" Yasha said, recognizing Dubina.

"A miracle of technology," Khrolov admired. "But how long before the batteries run out?"

"A long time," Dubina answered evasively. "By the way, I am permitted to replace my unsuccessful assistant with a private of my choice. Do you know of a suitable candidate?"

"Take anyone, everyone is tired. Just make sure you coordinate with the authorities to eliminate problems."

Khrolov sent the participants of the government experiment into his carriage and went himself with Yasha for deserts and dry rations to the distribution center. As always, before dinner, there was a little excitement. In the boring world of the carriage, the victory of the frail intellectual Yasha over the well-built Brick remained the main sensation. Taking advantage of the absence of Yasha, the round-headed Dandelion, for the umpteenth time, retold what happened.

"Brick, you see, had approached our director, and asked to show what he had in his pants. He tried to pull down his pants. Well, the Yasha, the artist, although much smaller than Brick, became furious, like a bull seeing red. He landed a strong blow to Brick's head and Brick flew up to the upper rack like a bird."

"Jews are generally weak, but sometimes they are very strong," commented one soldier, who was on guard duty that day. "For example, famous Grigori Novak, he lay down in the circus arena and cars drive over him like over asphalt and he is fine. Or Leonid Germain, the two-time European wrestling champion."

"And why does he have the name German if he is a Jew?" someone asked.

"Do you want his name to be a Jew? Deftly parried the guard. Everyone laughed.

Sergeant Khrolov and Yasha returned to the car with a box of dry rations for soldiers and a can of jelly. The Ensign went to Yasha and said something quietly to him. Yasha nodded his head and began hastily pack his duffel bag. The inhabitants of the carriage, busy with food, did not pay any attention. Warrant Officer Dubina led Yasha to Sergeant Khrolov and presented in a new capacity.

"Private Abramov expressed his interest to take part in the Ministry of Defense and the Academy of Sciences experiment."

"Okay, take the artist," the sergeant agreed. "Do the bosses care?"

"No problem," Dubina opened his secret briefcase and a bottle of vodka migrated into the hands of the Sergeant, and then just as quickly under his pillow. The Sergeant did not ask any more questions.

"What experiment were you talking about?" asked Yasha when they got out of the carriage.

"It is a play called The Experiment, which you will be staging." A cunning warrant officer had informed Yasha that he had arrived with an important assignment. Allegedly, the order came from the very top to create a soldier's folk theater. Yasha is to be appointed as the director.

The dreamer Yasha was happy. He was thinking about this future theater, his theater! He did not even ask Dubina why they should eat nettles and why they passed the 451st Kilometer Station, without waiting for the next train. They walked silently for twenty minutes in total darkness. Suddenly, a spotlight illuminated them from above. A helicopter hovered over them.

"Freeze! Put your hands up!" a thunderous command came from the heavens. "Any sudden moves and you are both dead meat!"

Yasha and Warrant Officer Dubina froze in bewilderment.

Chapter 16

DOCTOR ELLA AND VOLODYA PUTIN

SECRET REPORT TO GENERAL VOLOBUY:

An Agent, code name S-25, was delivered to the objective, a communal apartment, at 18 hours 45 minutes military time. At exactly 20 hours 15 minutes, I returned but was unable to locate Agent S-25. The interrogation of residents did not clarify the situation. Agent Badger, known in the district as Uncle Misha, was in a state of inoperability as a result of the holiday festivities and was not able to assist. Agent Rhapsody.

Junior Lieutenant Pyreeva was pissed off. "What kind of agents do we have working for us? He goes to an ordinary communal apartment, inhabited by old people, and disappears! What did they do, shove him in the oven, or flush him down the toilet? No, men cannot be trusted with anything! They have two problems, women and vodka. Only a woman can be a real agent like her, beautiful, athletic, and smart. And besides, these men are up to her neck."

Having read Agent Rhapsody's message, General Volobuy called a meeting. Suddenly, the Secretary of the Heritage Department showed up with his entourage.

"Comrade Shelepin expects answers at the meeting in only two days," the party organizer sternly warned. "If you fail in Abramovich case, the Party will never forgive you!"

Having finished his short but ominous speech, the secretary left. His retinue hurried after him, casting disrespectful glances towards Volobuy and Pyreeva.

"What are we going to do?" Asked Volobuy sadly after the Party operatives left. In his heart, he did not doubt that Pyreeva knew how to save the honor of his Department.

"Comrade General, I urgently need to fly out to the objective. Agent Rhapsody will take me to the Abramovich's apartment, the last place the Major was seen. I guarantee that it would only take me an hour to find our Major."

"Simple and sensible," thought Volobuy. "A wonderful employee of the underground front, although a woman. We must promote her to the next rank."

The general was worried and excited simultaneously. He admired Pyreeva not only as a competent worker, she had large breasts, a magnificent heap of hair, and a tendency to analyze any situation.

The general took off his tunic and hung it on the back of his chair. Then he went behind Pyreeva and rather briskly covered her breasts with his spacious palms. After that, he quickly unfastened the upper buttons of the subordinate's uniform and lowered his hand into the gap between her breasts, filling his palms alternately in turns with the left or right breast of the Junior Lieutenant.

She likes me, he thought, noticing that Ella blushed.

"Here's an old goat," Ella thought. "He sees nothing besides my tits. What kind of General is he?"

"Maybe you can rest a little before hitting the road?" the General nodded towards the secret room, where he occasionally spent the night during long operations. Here he sometimes had sex with female employees of the department.

"Well, I would have to wait half an hour until you get ready," thought Pyreeva, but said out loud with mock regret. "The plane leaves in an hour and a half, I can't be late."

"Yes," the general agreed, "The Party above all! We are indebted to the Party."

Two hours later, having overshadowed all flight attendants with her appearance, the Junior Lieutenant was already sitting in the cabin of the aircraft and thinking over the details of the upcoming operation. Inappropriately, a tipsy neighbor in the next seat started to court her. He introduced himself as the head of the supply department of a textile factory.

After twenty minutes of flight, the half-drunken supply man announced that he was in love with Ella. His meaty hand brazenly went over her blouse and skirt and went into the private space between her open round knees, where Pyreeva allowed only her immediate superiors—General Volobuy and Major Yanchuk.

Outraged, Ella, the karate champ and weight lifter, gently grabbed his impudent hand, made an elusive movement, and he, grimacing from the sharp pain flew into the aisle between the seats, almost knocking a stewardess off her feet.

"The Comrade lost his wallet, he's trying to find it on the floor," Ella explained to her. The humbled and bruised supply man silently returned to the chair, quietly folded his hands in his lap, and showed no signs of life until the end of the flight.

However, upon arrival, the pain in his body had subsided, and his feelings for Pyreeva flared up with renewed vigor. Ella allowed him to follow her up to the Toilet of Government Importance and told him to wait for her, but to his astonishment, she had never come back for him.

At the end of the female half of the restrooms was a door with the inscription "No Trespassing." Ella pressed the code letters "P" and "S", and the door opened. KGB veteran agent Rhapsody was waiting for her in the office. As always, she was wearing a double-breasted men's jacket with a medal on the lapel and a pistol in the inner pocket.

"Someone is obviously trying to disrupt us in this communal apartment," Ella said thoughtfully. "Clearly, the tenants know what happened to the Major, yet they choose to keep quiet."

"They all are counter-revolutionaries," Rhapsody replied, "just shoot one and the others will quickly confess."

"Here is the old revolutionary philosophy! She would be quick to shoot. But today, we have other methods at our disposal," thought Ella.

At the site of the stairs near the ill-fated apartment, they were being awaited by the best help available: Agent Badger (known in the district by the name Uncle Misha) and janitor Uncle Kolya. Uncle Kolya volunteered to accompany Ella to the apartment. Agent Badger and Rhapsody were left to wait for them downstairs. The door to the apartment was answered by a boy of about eleven.

"Volodia," said Uncle Kolya. "I need to speak with the grownups."

"No one is here, they all went to the store, and they are handing out buckwheat, only two kilos per person."

"We will have to return, comrade Pyreeva," the Janitor shrugged.

"Typical men, one little obstacle, and they give up immediately. No brains!" the Junior Lieutenant looked regretfully at the Janitor. "Wait, Nikolai Ivanovich, let's not rush."

She turned to the boy, "Volodia, did the journalist come here the day before yesterday?"

"He did," remembered Volodia. "But he turned out to be a thief. Bald Uncle Misha hit him over the head with a rolling pin!"

"Was he killed!?" Pyreeva was horrified.

"No, they didn't kill him, the driver said that he was in a coma."

"What driver?"

"The ambulance driver. He picked up the thief from the trash dump."

"Why the trash dump?"

"Bald Uncle Misha took the journalist to the dump since he was afraid that they would put him in jail if they found the body in the apartment."

"Volodia, do you remember where the journalist was taken to?"

"I remember, of course. To the Lenin Hospital."

"What good boy you are, Volodia," Ella praised "What is your last name?"

"Putin."

"You are going to be a great man someday, maybe even the KGB Colonel. To the Lenin hospital!" she ordered. Rhapsody's vehicle, disguised as a Confectionery van, drove off in a hurry.

In the Emergency Room of The Lenin Hospital, a patient by the name of Yanchuk was not among those listed. Ella rushed to the head physician and showed her formidable identification. Together they began to search the floors for the missing patient. At last, the

Major's motionless body showed up on a dirty mattress in the corridor next to the morgue. At the dumpsite, someone had stolen his wallet with his money and identification.

"Most likely Bald Uncle Misha." Ella thought. Nobody wanted to bother with the nameless patient, who was in a coma, so they put him closer to the final stop, the morgue. Not far from the Major's bed, the observant Pyreeva noticed a spacious vacant room with a TV and large ZIM refrigerator.

"Transfer the patient to this room!" Ella ordered.

"I am unable," the Head Physician said regretfully. "This is a special chamber, permission from the regional Party Committee is necessary."

"I see," agreed Ella. "Give me your hand, Doctor." She gently took the hand of the Head Physician, then an elusive movement followed and the Doctor, screeching in pain, was on the floor under the Major's bed.

"Do not mind me, Doctor. I have no time," Ella asked affectionately. "Transfer the patient to the special ward, and tomorrow, at ten in the morning, conduct a consultation with the best physicians."

"Thanks for the trust," said the Doctor from under the bed. "We will do our best."

The Head Physician, as one would expect, turned out to be a punctual person. At ten in the morning, he brought a candidate of medical sciences and a medical professor to the council. He even paid for the specialists to travel by taxi. The scientists carefully examined the patient, checked his pulse, squeezed his stomach, and twitched his fingers. The Major would not react to anything.

Afterwards, the Aesculapiuses sat down with Ella and Rhapsody and discussed the situation. Their opinions were divided. The Professor believed that the Major would stay in a coma for another ten years, and the Candidate thought he would remain in the coma for the rest of his life. They agreed on one thing, that modern medicine would be unable to help the sick Major.

"Again, these men," Pyreeva said with frustration. "They can't do anything. Professors, candidates, head physicians. Yes, I'll revive him in twenty minutes. Where traditional medicine is powerless, alternative medicine is omnipotent."

Ella waited for the useless scientists to leave, closed the door, and instructed Rhapsody to wait outside and not let anybody in. After that, she took the comatose Major's hand and placed it on her knee. Lifeless fingers hung in the air. Then, firmly pressing his hand to her hip, she lifted it, higher and higher...

She joyfully noticed that a little movement began to appear in his fingers.

To help the patient, she took off her panties and repeated the ascent of the hand again, then again and again. With each ascent, Major Yanchuk's fingers became firmer and more confident. And finally, the paper sheet covering his lower abdomen began to form a small tent.

This was exactly what the Junior Lieutenant was expecting. Without delay, she resolutely lifted her skirt, tore off the sheet from Yanchuk's loins and, like an experienced jockey, jumped on the reviving Major. Their bodies found each other and merged into one. As a connoisseur of alternative medicine and a traditional healer, Ella either slowed down or accelerated her rhythm until Yanchuk groaned and exploded right into her. After that, he opened his eyes and asked, "Am I in Heaven?"

"Mission accomplished, Operation Heir is saved," pronounced the Junior Lieutenant.

Chapter 17
SAFECRACKER YASHA

Yasha and Warrant Officer Dubina stood on the railway track with their hands raised. A helicopter, like a huge hammer with an iron handle, hung menacingly above them.

"Any sudden moves and you are both dead meat!" the voice from the helicopter warned them. A tight beam from the spotlight beat painfully in their eyes.

"Amazing!" muttered Yasha.

"What is amazing?" Dubina did not understand. "That they will shoot us now?"

"Amazing!" repeated Yasha. "The night. The spotlight. The column of light. Like in a theater. Someday I will stage such a performance. At the stadium."

"When they shoot us that will be a real performance."

"This must be some mistake, they'll see," Yasha said with conviction.

The helicopter slowly began to descend. The searchlight beam continued to bore the Ensign and his subordinate. Suddenly, like an expert sky jumper, the helicopter landed deftly, placing its landing skids on the railway tracks. The helicopter door did not immediately open. Apparently, something was stuck. Finally, the door opened with a loud clang. The pilot and an officer, wearing the uniform of a lieutenant, appeared in the doorway.

"Lieutenant Turkin!" ordered the Pilot. "Proceed to detain the criminals."

"Yes, Sir!" Lieutenant Turkin said uncertainly.

The gun trembled slightly. He peered intently at the criminals who stood with their hands up. The Lieutenant had only recently begun his service after finishing the military academy. This was the first detention of his career.

"You are under arrest!" Turkin announced, stuttering slightly. "Hands up!"

"We have been holding them up for a long time," Yasha said. Silence reigned. The Lieutenant did not know what to say or do next.

"Put them on the ground and search them," the Pilot advised in half-voice.

The lieutenant jumped out of the helicopter, ran to the detainees, and yelled, "Lie down!"

"Right on the rails?" Dubina was surprised. The Lieutenant's eyes filled with blood.

"You want me to make a bed for you?"

He put his gun behind his belt and tried to hit Dubina in the face.

An experienced boxer, Dubina easily ducked his punch. The Lieutenant's hand passed by, he slipped on the wet rail track and awkwardly fell on his back. Yasha and the Ensign watched curiously as he tried to get up.

"Do you need help?" asked Dubina ironically.

The Lieutenant's eyes filled with blood again, he was about to answer when the piercing whistle of a train engine sounded. Yasha looked around. A freight train was coming right at them. Flakes of white smoke, like huge pieces of cotton wool, hung over the steam locomotive. It was less than a minute before a collision would occur. The helicopter pilot was not going to wait for that. The helicopter's propellers spun intensely; the co-pilot rushed to close the door.

"The door is stuck again!" he shouted.

"F-ck it," shouted the Pilot, "we will fly with it open!"

Turkin managed to shove the prisoners inside and jumped in himself at the very last moment. The helicopter twitched and slowly went up. The steam locomotive rushed right under them, almost cutting the belly of the helicopter with the steam pipe.

Yasha, looking into the illuminator, saw the frightened face of the locomotive engineer. The entire helicopter was shrouded in smoke. A loud wind burst into the open doorway. Everyone held

onto the handrails tightly so as not to fly out. Turkin, holding a gun near Yasha's head, decided to begin the interrogation right there in the helicopter.

"Where did the money go?" he cried.

"What money?" a surprised Yasha answered.

"He robbed two banks but doesn't know about the money!?" Turkin's eyes once again turned bloody. "Confess!"

The helicopter swayed. The interrogator lost balance and with cry disappeared into the doorway.

From the newspaper "The District Truth":

Two hardened criminals robbed a savings bank in the village of Murkino, and then in the working-class village of Kluch. They were going to rob a third savings bank in the village of Maramyrochka, but Lieutenant Turkin stood in their way. In carrying out his duty, the fearless lieutenant died, but with his life, he saved our people from two seasoned criminals. The memory of the young Communist and the patriot of the Fatherland will remain forever. At the request of the workers, the village of Murkino will be renamed to the village of Turkino. The community of the district demands to fulfill the last will of the lieutenant-hero and to sentence the criminals guilty of his death to execution.

"You see, the people are demanding your execution."

KGB investigator Parashin, who summoned Yasha for questioning, showed him the article from the regional newspaper. Due to its importance, the case of the bank robberies was transferred from the local Militia to the KGB.

"Execution?" Yasha said dumbfounded.

"If you truthfully admit to your guilt, you may get off with only 25 years in prison," the investigator reassured. The prospect of spending 25 years in prison did not please Yasha.

"This is a mistake; I want to talk to a lawyer!" he demanded.

"No problem, after you confess, we will provide you with a lawyer," the investigator said mockingly.

"We are not guilty of anything!"

"You say so. But your accomplice already confessed to everything!"

"Who is my accomplice?"

"Ensign Dubina. He even told us where you buried the stolen money. Near the house of Colonel Grom. Remember now?"

"I am not guilty of anything," stubbornly repeated Yasha.

"An investigation is scheduled for tomorrow. Near the house of the Colonel. Dubina will show us where you buried the money. You will have to confess to everything."

An investigation was scheduled for six in the morning to avoid the attention of military personnel. Yasha and Ensign Dubina, handcuffed, were taken to the house where Colonel Grom and his wife Nadezhda lived. Then everything happened just as the sharp-witted Ensign planned. Upon seeing the arrested, Nadezhda ran out of her house. As she usually did on early mornings, she was up reading her cards.

"Dubina, my dear, what is going on? Why have they handcuffed you?" She screamed, "Is that Yasha with you, the Jack of Crosses?"

"You may not speak with the detainees," said Captain Parashin sternly.

"Oh, yeah, chicken shit," said Nadezhda. "This is the garrison of my husband, Colonel Grom, and I am the mistress here!"

"These are very dangerous criminals," said the investigator conciliatorily. "They pushed an officer out of a helicopter and robbed several savings banks. Dubina, show me where you buried the stolen money."

"I do not remember! I need time to think," said Dubina.

"Don't fool around with me. I'll bury you myself."

"Where are you going to dig, there's only asphalt here," Dubina reasonably said. The Captain waved his hand. The investigation was over.

"About face! Step march!" He commanded. "I'll show you. Prepare for the tribunal."

The community vocally demanded the execution of the criminals. Investigator Parashin was in a hurry. Dubina and his former subordinate were no longer summoned for interrogations, and the outcome of the case was becoming clearer. Captain Parashin hoped for a big promotion. He even relented and allowed the defendants to be in the same cell. The night before the tribunal, Yasha and his friend could not fall asleep.

"It's a pity if they shoot us," Dubina sighed. "I was going to become a doctor. I thought of treating children." Yasha was going to say something, and suddenly the door opened. Colonel Grom and Captain Parashin entered the cell.

"Good morning, Comrade Colonel!" the prisoners said in one voice. From the smile of the Colonel and the gloomy grimace of the Investigator, they realized that something good had happened.

"You are free," said the Investigator. "An error occurred due to the mistakes of the late Lieutenant Turkin."

"Thank my wife for everything," the Colonel said in a half-voice when the investigator went out. "She sent you some apple pie." He handed the still-warm apple pie into the happy hands of future pediatrician Dubina.

Chapter 18

"DO NOT STICK FINGERS
AND EGGS IN A SALT SHAKER"

(From the rules of public catering)

Once upon a time, Colonel Grom was a cadet at the military academy. He was plump, rosy-cheeked, and very lazy. The cadet Grom had a unique gift, the ability to fall asleep anywhere. He could sleep during marching, in class, or in an open truck. Even during practice parachute jumps, he managed to take a nap during a free fall. So imperceptibly, like in a dream, passed years of Military service.

The Academy, admission to the Communist Party, and the first years of service. He received the rank of Lieutenant, the rank of Senior Lieutenant, but then all promotions stopped. His friends at the school became Captains, some made their way even further.

Then suddenly everything magically changed. Promotions poured on him, he was awarded the rank of Captain and then was appointed to the position of Major. The puffy and sleepy Vasya became the ardent servant, Captain Vasily Grom.

As the French people say, "chercher la femme", and in this case they were right. La femme was an elementary school teacher by name Nadia. One day, Vasya was summoned by the regiment's Chief Political Officer, Major Nechaev.

"It's not good," said the Major. "You have demonstrated immoral behavior!"

"Did he find out that I was playing cards or drinking while on duty?" thought Vasya.

The Chief Political Officer opened the door and said, "Nadezhda Ivanovna, please come in."

Nadezhda Ivanovna happened to be the young teacher Nadia, his former girlfriend. They separated two months ago, he got another girlfriend and completely forgot about Nadia. But she did not. Especially since she found out that she was pregnant. She was crying.

"Is that him?" the political officer asked, menacingly looking at Vasily.

"It's him!" confirmed Nadia.

"He promised to get married?"

"He did!" Tearfully confirmed Nadia.

Vasily wanted to explain that he didn't know about the pregnancy and that he was not sure that he was the one responsible, and that he loved now new girl. But in the eyes of Major, he saw that he was guilty of moral indecency and behavior of unbecoming of a Senior Lieutenant and a member of the Communist Party.

He admitted his defeat and went right away with Nadia to register their marriage. Thus, Major Nechaev, Chief Political Officer, helped to create another healthy Soviet family. Nadia became head of the family right away.

"You have no ambition, you need to become Captain," she said. "We need to move. We'll go to Moscow to my uncle Bolivar, he will help."

"Yes, but I have a vacation just next year," complained Vasya. Without saying a word, the combative Nadia went to Major Nechaev, and he arranged a weeklong vacation to Moscow for family reasons. The stingy Vasya wanted to ride in a Third-Class carriage, but his wife insisted on the First-Class. As soon as they boarded the train, she immediately took him to the dining car and gave him a lesson in proper manners.

Vasya ordered hard-boiled eggs and a cup of sour cream. He peeled an egg and dipped it in an open salt shaker, but his wife-teacher severely wrinkled her eyebrows and pointed to a large poster: "DO NOT DIP FINGERS AND EGGS IN THE SALT SHAKERS".

Vasya was embarrassed. He poured salt in his palm and adapted to dunk a flaky egg there. Having finished his eggs, Vasya went to the buffet and bought himself a mug of a draft beer. A good half of the mug was filled with foam.

"This is not acceptable. Let those crooks add beer after foam settles down," The strict wife demanded, and showed him another poster: "CUSTOMERS, REQUEST FOR TOP OFF AFTER FOAM SETTLES".

Uncle Bolivar lived in Moscow in a government house on Granovsky Street. He received the newlyweds in his kitchen, from which the Tower of Kremlin was visible.

Bolivar had an important position; he was responsible for the correct political behavior of the horses during the military parade on Red Square.

When the Marshal conducts the troop review during a military parade, the enemies of the young Soviet state hoped that the mare under the Marshal would suddenly lift up its tail and put some souvenirs on the sacred cobblestones of Red Square.

Corrupt Western correspondents were ready to spend miles of film on each atom of manure. To prevent this from happening, uncle Bolivar stood guard over the gastrointestinal tract of Marshall's mares. He and the famous Academic Lysenko were personally responsible for mare's intestines before the Communist Party.

Far away in Siberia, Uncle Bolivar built a model of Red Square and trained the horses over there. If a mare pooped in the wrong place, she was mercilessly beaten and not fed for three days. But as soon as the natural process happened in the right place, the horse received a ration of sugar and encouragement in the form of a love affair with a dashing stallion. Horse whisperer Bolivar was accustomed to talking with horses, so he was brief.

"I can bring Vasily up to a general's rank, but any further ranks, he will have to do himself."

But he would not be able to make a general out of Vasily. The technological revolution knocked all mares out of military parades and replaced them with huge convertible Chaika automobiles, made exclusively for top Soviet brass, in which Marshals were driven on Red Square. The stomach of the Marshal's mares lost its former significance, and with it, the influence of Uncle Bolivar gone.

Although Vasily managed to become a Colonel during Bolivar's good times, for the ambitious Nadia it was not enough. She was very jealous of her girlfriend Lyudka, wife of general Zhivoh, and she started vigorously reading the cards. They showed the government house, the fulfillment of desires and the rank of general. They also showed that a Jack of Crosses would come to help.

"Who is this unknown Jack of Crosses?" thought the wife of the Colonel.

Once, her husband told her about an amazing rookie soldier who managed to get a scarce nylon shirt for Ensign Dubina. Even General Zhivoh failed to acquire such a scarce shirt.

"Is he a brunette or blond?" Nadia asked with bated breath.

"I think he has black hair," the Colonel recalled.

"Yes, this is the Jack of Crosses," gasped Nadia.

Thus, Yasha Abramovich turned into the Jack of Crosses. Hopes of becoming a general's wife flashed before Nadia's eyes with a renewed vigor. Suddenly one morning, right in front of her apartment window, she saw Yasha and Dubina in handcuffs. Some Lieutenant had accused them of robbing a savings bank in the village Murkino, which they had never been to. She rushed to General Zhivoh for help. Meanwhile, it turned out that this idiot Lieutenant fell out of a helicopter, and his stupid accusations crashed with him. Soon after, the real criminals were caught. Colonel Grom himself came to pick up Yasha and the Ensign from custody.

"I am going to direct your Jack of Crosses to grow corn," said Grom at the dinner. "Corn is now the most important thing in the country. Here the order came to the commander of our Army: *"At the moment, the Party and the Government are paying extreme attention to the production of corn. I order all army subsidiary farms to immediately start the cultivation of corn."*

Soviet agriculture was in terrible shape since times of Stalin, when all rich farmers, those who have more than one horse or cow, were exiled or killed. When Khrushchev visited the USA in 1959, he realized that all great American agriculture was based on corn production. After returning home, he started the "cornization" of the Soviet Union. Next year he traveled all over the country to see corn plantations, but in most areas, corn didn't do well.

Yasha courageously took the exile to corn, although he had never seen corn before. He called his brother Simon, the well-known journalist, and asked for help. Three weeks later, the kind brother Simon arrived with the chairman of the Rimsky-Korsakov collective farm, who brought three bags of selected seeds of corn as a gift. Corn was planted, as expected, by the square-nesting method. Two or three times, a professor at an agricultural institute, a personal friend of brother Simon, came by.

A long column of government vehicles stretched along the highway in the Leningrad Region. Underdeveloped corn growing on both sides aroused compassion for its bad appearance. And suddenly, behind a thread of barbed wire, a wall of seven-foot-tall corn plants appeared. It was a mighty corn forest. Sitting in the first car, Nikita Khrushchev clapped his hands in joy and ordered the driver to turn.

"You see, Anastas Ivanovich!" he said to his seatmate. "And you did not believe in our northern opportunities."

The motorcade turned off the highway and stopped at a checkpoint. In five minutes Yasha was under the vigilant eyes of Khrushchev's bodyguards, showing the omnipotent First Secretary his corn kingdom.

The car of Colonel Grom, warned of the important visitors by the guards, was approaching the subsidiary farm at breakneck speed. He saw from a distance Yasha being surrounded by the important visitors. Khrushchev looked happy and was chewing a cob of yellow corn.

The brakes screeched. The Colonel jumped out of the car and stood at attention before his great visitor.

"Comrade Chairman of the Council of Ministers, First Secretary of the Central Committee, Colonel Grom!" He introduced himself, trying to suppress his excitement and shortness of breath.

"Major General Grom!" corrected him Khrushchev. "You grew excellent corn, Comrade Major General!" Standing in the distance, the main corn man Yasha smiled.

"He didn't let me down, The Jack of Crosses," the freshly minted General Major thought.

Chapter 19
SHAMAN'S DAUGHTER

There were two people in the ward of the city hospital, Junior KGB Lieutenant Ella Pyreeva and her boss, hospital patient Major Yanchuk. Ella looked at the patient with a triumphant smile. She had something to be proud of, simply applying her methods of alternative medicine, she managed to get her commander out of a coma and maybe out of the morgue.

"My head hurts terribly," complained Yanchuk.

"After a coma, that is a common occurrence," Ella authoritatively confirmed.

Overcoming his painful headache, the Major tried to open his eyes and immediately closed them. What he saw did not fit into his consciousness.

Again, he barely raised his eyelids, but the picture was not changed. He was lying completely naked on a hospital bed. On the other side of the bed was Ella. She was wearing only a large amber necklace. A waterfall of blond hair scattered over her bare shoulders, lightly touching large juicy nipples. Golden hair in the lower abdomen sparkled fervently in the morning sun. Trying not to look at Ella's body and wincing from pain, the Major asked,

"Where are we?"

"In the city hospital, in the regional Party Committee recovery room."

"Why am I, why are we, without clothes?" Yanchuk asked the question which was puzzling him.

"This is a requirement for medical treatment," Ella answered vaguely.

"Medical treatment for what?"

"You were in a coma. Someone in the Abramovich's apartment hit you over the head with a blunt object."

"And where are the doctors, nurses?"

"The doctors gave up on you. They said that the situation was hopeless. I called the best medical professionals, a professor and an associate professor, but in vain."

Yanchuk ran a hand over his unshaven cheek and remarked. "My beard has grown in!"

"Everything is provided for in the special Regional Committee room."

Ella lowered her legs to the parquet floor, threw on a hospital gown, picked up a bright box from the nightstand and handed it to the Major. In the box was a Sputnik mechanical razor, a novelty of Soviet technology. Yanchuk took the technological miracle of out of the box, wound it several turns and began to shave. Recently, he had seen famous actor Sergei Filippov advertising the Sputnik razor on television.

"Who cured me? How?" he asked, trying to break through the clearing in his stubble.

"I cured you!" Ella suddenly announced.

"You?" the Major was surprised. The mechanical razor in his hand suddenly died out.

"In the whole world, only two people can get a person out of a coma, the great shaman Hugui-Batyr and I. I am his daughter."

"A KGB Officer, the daughter of a shaman?" Yanchuk was dumbfounded. The Sputnik mechanical razor in his hand suddenly started to work again.

"Yes! I am the daughter of the legendary Hugui-Batyr. My mother was 19 years old when she fell into a coma. No doctor could help. Someone advised to go to Hugui-Batyr. And the great shaman cured her. I was born as a result of the treatment."

Only now did the Major realize how Pyreeva had cured him. Ella's robe suddenly opened under the pressure of her high breasts, and they, like two guns, stared at Yanchuk. Part of his body felt an irresistible desire. It was obvious to Ella. She said encouragingly,

"A second course of treatment protects against remission."

"But won't they disturb us?" the Major asked.

"Agent Rhapsody at the door. No one will come."

"Comrade Major, you served in foreign countries," Ella asked after finishing the treatment. "How do foreign women differ from ours?"

Yanchuk thought for a moment.

"They shave under the armpits and below the navel."

On the nightstand next to the Sputnik mechanical razor was an ordinary old-fashioned safety razor. Ella took the razor and put it on her stomach.

"Foreigners, under the arms and below the belly button? We can do that!"

"Don't cut yourself!" Yanchuk said patronizingly. He took the razor and leaned over the belly button of his subordinate. Suddenly the door burst open. An angry General Volobuy appeared in the doorway.

"We have to report to Comrade Shelepin tomorrow, and you two are shaving each other!?" he thundered. "Rhapsody told me that Pyreeva treated the Major with special methods. Now I see these methods for myself."

Ella grabbed a dressing gown and flew into the bathroom like a bullet, and the embarrassed Major pulled a blanket over himself. The enraged General measured the room with great strides, pondering how to punish the perpetrators.

"Comrade General, there are scientists here for you," the sentry Rhapsody said.

"Let them in, Rhapsody, this can't get any worse."

Knocking gently, a professor and his assistant entered the door. They had a blood pressure monitor, test tubes, and other medical devices. They immediately rushed to Yanchuk and began to measure his pressure and pulse. The Major, to their great surprise, was perfectly healthy.

"Your employee has done the impossible," said the astounded Professor.

"Our employees do the impossible every day, as comrade Lenin prescribed." said Volobuy.

"What did she use? Ultrasound, paramagnetism, isotopes?" the Associate Professor tried to determine.

"She applied folk methods from the far North along with the latest scientific advancements," Yanchuk said from the bed.

The General glanced at his watch.

"Goodbye, scientists. We have an operational meeting," he escorted the curious guests out.

Ella Pyreeva appeared in the bathroom door. Mentally, she was prepared for dismissal from the KGB for the manifestation of shamanism. But surprisingly, the General became very friendly.

"Well done Pyreeva, you did a great job! You wiped the nose of those medical professors. Now, they will be wondering for a hundred years how you cured Yanchuk. Tomorrow I'll file a report to assign you the rank of Senior Lieutenant."

"I serve the Soviet Union!" said Ella, standing at attention and pressing her hands to her robe trying to keep her tits put away.

"For your attention!" agent Rhapsody opened the door and handed the General a brown package with a massive wax seal. On it was the bas-relief of Lenin. The General broke the wax seal and threw it into the bin. Then he changed his mind. He took the wax with the bas-relief of Lenin from the bin, wrapped it in a handkerchief and carefully put it in his pocket.

Inside the package was a small piece of paper. Something was typed on it, but the general could not make out. He handed the paper to the shaman's daughter.

"Read what it says. I don't have my glasses."

Taking a sheet with one hand and holding back the wayward robe with the other, Ella read:

"In response to your request, we inform you: Private Yakov Abramovich is in active military service in unit 03216. PV troops. Location: 5 kilometers south of the village of Taramyrino, Tyumen region."

"What are these PV troops? I've never heard." Pyreeva asked.

"They study the effects of a nuclear explosion. Guinea pigs," explained Yanchuk.

The head of the Rhapsody again appeared in the door, "An important message from Moscow, turn on the radio."

The radio was on the nightstand next to the bed. Yanchuk turned the knob and Levitan's voice came in the chamber.

"In the Presidium of the Central Committee of Communist Party. Comrade Semichastny Vladimir Efimovich has just been appointed Chairman of the KGB. Comrade Shelepin Alexander Nikolayevich was relieved of his duties in connection with his transfer to another assignment."

The General was intently looking at the radio, as if processing what he had heard. Ella diligently pulled the sides of the robe, so they would not disperse. The Major climbed back under the blanket. Everyone was thinking about how the dismissal of Iron Shurik would affect their lives. Finally, the General said,

"I know Comrade Semichastny well. He is a faithful follower of Dzerzhinsky. We can work with him. I urgently need to return to Moscow. Changes are coming. Our report will be postponed."

The General's mood improved. For shortcomings in the Abramovich operation, he was looking at a severe reprimand from Iron Shurik. Now the matter had been postponed indefinitely. Now they could make up for lost time.

"You two will fly today to the place of service of this Tsyperovich, or rather, Abramovich. Upon arrival, you will immediately notify me. Clear?"

"Yes! Comrade General!" Yanchuk reported from the bed. With a brisk military step, the General left the room. Suddenly he returned.

"And no more medical treatments, okay?" he added.

"Yes!" unanimously answered Yanchuk and the daughter of the shaman.

Chapter 20

THE CONSPIRACY AGAINST KHRUSHCHEV

The story spread throughout the military districts with the speed of a missile. Details changed from storyteller to storyteller, but the backbone looked something like this: Omnipotent Communist Party chief Khrushchev drove along the roads of the Leningrad Region. As always, he carefully examined the harvests of his favorite crop, corn, and they were in miserable shape.

Suddenly, Nikita Sergeyevich saw a powerful seven-feet forest of corn plants with burly ears of milk-wax ripeness. As it turned out later, it was a subsidiary farm of the brigade of Colonel Grom. The rapturous Khrushchev immediately sent his motorcade to the farm. There, the highest guest was met by Colonel Grom. Khrushchev praised the Colonel for his great corn crop and immediately promoted him to the rank of general. Thus, Grom became the first Colonel in military history who was promoted to the rank of general for his achievements in the cornfield, not on the battlefield.

The story, which the officers passed around was true except for some details. First, Khrushchev was only presented Grom to the rank of general, the official promotion was to be done by the Minister of defense. Second, when Khrushchev came to the cornfield, Grom was not there at all. Yasha managed to delay the leader until the arrival of the Colonel. He demonstrated to the First Secretary the magnificent plants with three ears on one stalk. The seeds of this triple corn were brought from Japan by his brother, the well-known journalist Simon Abramovich.

Triple Japanese corn brought Khrushchev complete delight. With an appetite, he ate one ear of corn and loudly said: "With such corn, we will leave American agriculture far behind."

The members of the entourage smiled and obediently applauded the words of the leader. In the evening, as required by army tradition, Colonel Grom poured a full glass of vodka, threw a general's star to the bottom and drank the contents in one gulp. The next day he invited relatives, again made a cocktail from the general's star with vodka and again drank it in one gulp to the applause of those present.

A whole month had passed. Colonel Grom remained steadfastly on his diet—a glass of vodka with a general's star per day, however, for some reason, an official order from the Ministry of Defense to confer Grom to the general's rank didn't come yet. If at first Grom drank in anticipation of the happy event, a week later he was drinking from unhappiness with bureaucratic delay.

His wife Nadezhda, wanted to become a general's wife even more than her husband himself wanted to become a general. But if Grom sought an answer in the vodka, she was looking for one in the cards. The cards clearly showed that the Jack of Crosses would come to the rescue. The image of the Jack of Crosses was firmly connected in her mind with Yasha. It is necessary to send the Jack of Crosses to the government, stubbornly dictated the cards. Nadezhda just had to follow the cards. She invited Yasha to her house. As always, there was tea and apple pie.

"Yasha, do you remember how Khrushchev came to visit us?"

"Of course." Yasha confirmed.

"A month has passed, but there is still no official order."

"I also thought about this," Yasha said mysteriously. "Something is wrong."

"What do you mean?" Nadezhda did not understand.

"I think it is a conspiracy." Yasha said clearly.

"Against Grom?" the Colonel's wife was alarmed.

"No, it goes much higher, much higher."

"You mean against Khrushchev?" she whispered with fear and looked around. Yasha did not say a word. It was time for Nadia to act.

"In the meantime," she said. "I will arrange a vacation for you and a ticket to Moscow. Go with your brother. Warn who you should. If you think that is a conspiracy against..." She stumbled because she was afraid to pronounce the name of the head of the country.

She remembered that at the beginning of his reign, Khrushchev reduced the Soviet military by mindboggling three million people. He forced a lot of honored commanders to retire. Many were dissatisfied. Nadezhda Ivanovna thought that over the years everything had been forgotten, but apparently, it was not.

Right from her apartment, Yasha called his brother Simon. He, as always, was in a fit of inspiration.

"I'm going to Minsk, brother to write about the new tractor factory over there."

"Both of us need to go to Moscow urgently." Yasha said firmly.

"I can't, brother. They already assigned a business trip for me."

"This is very important," Yasha insisted, "I cannot speak on the phone."

Simon line thought for a moment at the other end of the. His extraordinary kindness and inability to refuse to his brother prevailed.

"We'll talk, brother. Yuri Ukhtomsky is going to Moscow to write about the Exhibition of Achievements of the National Economy. Maybe he will trade with me. Especially since I gave him a rare two-volume of short stories of O. Henry."

The famous American writer did his job. Or maybe the thing was that the other journalist wholeheartedly loved Simon, who in turn always helped everyone. In short, Yuri Ukhtomsky went to Minsk, and Simon Abramovich went to Moscow.

As befits a famous journalist, Simon flew to Moscow by plane. Yasha went by third-class carriage. The journalist met his brother at the Leningrad Railroad Station in Moscow and they took a taxi. Caring Simon brought for his younger brother his favorite treat, almonds in chocolate. Tired of the harsh army food, the sweet tooth Yasha immediately ate candies in the taxi.

"Well, what happened to you over there?" asked Simon, watching with pleasure as Yasha emptied the box.

"A conspiracy," said Yasha, glancing at the driver.

"Against who?"

"Against le pere cosmique."

"What kind of leper cosmique?" Simon was surprised.

"It's in French. It means 'space father'".

"The space father" was a flattering nickname, how newspapers called Nikita Khrushchev. During his reign, the Soviet Union launched the first satellite "Sputnik" and the first man, Yuri Gagarin, into the space.

"Oh, it's not our Jewish business to interfere in conspiracies," the journalist became sad. "Well, tell me. What the story?"

"So, le pere cosmique came to our military brigade," Yasha continued.

"He was delighted with the corn I raised with your help. And then he awarded Colonel Grom the rank of general."

"I know this story," Simon smiled. After all, it was he who informed his old friend at the Moscow State University, Lesha Adjubey, Khrushchev's son-in-law, about unusually great corn. And there, apparently, Khrushchev ended up in the military base farm and made Grom a general.

"And what is the plot?"

"Very simple, a month has passed, but there is still is no order from the Minister of Defense." Yasha pulled out a sheet of paper, drew several men and circled one. "This man," he explained, le pere cosmique, and this is his environment."

"An interesting scheme," the journalist confirmed. "Well, what does the plot have to do with it?"

"Look, if the order had reached the minister, then he, like a military man, would have immediately executed it. Right?"

"That's right." Simon agreed.

"It didn't get to him!" Yasha concluded triumphantly. "So, someone from the circle intercepted the order."

"We will never know who did it," the older brother shook his head.

"But I seem to know!" exclaimed Yasha. He leaned over and started whispering something in his brother's ear. His words must have made a big impression. The journalist turned to the driver and said.

"Take us to the editorial office of the All Union Newspaper Izvestia!"

In the lobby of the editorial office, Simon went to the window and told the gloomy watchman. "I need to see Alexei Ivanovich urgently."

"Urgently? Adjubey?" the watchman was surprised. "Some ministers have been waiting to see him for weeks! Write an application! Maybe in a year, you'll see him!"

Simon had no choice but to start writing a spacious application. "Simon, what are you doing here?" he heard a familiar voice. Simon looked up and saw that Adjubey himself was smiling at him.

"I am writing an application to see you!"

"Consider yourself first, come in! Who's that? Private security?" he nodded at Yasha, who was in his soldier's uniform.

"This is my brother. He has a very important message for you."

"Speak!" ordered Adjubey as they entered his office. "You have twenty minutes; in half an hour I have to meet with the Ambassador of Portugal."

"Remember, I wrote to you about corn on a military base?"

"Of course, I remember. My father-in-law was delighted and granted the general's rank to the Colonel."

"So, a month passed by, but the official order did not come yet." Simon said. "Some kind of sabotage."

"Ah, I see!" Adjubey became very serious.

"My brother thinks that it is a conspiracy. Incidentally, he was present during your visit to the cornfield."

"Yes! I remember him, he stood between Tolstikov, who was Leningrad party boss, and Brezhnev." Adjubey had a very good visual memory.

"Yes!" Confirmed Yasha. "And Tolstikov wrote everything that Krushchev said in a special notebook, to execute Khrushchev's orders."

"He was a human tape recorder," smiled Adjubey.

"Tolstikov and Brezhnev stood with their backs to me," Yasha continued to recall. "When everyone began to leave, Tolstikov leaned towards Brezhnev and said 'This shame must be stopped. We cannot give the rank of general for achievements on a cornfield. It's time to take the old man out.' Brezhnev thought a little and answered in a whisper, 'I have already spoken to some members.'"

At that moment, the office door opened and Nikita Sergeyevich Khrushchev himself appeared on the doorstep. Chairman of the Council of Ministers and father-in-law of Adjubey.

"Look, Leshka, my foot got hurt for some reason." The father-in-law lifted his right pant leg. "Who's that?" Khrushchev noticed the visitors.

"Remember, Nikita Sergeyevich, you visited a cornfield on a military base?"

"Of course, I remember, it had that wonderful triple corn!" Khrushchev lowered his right pant leg.

"There was something else," Adjubey remarked ominously and retold what Yasha had just said. Khrushchev's eyes filled with anger.

"Leonid Ilyich Brezhnev loves me, he couldn't say such a thing, your soldier made a mistake," he said, "but Tolstikov is a different story. We will send him to be ambassador to Mongolia and may be further, much further."

The enraged Khrushchev left the room. Adjubey glanced at his watch. "Well, I have to go, the Portuguese ambassador is waiting for me. Today we'll send a special messenger with an order for Grom, and at the same time, we will promote Yasha to the rank of Sergeant," Adjubey smiled.

"And what about me?" jokingly complained Simon. "Grom will become a general, my brother a Sergeant, and I?"

"And you will remain an outstanding journalist!" Adjubey laughed and said goodbye to the guests.

Chapter 21
THE PRODUCT-22

Stove-maker Abramov ran along the street, a Militia detachment was chasing behind him. The clatter of forged boots grew louder. "Stop!" they shouted to him, but he did not stop. His heart was beating furiously and had sunk into his stomach. He tripped and fell. A cop put a boot on his head. Abramov grabbed the boot with both hands and woke up. Someone had put their hand over his mouth. The former stove-maker pushed the hand away and saw his neighbor, Private Murlo.

"Why are you screaming, kike snout," he hissed angrily. "Not letting anyone sleep?"

"Why kike snout?" thought Abramov, and then he remembered. Two months have already passed since Ensign Dubina made him a Jew. He asked Dubina to doctor his documents to hide from the Militia, who were looking for him for theft of two truckloads of bricks.

Before his last name was Abramov and now he became Abramovich. But either on purpose or by mistake, Dubina made him a Jew. Initially, a soldier's document book with the name of a Jew, Abramovich, burned in his pocket. But now it warmed his soul. After all, he became invisible to the cops. The abductor of socialist property Abramov disappeared, and an innocent Jew Abramovich appeared in his place. Ha-ha! That is what a simple bottle of vodka for 3 rubles 62 kopecks can do!

And everything was fine, but in their new place of service, problems began. His neighbor Private Murlo turned out to be a terrible anti-Semite. On any occasion, he would call the stove-maker a Kike face, give him a poke in the ribs, and threatened to break his Jewish nose. The stove-maker would be happy to explain that he himself does not like those Jews, but he had to keep quiet and endure the insults. Thus, along with Jewish nationality, he also received the sorrows of the Jewish people.

"Okay, I will not scream," humbly promised the imposter, rolled over and fell back asleep, but not for long. An alarm sounded. Apparently, something important had happened. Major Tetradze, the division commander, along with some generals, appeared in the barracks. Soldiers had never seen generals in their barracks. It was only 6 a. m. and Tetradze was very excited.

"Soldiers, comrades!" the Major thundered. "Just yesterday, our troops shot down a spy-plane from America. The pilot, Harry Powers is in captivity. Therefore, we have been ordered to test Product 22. We are witnesses of a great event. In three hours, at exactly 9 o'clock in the morning local time, Product 22 will be blown up. From this explosion, Earth and Heaven will be shaken." Major Tetradze stopped to take a breath. "Yes, the Earth and Heaven will be shaken." He repeated menacingly.

The soldiers looked sleepily at the Major. The fate of Earth and Heaven clearly did not bother them. "But even more than the Earth and Heaven, the American imperialists themselves will be shaken," the Major continued. "They will be terrified that we have such powerful weapons as Product 22."

The stove-maker was puzzled. He remembered how in their rural pharmacy, to hide information from children, they called condoms Product 22. He understood it was possible to shake while using them, but not why it was necessary to explode them.

"What is Product 22?" he asked his neighbor.

"You don't know?" he was surprised. "Well, it is the atomic bomb."

"And when the American imperialists see that you are marching over the blast site, they will tremble with fear," thundered Tetradze.

Following the Major, the General spoke. "Comrades soldiers! Your homeland is looking at you. You will carry out the most important task of your lives. The Party appreciates what you are doing. Upon return to the barracks, everyone will receive a bottle of beer and a glass of vodka."

At the word beer, the soldiers instantly woke up. Neither the impending atomic explosion, nor the imperialist intrigues made any impression. But a bottle of beer and a glass of vodka lit a fire in their eyes. Now they were ready for any task set by the Party.

The personnel rushed into the underground bunker. They donned gas masks, atomic stockings and suits, and prepared to dash through the heavily contaminated area. However, for unknown reasons, no atomic explosion occurred at 9:00 AM.

False Abramovich did not suspect that a KGB team was hunting him along with the police. Major Yanchuk and his assistant Ella arrived at the airport the day before the atomic bomb explosion was scheduled and settled in a military hotel. The next day, they were finally going to meet with Abramovich.

But the explosion of Product 22 disrupted their plans. In addition, Yanchuk was urgently recalled to Moscow and Ella was left alone. The hotel was overcrowded. There were academicians and scientists with the task of collecting data about the nuclear explosion. The hotel itself was located deep underground, with only periscopes were sticking out, so that the scientists could monitor the area.

Exactly at nine in the morning, the scientists clung to the periscopes to see the explosion of Product 22. But for unknown reasons, the explosion did not occur.

A city was built at the future epicenter of the explosion. The houses were unfinished, there were no doors, no windows, gaping holes in the walls and ceilings and inhabitants of the doomed city were only cows, sheep, dogs, and rats. The hungry cows mumbled, the sheep bleated piteously, the dogs barked, and only the rats kept quiet.

At 9:00 AM, the poor animals were to be killed, to help the voracious scientists study the impact of the explosion on living organisms. Thus, the failure of the explosion saved thousands of poor animals.

The pilot of the TU-16 aircraft gained a target altitude of 14 miles. Product 22 was attached to the fuselage belly. Exactly at 9 AM, per a radio command from the command center, the pilot turned the bomb drop lever and donned safety glasses. Product 22 had unhooked and the plane bounced in the air. A bright flash of light with a force of a thousand suns was to blind the pilot from behind. He even closed his eyes. But for unknown reasons, the explosion did not happen.

USSR Foreign Minister Andrei Gromyko was preparing to address the UN General Assembly. He was to come up with a new peace initiative. Gromyko liked to talk about peace after testing atomic weapons. The imperialists would better understand the peace initiatives of the Soviet government. He was looking forward to hearing about the next successful test. But for unknown reasons, the explosion never happened.

A lot of unexploded bombs from World War II were left in the long-suffering Russian land. And now, an unexploded atomic bomb was added to them. The situation was extremely dangerous. A special government commission was created. Nikita Sergeyevich Khrushchev called the new head of the KGB, Semichastny, and gave him instructions. The bomb had to be found, defused, and delivered back to the manufacturer as soon as possible. Upon his return, Semichastny convened his generals and department heads. "We can't rest," he said. "Until that bomb has been defused. What are the proposals?"

Unexpectedly for all, the head of the Heritage department, General Volobuy, stood up. "My subordinate, Lieutenant Pyreeva, is at the very epicenter of the explosion. She is at the bunker-hotel where scientists are staying."

"Very good," Semichastny rejoiced. "I order to vest Lieutenant Pyreeva with the powers of a KGB Colonel. Let her immediately begin to interrogate the academicians and scientists about the non-explosion. Can she handle it?"

"I have no doubt, she always succeeds."

"Perfect. I will immediately send two or three Majors to help her begin working. Report back to me every six hours."

Pyreeva received a teletype message with the order of Semichastny and was not scared of her immense new powers. She ordered a special room to be allocated to interrogate scientists and specialists. She also summoned Major Tetradze and ordered him to immediately begin the search for the unexploded bomb.

The initial interrogation did not get any results. Academicians and specialists mumbled something about gamma and beta rays, about the size of the critical mass and some other scientific problems that she did not understand and which, in her opinion, had nothing to do with the case.

The chief designer of the bomb did not say anything intelligible either. He could not understand what had happened. Pyreeva demanded a bomb passport and other technical documentation from him. It turned out that all the documentation remained in an underground factory in the Siberian city of Omsk.

Pyreeva ordered a special plane to be sent for the missing documentation. In the evening, Major Tetradze informed by radio telephone that the atomic bomb had been found. It was buried at a depth of 20–22 feet. Pyreeva immediately wanted to start digging out the bomb but decided to first measure the level of radiation at the crash site.

Two professors were sent to measure radiation and deliver a soil sample. They came back with good news. The radiation was within normal limits, and the soil was medium-hard. Pyreeva immediately ordered Tetradze's division to begin carefully unearthing the bomb, the way archaeologists do it, with bare hands. She banned the use of shovels and other iron objects.

The next day, when members of the government commission arrived at the scene, they discovered that the work was going full speed under the leadership of Pyreeva.

Tetradze's soldiers had already removed three feet of soil above the bomb, the bomb's passport was delivered to Pyreeva, but the scientists still could not determine out the reasons for the non-explosion.

After three days, Pyreeva called a general meeting. It was attended by scientists, designers, and military pilots. Physicists testified first, then chemists. The reason for the non-explosion was still unclear to them. But they believed that the pilots who incorrectly dropped the bomb were to blame. The pilots said that they accurately followed the instructions and the matter was most likely due to the flaws in the design of the bomb. Then the designers spoke. They too did not know the reason for the failure but believed that it was the fault of scientists. The circle was closed.

Everyone was ready to leave, but then Pyreeva asked to speak. Scientists and pilots looked at her with a smile. What could this beautiful blonde understand about these complicated scientific matters? Pyreeva immediately took the bull by the horns.

"This bomb was doomed not to explode," she said to the crowd. Her words exploded like a bomb.

"Why?" Asked academicians, designers, and pilots in one voice.

"It's all in the bomb passport," said Ella and handed the passport to the commission members. "As you may see, this bomb was made on December 31st."

"So what?" The commission members were surprised.

"What do you mean, so what?" Pyreeva was in turn, surprised. "It would be okay if it were the last day of the month. But this was the last day of the quarter and of the year. Was the atomic bomb manufactured under the pressure of being late?" she asked point-blank of the Chief Designer.

"Yes." He confessed after a little thought.

"Did the annual bonuses depended on the timely production of the bomb?"

"Yes."

"So, everybody was in a rush?"

"Yes!"

"This bomb is defective, made in a hurry, to earn a bonus. Tell me if a refrigerator is made on the 31st of December, will it work? 99 % not! A TV made on the last day of the year would work? 100 % not! This bomb if no more dangerous than a barbecue grill. It can be safely excavated and then sent to the manufacturer to fix the defects!"

The members of the commission applauded. The mystery was solved, and the report was sent to comrade Semichastny. Now Pyreeva could return to the original purpose of the trip, the long-awaited meeting with Private Abramovich on the issue of his American inheritance. Pyreeva contacted Major Tetradze by radio and asked to bring Private Jacob Abramovich to the hotel. An hour later, Major Tetradze called back and said that Private Abramovich had disappeared.

Chapter 22
YASHA IS FLYING TO MIAMI

Major Tetradze, wrapped in his overcoat, sat in his office dozing lightly. His round-the-clock duty of the unexploded A-bomb had thrown him off balance. Someone scratched at the door. "Come in," said the sleepy Major. The orderly stood on the threshold. That day it was Private Murlo, pseudo-Abramovich's barrack mate.

"Phone call for you!" the orderly reported. "A KGB woman."

With his gummed-up eyelids closed, the Major picked up the phone. A female voice was asking about an Abramovich.

"Abramovich? Listen, what Abramovich?" Tetradze asked drowsily. "Ah, yes! We have a Private Abramovich," the Major finally remembered. "He repairs monuments to Lenin. Deliver him to your hotel? Who, Lenin? Abramovich! Of course!"

When the stove-maker came to a new place he found a familiar monument to Lenin. And this Lenin has the same problem of losing parts. He told Major Tetradze that he knows how to fix Vladimir Illich. Tetradze was very happy, and Lenin got a new healer. The Major opened the door.

"Orderly!" he barked. "Go get Abramovich! Quick!"

"Aye aye!" Murlo saluted and rushed to the barracks.

As expected from an orderly, he had eavesdropped on the Major's entire phone conversation. "Aha! Your time has come, you kike!" he thought gloatingly of Abramovich. "The KGB will knock your filthy liver out soon!"

The former village stove-maker, who by the quirk of fate had turned into an Abramovich, was snoring peacefully in his bunk after a night watch by the unexploded A-bomb. Murlo triumphantly stripped his blanket.

"Get up!" he yelled. "The KGB's come for you."

"KGB?" asked the sleepy soldier, startled. He knew he would have to answer for stealing collective farm bricks, but he did not expect the KGB to be involved.

"The KGB!" the orderly confirmed. "I bet they'll give you twenty years in prison!"

The phone rang, and Murlo, performing his duties as orderly, rushed to pick up. The frightened soldier watched him with hatred. "They're not getting me alive," he thought, pulling on his boots and blouse. He looked into his nightstand. Inside was a paper-wrapped thick slab of bacon his mother had sent him. "Ah, I shouldn't have given the new address to my mother," the stove-maker realized. "Now the KGB is here!" He tucked the bacon under the shirt, quickly ducked under the neighboring bunk and crawled towards the store-room. "They're not getting me alive," he thought again.

"Abramovich! Where the hell are you?" Murlo returned to his neighbor's bed, but he was nowhere to be found. In the bunks, soldiers were sleeping after the night shift, and the commotion caused by Abramovich's disappearance did not wake them up.

Meanwhile, the stove-maker had already crawled to the last bunk and was watching his adversary from under it. He still needed to make a short dash to the store-room door. Luckily, the phone rang again and the orderly ran to answer it. Those ten seconds were enough for the stove-maker to reach the store-room and unlock the door. One month before, Tetradze gave him the key to the small room where he kept tools for repairing Lenin. He looked around, knocked out the high store-room window, and standing on a stool, clumsily fell outside.

Now the entire barracks were astir. He heard from a distance the noisy orders of Tetradze, he could figure out that the soldiers had checked the latrine and turned over all the beds in the barracks. The fugitive had vanished. Now they're coming to the store-room. "Where do I go?"

His heart pounded like the Kremlin chimes on central radio and television. He had no escape plan. The stove-maker recalled that, while repairing the Ilyich monument, he discovered that the armored car on which Lenin stood was hollow, it had a tiny room inside, fit for a school child.

Behind him, he heard his pursuers yell in the store-room. There was no time for deliberations. He rushed to the monument. "Lenin, dear, help me!" the stove-maker prayed, then ran to the armored car and dove desperately into the tiny hole.

Lenin must have been smiling at him from the otherworld, since the fugitive managed to get into the little space somehow. Or maybe, the good-natured leader was smiling because he knew that the unfortunate stove-maker would never be able to get out of the narrow hole. An hour and a half later, the pale Tetradze appeared before the KGB lieutenant Pyreeva.

"So, where is Abramovich?" she asked, perplexed.

"The search is underway! He vanished! Completely vanished!" the Major shrugged. "But his file is here." He held out the folder to Pyreeva.

Ella opened the first page, looked at the photo, and said disappointedly, "This is the wrong Abramovich! The KGB doesn't need this one!"

* * *

Yasha came back from Moscow with a bagful of scarce goods. He brought, as ordered, a jar of instant Brazilian coffee for warrant officer Dubina, toothbrushes for Nadezhda Ivanovna, Grom's wife, and some laundry soap for the officers' wives, one piece for each, which were not available in local shops.

He also brought thermometers and bandages for doctor Petrov. But Petrov was not there. Senior Lieutenant of Medical Service Arkady Guralnik had taken his place. The young doctor was the same age as Dubina. He was very happy to get the thermometers and immediately offered Yasha a position in the medical unit under his supervision. That was a dream position. It enabled Yasha to prepare for the entrance exam at the theater institute. Guralnik talked with his roommate, the all-powerful warrant officer Dubina, who arranged commander Grom's order to transfer Yasha to the medical unit.

One day, Guralnik invited Yasha to his place. He shared a two-room communal apartment with another bachelor, warrant officer Dubina. Shelves full of medical books covered the walls in his little room. Guralnik offered his visitor some tea. For himself, Yasha noticed, the Senior Lieutenant poured vodka. They engaged in a conversation about books. Both, it turned out, adored Hemingway and Remarque, and also the young poet Evgeny Evtushenko. Arkady moved aside a thick opus on internal diseases and drew a bunch of postcards. A coastal city with tall white buildings was pictured in one of them.

"So, this is where I'll be living in som-me ten years," said Guralnik, half-drunk. Alcohol somehow made it hard for the doctor to articulate the 'm' sound.

"What is it, Sochi?" Yasha asked.

"No, M-miam-mi!"

"But how will you get there?" Yasha wondered.

"Don't know yet, but don't tell anybody!" begged the doctor.

The soldier reassured him. He kept silent for a moment and then confided his biggest secret to the doctor. "My aunt lives in Florida."

"In M-miam-mi?"

"No, but somewhere close. In Key West."

"Key West! It's the m-most am-mazing place on earth!" Guralnik drew another postcard. "See, this seven-m-mile bridge is a technological m-marvel. It lies on the road to Key West. There are fam-mous coral reefs around Key West, they're so charm-ming they look like underwater gardens. Scuba divers spend whole days there and can't see enough of them-m. And the building where the very Hem-mingway lived is in the center of Key West. He wrote his best books there. And in the evenings the whole city watches the sunsets, the m-most m-marvelous sunsets on earth."

"How do you know all this?" Yasha was startled.

"M-my research supervisor had a conference there. He infected m-me with his love for Florida."

"Ostap Bender wanted to live in Rio de Janeiro," Yasha recalled.

"Because Ostap didn't know about M-miam-mi!" the doctor retorted.

Bidding Yasha goodbye, the doctor gave him the magazine *America* as a token of friendship, with a warning that nobody was to see it.

As soon as Yasha left the doctor's room, the alarm set off. Yasha, who was a part-time altimeter operator, rushed to the command post. As usual, the cause of the alarm was the milk plane belonging to Finland. Everyone knew about the plane. It hopped from one borderline farm to another collecting milk and other dairy products. Occasionally it would hop onto the USSR territory by mistake. Then a general alarm would be raised, interceptor planes would take off, rockets would aim menacingly at the baby plane.

This time the alarm lasted about thirty minutes. Having teased the Soviet air defense, the milk plane buzzed off to its home country. The alarm was off. Along with other soldiers, Yasha marched to the barracks. Only in bed did he realize that he had forgotten the *America* magazine at the command post. Next time Yasha saw his magazine at the morning formation, in the hands of the political officer Major Kusko.

"We have an emergency," the Major announced. "This *America* magazine that I'm holding in my hands is prohibited in the Soviet Army. It's a corrupt organ that the CIA uses to slander the Soviet Union and praise its American swamp in all kinds of ways. And some bastard is reading this. We're going to expose him, this bastard, we have modern methods. He'd better confess, this will buy him some indulgence."

Nobody hastened to admit reading the prohibited magazine.

Making a brief pause, Kusko added, "You have twenty-four hours."

Yasha did not follow the political officer's advice. He had talked with doctor Guralnik, who comforted him saying it was impossible to find him out. Twenty-four hours passed, but no one turned up with the confession.

"The emergency continues!" the Major announced at the next morning formation. "The damned turncoat didn't confess. But today he'll crack for sure. We will use our special methods..."

The Major's special methods turned out to be the working dogs he had borrowed at a local police station. In the evening before lights out, when everyone was in the barracks, Major Kusko came with two dogs and the person in charge. Making sure that all the servicemen were present, he got the dogs to sniff at the calamitous magazine and released them into the aisle between the beds.

Yasha, tense with anxiety, watched the trained animals circle the barracks sniffing around. One of them ran towards him and started barking. Major Kusko rushed to the "hot spot." The dog came close to a nightstand between two beds. It was the one Yasha shared with Private Gurin.

The Major opened the nightstand, expecting piles of *America* magazines and other propaganda literature. There was nothing but a lone piece of sausage. The tracker dog grabbed the sausage and dashed away. Private Gurin tried to snatch his favorite sausage out, but to no avail. A burst of laughter followed the dog. Yasha's sigh of relief passed unnoticed.

The stubborn Major did not give up after that failure. A week later, he announced the arrival of a KGB fingerprints expert, whose task was to compare the fingerprints on the magazine with the fingerprints of all the enlisted servicemen, thus fishing out the renegade traitor.

The KGB expert who arrived at Kusko's request was Senior Lieutenant Pyreeva. That was her first big assignment after completing the course in dactyloscopy. As always, Pyreeva got down to work straight away. Together with her assistant, warrant officer Dubina, she took the personnel's fingerprints. Kusko allocated her a separate office in the headquarters.

Pyreeva spent two days analyzing the fingerprints. Then she summoned Dubina. "Warrant officer," Ella asked. "Do you have Private Abramov among your servicemen?"

"We do," Dubina confirmed.

"A week ago, I visited the apartment of conscript Abramovich, who was assigned to your brigade a while ago and took his fingerprints. And you know what?"

"What?" Dubina asked with fake interest.

"They are identical. Private Yan Abramov, who is now in your command, and conscript Abramovich are the same person! But their last names are different!"

"What a surprise!" Dubina exclaimed. Not a single muscle on his face twitched.

"There's more," Ella proceeded. "There is a Private Abramovich serving in the PV troops. I visited him. And I visited the village he is from. He is a stove-maker and he used to serve here, and he used to repair the statue of Lenin in your brigade.

"You understand what I am talking about?"

"Not exactly."

"Don't pretend you don't know. You issued papers for both. You 'swapped' them for some reason. The Jewish boy Abramovich became the Russian Abramov, while the former Russian Abramov is now Abramovich! You have committed a crime against the state!"

Shattered, Dubina sat silent. He was in that woman's power. Having delighted in his fear, Pyreeva continued:

"Anyway, I'm not going to put that on your file and send you in jail, which you deserve, by the way. I need Yasha, but it has nothing to do with this stupid magazine. His Jewish aunt has left him a fortune in the USA. Turn him back into Abramovich and a Jew, quickly, and we'll be done for the time being. Get his papers ready by 5 p. m. Clear?"

"Clear," Dubina said with relief.

"And you know what?"

"Yes?" Dubina grew wary.

"With your talents, you should be working for the KGB. I'll mention you. Meanwhile, bring Abramovich here."

Dubina found Yasha in the medical unit and told him what had happened. To his amazement, Yasha was happy at the news. He was sick and tired of disguising under another man's last name and ethnic background. At last, he would be himself again, Yasha Abramovich. Yasha felt great relief.

"I suspect that Dubina has already told you everything?" Pyreeva said when Yasha turned up in her office.

"Yes Ma'am!" Yasha replied.

"I'm sorry to say that your aunt in America has died. But she has left you a large fortune."

"Why me?" Yasha asked, surprised. "I have brothers, Zakhar, Simon, Mikhail. They are better than me."

"I'm afraid your aunt won't be able to explain this," Ella snapped. "And this stupid trick with the papers has cost us a lot of time. The case has gone to court, and the judge in this Miami wants to see you in person. Got it?"

"Got it," said Yasha, who did not get anything whatsoever.

"So, in three days we are flying to the USA, to Miami. I will be your cousin, Major Yanchuk, your uncle. Don't tell anyone, not even your family, not even your brothers. You can go now."

"Yes Ma'am!" Yasha saluted.

"By the way. I know who the fingerprints on the *America* magazine belong to!"

Yasha sensed a hidden threat in her voice.

Chapter 23
DUMTSEV'S DUMBBELLS

Only three days remained before their departure to Miami. In the meantime, there was a long list of errands to run: to procure travel passports, to obtain American visas, to pass the vetting by the Old Bolsheviks' Board, a mandatory procedure for all outbound travelers heading to capitalist countries, to buy flight tickets to the US, to approve the foreign exchange budget, agreed upon with the Ministry of Finance, and finally, to draw some currency from the State Bank.

If there was a person capable of pulling all that off, it was KGB lieutenant Ella Pyreeva. As secretary to General Volobuy from the State Security Committee, she had long understood that, in the bureaucrats' world, everything depends on secretaries. These quiet, unassuming mistresses of typewriters were equally capable of making one's life as blissfully carefree as a fairground ride or as unpleasant as a trip to the dentist. A couple of sympathetic remarks on "these bloody men", an imported bottle of nail polish or a pair of panties—and yet another secretary would become Ella's trusted friend for life. Pulling her secretarial strings, Ella managed to negotiate the passports, collect the currency, and arrange the tickets for an overseas flight in just one day.

The biggest challenge was navigating the unfamiliar world of the American embassy. Strictly speaking, Yasha and Pyreeva were the only ones who needed visas. Major Yanchuk had been hopscotching across the globe for years under the guise of a foreign trade representative and held a diplomatic passport. After a long wait, they were received by an Embassy employee named Mrs. King. She was a lady of monumental proportions. Never in his entire life had Yasha seen anyone quite as voluminous as her. A saying has it that between two chairs one falls to the ground. In manifest defiance of the saying, Mrs. King was sprawled quite comfortably across three chairs at once. To Yasha's surprise, the fat lady had pretty decent Russian.

She asked Yasha and Pyreeva a bunch of questions and ordered them to come back the next day for the results. The following day it turned out that Ella's visa had been granted, while Yasha's was declined.

"Mr. Abramovich's earnings are a mere 5 rubles per month," Mrs. King justified her decision.

"But he is a soldier," Ella reasoned.

"And he is homeless, too," Mrs. King interrupted, talking over her.

"He is not homeless—he lives in a communal apartment."

"Well, all the same!" Mrs. King rebuked. "He's probably not coming back. It's a risk for the United States."

"He will soon receive a big fortune," Ella objected.

"That's a big if!" Mrs. King snapped out. To make it clear that the conversation was over, she pushed the button and announced: "Next!"

That king-sized Mrs. King was ruining their plans. Lieutenant Pyreeva was itching to get her claws right into the woman's enormous face. In an instant, however, the door swung open and a man of fifty, handsomely silver-haired and dressed immaculately in a suit and tie, walked into the room. Ella recognized his face from newspaper photographs: that was the Ambassador himself.

"Mr. Abramovich!" the Ambassador said, throwing a glance at the papers. "I've read the article in The Miami Herald, titled 'Russian Soldier Inherits a Fortune from American Aunt!' Congratulations! Mrs. King, could you please move his visa along. Let him flash his cash in the US!" the Ambassador concluded with a smile.

Begrudgingly, Mrs. King raised her huge hand and hammered the stamp into Yasha's passport with ill-concealed contempt. The only thing that remained was the vetting by the Old Bolsheviks' Board. Shortly before the interview, Ella furnished the old men with vouchers for salami. That softened the hearts of the faithful Leninists. They only asked Yasha one tricky question:

"When did Vladimir Ilyich Lenin visit America?"

"Lenin never went to America," Yasha replied.

"Correct!" Old Bolsheviks nodded in agreement.

The door to Miami was open. Right before their departure, General Volobuy gave Major Yanchuk a final briefing.

"Major, the Party has entrusted you with a very important mission. You must provide Abramovich with moral guidance. He has to understand that the greatest fortune in the world is to donate a fortune for the good of Communism. We expect him to be more than happy to oblige. However, should he be stubborn," the General opened a small briefcase containing a pair of gym dumbbells and said, "Dumtsev's dumbbells, and the latest brainchild of our scientists!"

"Do I peck him on the head with the dumbbell?" Yanchuk wondered.

"That's a crime, isn't it? Might get the electric chair for that kind of cute thing. No pecking. We're no amateurs," the General smiled, pulling a lighter out of his pocket. "Soviet science is humane in its ways and means. Each dumbbell is a true engineering marvel, it has an ultra-low frequency generator concealed inside."

"So, how does it work?"

"This dumbbell generator is switched on remotely with this lighter. 2–3 seconds—and a person gets overtaken by a fit of desperate terror. Another 2–3 seconds—and the heart breaks apart. No traces, no crime."

"Poor boy," Yanchuk thought to himself. "But what an elegant murder!" Following the General's instructions, Yanchuk began Yasha's moral guidance as soon as they boarded the aircraft.

"What is happiness?" he said musingly, gazing out of the window. Ella took the hint at once.

"Happiness is to give everything to your homeland," she picked up the thought, "like the collective farmer Golovaty, who gave money for two military planes during World War II."

"And the school kids from the village Voronya Dyra, who picked leftover crops enough to buy three Kalashnikovs for our infantry!" the Major continued. "What a great initiative."

"And just imagine how many missile launchers Yasha could donate to the state!" Pyreeva said dreamily and shot a glance at Abramovich through the corner of her eye. The heir, however, was sound asleep, exhausted on a long-haul flight. The Major, too, cast an eye at Yasha and began rapping his fingers frantically on the little briefcase hiding the secret dumbbells.

At Miami Airport, they were met by Mr. Steve Dworkin, a lawyer. He was retained by the Russian Bar Association for Foreign Affairs to represent the interests of the Russian soldier and heir to the rich aunt. Yasha was the first to spot someone holding a sign with his last name spelled in Russian, only that letter "b" was upside down.

"Tovariches!" Steve exclaimed. "Tovariches! Mr. Abramovich! Zdarastvu-vuite. Sputnik. Gagarin. Kharasho!"

At this, lawyer Dworkin's Russian vocabulary had run dry. The talkative lawyer explained that his grandfather was a devout Jew, born in Russia. Dworkin could not recall where exactly—might've been Minsk, Pinsk, or Dvinsk. Although that Minsk and Pinsk had never been a part of Russia, Yasha did not say a word.

The famous Miami Beach turned out to be a narrow long island, separated from the mainland by the scenic Biscayne Bay, with picturesque palm groves in between. In around twenty minutes, Dworkin's Cadillac pulled up at a small three-story hotel in the southern part of the island. Pyreeva and the Major helped Yasha get settled in the hotel and, saying goodbye to the lawyer, headed off to the post office on Washington Avenue. The post office was a long single-story pre-World War II building. To the right of the entrance, there stood a rather large garbage can, which was used as a secret dropbox by Soviet agents.

Casting a sly look around, the Major rummaged in it and fished out a plastic bag, tightly bound with a blue elastic band. Inside was a secret dispatch from the Center. Pyreeva, a cryptologist, deciphered the message straight away. The dispatch instructed Yanchuk to travel immediately to New York. Pyreeva was to stay in Miami and handle Yasha. Besides, Pyreeva was instructed to attend to the lawyer Dvorkin most thoroughly.

Obeying the Center's orders, the Major collected his dumbbell briefcase and set off to the world's capital. Ella, in her turn, embarked on her mission, keeping a close eye on the God-fearing lawyer. Dworkin seemed to have no objections to such keen attention. Almost every other evening, he would take Ella sightseeing around Miami. To win his trust, she even visited his favorite synagogue, Temple Emanu-El, having obtained permission from the Center. She later declared to Yasha that all religions were, no doubt, the opium of the people, but Judaism, she thought, was better than others because every Saturday was the Sabbath, a day of rest.

Meanwhile, the battle for the auntie's inheritance intensified dramatically. The other party produced the aunt's will from five years ago and was now trying to prove that Yasha had no right to a single penny. Lawyer Dworkin, however, swore that he would win the case, and Yasha would receive his inheritance in full. A month went by, followed by another. The court case ran into a stalemate.

Ella Pryeeva's cryptic messages were getting shorter and shorter and gradually came to a halt. The Center went into frenzied commotion. In contempt of all rules, General Volobuy made a phone call to the hotel. Yasha answered instead of Ella, who was not around. He explained that Ella had checked out of the hotel and moved into a private house, which Mr. Dworkin had rented for her.

"Seems to me all this winning the religious Jew's trust has gone far enough." The General thought and rang Mr. Dworkin's house. A housemaid picked up.

"Speak to Mrs. Ella?" the puzzled housemaid echoed. "She's keeping the Sabbath and not taking calls today."

"Keeping the Sabbath!?" the General roared, utterly shocked. "I'll show her the Sabbath!" He called New York and ordered Major Yanchuk to report immediately back to Miami, bringing Dumtsev's briefcase along.

Chapter 24

ANIMAL TORTURER WALKS FREE

Major Yanchuk flew to Miami on an important mission launched by the Center. He was supposed to find all the details and step-by-step guidelines in the special cache at Miami Beach Post Office. At the airport, he had a gut feeling that he was being followed. Just in case, he zigzagged up and down between floors to lose the tail and got the last cab in the line.

The driver seized his gym bag and suitcase and was about to put them in the trunk, when suddenly the little suitcase slipped out of his hands, fell on the ground and opened, letting a pair of old dumbbells roll out. To the cabbie's surprise, the incident strongly upset the passenger, who picked the dumbbells himself, put them back in the suitcase, and held it tight till the end of the ride. The entire ride went in silence.

Upon arrival, the driver's worst expectations came true: the passenger paid the exact fare, finding small change and leaving no tip. The indignant driver waited for the suitcase owner to disappear through the post office front door, spat in his direction, and spewed out a longish curse in Spanish. He would not know that to save foreign currency, the KGB had strictly prohibited any tipping by its agents.

The post office was crowded. The KGB cache was in the garbage can by the entrance. At the right moment, Yanchuk dropped his pen "accidentally" into the garbage container and pulled it back immediately, along with a tiny plastic bag bound with a blue elastic band.

From New York, he had wisely made a reservation at the Clinton Hotel, which was not far from the post office. Making himself comfortable in his room, he unfolded the plastic bag. Two used-up pencils were inside. The scribbling on them was the dispatch from the Center. Sergey Andreevich took out his magnifying glass and read the encrypted message tattooed on the pencil stubs.

The order concerned the agent Pyreeva. She was accused of connections with Zionist elements represented by the lawyer Dworkin and charged with treason. Major Yanchuk was instructed to double-check the facts and, upon confirmation, terminate the offender with Dumtsev's dumbbells. Those were the very dumbbells that unbagged themselves at the airport. Each was stuffed with a super low-frequency generator, which killed everything within a five-yard radius, the new secret weapon of the KGB. The Major dialed the number of Pryeeva's current residence. A housemaid picked up the phone.

"Miss Ella is out, she's having her bat mitzvah at Temple Emanu-El," she said.

"What's that?" Yanchuk wondered.

"That's a special ritual, when a girl reaches the age of twelve, and she..."

"Our girl's over twelve, I believe," the Major observed sardonically.

"It's never too late, no matter how old you are." the housemaid retorted.

"So, Komsomol secretary Lieutenant Pyreeva is having a bat mitzvah," the Major concluded silently. "Very well, Comrade Miss Pyreeva, you've condemned yourself to Dumtsev's dumbbells."

However, after their fall at the airport, the Dumtsev's dumbbells may have gone out of order. Therefore, the Major decided to test them on a stray cat first.

* * *

At 10 a. m. sharp, Mrs. Kulmacher showed herself on the ocean shore. She was walking with great difficulty: her right hand was supported by a metal cane, while her left held a heavy shopping bag with canned pet food. Cochise, the impertinent fat tomcat with a cunning glow in his eyes, habitually came out first to see her. Cochise must have taken pride in being one of the few Miami toms that had avoided a veterinary knife and kept their noble masculinity.

The pussycats, Cochise's coastal girlfriends, waited patiently till he was full to surround Mrs. Kulmacher and take their turn.

Satisfied, Cochise lay aside and watched his harem fed. He had grown so arrogant that he was totally off guard. A man cast a plastic bag slickly over the tom and shoved him into a gym bag. Despite her myopia, Mrs. Kulmacher was quick to detect the abduction of her favorite pet. Thrusting the half-empty cans back in the bag and supporting herself with her cane, she chased the cat thief. She recollected rumors that some cultures considered cat meat to be a gourmet food. No surprise that the dear fatty Cochise was their choice. Her hatred of the cat-eating barbarian was so great that Mrs. Kulmacher had forgotten all her ailments and pursued the kidnapper steadily.

For the first time in his life, Major Yanchuk failed to register a tail. Cochise, who was pirouetting and mewing loudly in the bag, distracted the agent and paralyzed his habitual vigilance. Pushed forward by Cochise's restlessness, the Major literally flew into his hotel room. He rushed to open the suitcase and put the dumbbells on the windowsill. Then he shook Cochise out of the bag. Cochise dashed for the door, but Sergey Andreevich was ahead of him, tossing the cat skillfully back in and slamming the door from the outside, right in the animal's muzzle. The guinea pig Cochise was left alone with the Dumtsev's dumbbells.

After securing the door, the Major got out a cigarette and lighter from his pocket. The lighter was the disguised remote control for the Dumtsev's dumbbells. He flicked the lighter and lit up. A minute passed. Nothing happened. The puzzled Major flicked again—to no effect. He flicked another time, and another, and once more. Suddenly, there came the sound of shattering glass, then a hair-raising scream from Cochise; then something fell, and everything was quiet.

Intrigued to know Cochise's fate, the Major opened the door. Within a few seconds, the animal had managed to tear down the curtains, break a flower vase, and pull the blanket off the bed. Now it lay motionless under the window. Its head was bleeding. Evidently, one of the dumbbells had fallen off the windowsill right on the cat's head, now resting next to the prostrate Cochise.

Yanchuk leaned over Cochise to have a better look at what had happened, when two cops charged in, with pistols in the hands. Mrs. Kulmacher, leaning on her cane, was following them hastily. She had dialed the magical 911 number earlier, so five police cars plus a fire truck and an ambulance were now jamming the street by the hotel. They were honking, blaring, and blinking in all kinds of manner, forming an incredible light and noise orchestra.

"You are charged with animal abuse, conversion of dumbbells into instruments of torture, and reserving a hotel room for criminal purposes! You have the right to remain silent and contact your lawyer!" one of the cops gasped out, and handcuffs slapped on the Major's wrists.

Mrs. Kulmacher, who was a former hospital nurse, pulled a stethoscope out of her bottomless bag and galloped to the immobile Cochise.

"He's breathing!" she announced happily to the cops. Two orderlies with a stretcher ran into the room. Misjudging the situation, they grabbed Mrs. Kulmacher, turned her promptly into a horizontal position, and fastened her to the stretcher.

"It isn't for me!" the lady shrieked. "It's the cat who's in danger!" The orderlies unfastened Mrs. Kulmacher obediently and set her back to a vertical stance. Then they lifted Cochise and fastened him to the stretchers. The ambulance headed to the veterinary clinic. Mrs. Kulmacher followed by taxi. Her heart was breaking with anxiety over Cochise's destiny. The police searched the hotel room, but, strange as it were, discovered no traces of other tormented animals. They took the dumbbells as material evidence, while the handcuffed Yanchuk was led to the hotel lobby. A flock of aggressive reporters had already been waiting for him there. Questions showered over him.

"How many cats have you killed in your life? How old were you when you tortured your first animal?"

The confused torturer, who had not expected such an outburst, kept silent. Escorting Yanchuk between the rows of journalists, the cops had him get into a car and took him to the District Court. The duty judge was quick to get rid of him.

"This is a serious and unconventional crime. Animal torture with aggravating circumstances. Criminal use of a hotel room. For release on bail until trial, twenty thousand dollars."

"The greedy KGB Accounts won't find this sum for me," the Major reflected in sorrow.

Meanwhile, his arrest had an international resonance. Without a clue, Mrs. Kulmacher and her beloved Cochise ignited an international scandal for the State Department, the TASS agency, the newspaper *Pravda* and the Soviet embassy to contribute to. The KGB reacted harshly. On the following day, they arrested American embassy secretary Mr. Tort. He was caught red-handed in Sokolniki Park while trying to stroke a dog, Nikolai, of a pensioner, Grodnick.

The Soviet Ambassador paid a visit to the Department of State and shocked everyone by hinting that another five American diplomats were going to be arrested and charged with the same crime as Mr. Tort.

The day of the trial of the Number One Enemy of the Cat World, as one newspaper labeled Yanchuk, was approaching. He was so notorious that Hollywood promised to give a million dollars for a biopic based on his life. Mrs. Kulmacher appeared on several TV shows and related how she had tracked Yanchuk. On top of that, she signed a contract for a book about her life, indicating a decent amount as her honorarium.

The publicity was working. America's most celebrated lawyers lined up to offer Yanchuk their services. After some doubt, he chose a defending genius, Steve Smuglowitz. Steve had never lost a single court case. In every trial, he would find the only possible winning move and, speaking in chess terms, checkmated the witless prosecution.

This time also, everyone was waiting anxiously, what kind of victorious move Smuglowitz would select. The lawyer let nobody down: the trial lasted less than one minute.

"Officers," he addressed the policemen. "Do you remember the moment of my defendant's arrest well?"

"Yes," the cops replied.

"Did you inform the suspect about his rights? Did he understand you?"

"We did. That's the law!"

"Well, did you know that he was a native speaker of Russian?"

"No, we did not!"

"Was an interpreter present at the time and place of the arrest?" the lawyer pressed.

"No," the officers admitted.

"An inexcusable violation of the law!" the defense glanced at the judge triumphantly.

The judge hammered smartly with his gavel and announced, "Case dismissed. Release the accused!"

Learning about the unfair court decision, Mrs. Kulmacher cried bitterly. Her sole consolation was that Cochise had recovered and returned to his harem on 8th Street.

Chapter 25
ESCAPE TO HORCON

After a month in America, Yasha discovered a new law. He called it the "Law of the Stranger." The law was as follows: if a stranger were to call you out, it means he or she needs your money. No other way around. They may call anywhere—on the beach, in the store or on the street. But street intersections were a favorite hunting ground for local beggars, where they would attack motorists who stopped at a red light.

Yasha got used to the fact that Soviet beggars were much more modest. Usually, they were miserable crippled old persons staying at the same place every day, who patiently and silently were waiting for the attention of passers-by and afraid of Militia.

American beggars were surprisingly healthy men and women, who smelled of beer and lacked money for some mythical bus. During his first day on American soil, Yasha gave a quarter to one such an outcast and immediately got a scolding from him, because the donation was so small. The disappointed beggar angrily threw the coin on the asphalt. However, as soon as Yasha turned away, the beggar picked it back up.

That is why, when some unknown man called him in the hotel lobby, Yasha did not even flinch. The man called him again, and this time by name. He was a well-dressed man in a white shirt with a tie and a straw hat.

"Do you know me?" a surprised Yasha answered.

"Jacob Abramovich!" repeated the man. "Hotel Carlton, room 222!" he read from the paper.

"Exactly! I live there!" Yasha was astonished. "But this is some kind of mistake. I did not call anyone."

"No mistake. I am in Real Estate. My name is Dick Critini. We want to offer you a beautiful home. Right on the ocean."

"A home on the ocean? For me?"

"Yes! For just a half million. Just a gift. The best place. Golden Beach. We will send a limo for you."

"Limousine?" Yasha was even more surprised. "What for?"

"So that you can personally see your future home."

"Some kind of psycho," Yasha thought "He will probably ask for a quarter now and get out."

But Mr. Critini did not ask the quarter and did not think to leave. He took out a catalog of houses for sale from his voluminous portfolio. The 'future' house of Yasha had two columns, under which the bronze lions dozed, was on the front page of the cover. The house resembled a 19th-century mansion. The only exception was a three-car garage. There were no car garages in the 19th century.

"And by the way, it's nice to put a Cadillac your garage!"

Yasha had not noticed, that one more seller joint them. He was also in a snow-white shirt with a tie, but without a hat.

"And don't forget about furniture for your new house!"

"And electrical appliances! Refrigerators, washing machines!" Sellers appeared one after another.

"I don't have money, I don't even have credit cards," Yasha disappointed the sellers. "This is an obvious mistake. You need another person. With money."

"No mistake!" said Mr. Critini. "It's the American way; buy now, pay later."

He took out a newspaper from his vast portfolio and read an excerpt from the article: "The trial of the case of the inheritance of Feigi Pechenyuk is coming to an end. Most observers are inclined to believe that the largest part will go to her nephew Jacob Abramovich, a Private of the Soviet Army."

"Ah, that's where the wind blows from!" realized Yasha.

"Listen, my son," the car dealer friendly hugged Yasha. "Our best Cadillac is next to the hotel. Ride it, have fun, and pay later when you get your millions."

"Firstly, there is a mistake in the newspaper," said Yasha.

"What is the mistake?" the sellers were wary.

"I'm not a Private, but a corporal, and second..." Yasha wanted to say that the Soviet Union would take all money from him for the construction of communism, but when he thought it over, he added like a real American, "I have to talk to a lawyer."

"That's right, talk to your lawyer," the sellers supported. "And we'll be back tomorrow."

They turned and headed for the exit. Yasha looked after them and was horrified to notice that a new wave of sellers in white shirts rolled into the hotel lobby through the revolving doors. They also had newspapers in their hands. They were heading towards him. It was necessary to be saved. Yasha threw himself into his room, put on a bathing suit, and headed through the emergency exit to the ocean. The beach was full of swimmers. He opened the catalog and began to examine the palace that Mr. Critini had offered him.

"Excuse me, what time is it?" suddenly asked a female voice.

"Quarter is needed again?" Yasha thought with displeasure and took his eyes off the catalog. In front of him stood a miniature girl with fluffy hair to her shoulders and with huge eyes. Yasha did not mind such strangers.

"Yasha!" he introduced himself, instead of answering.

"Juanita!" the girl held out her hand. She seemed to have forgotten her question too.

"Juanita! Let's go swimming!" a curly-haired boy of about five embraced the legs of the girl and looked into her face. Yasha got the idea that he would love to swap places with the boy.

"Is he your son?" he asked in a sinking voice.

"No," Juanita smiled. "His name is Gianni. This is my job. I am with him every day from eight in the morning until ten at night."

Gianni pulled Juanita to the ocean, and Yasha went after them. Ocean waves cheerfully jumped ashore and immediately jumped back. Gianni began to compete with them and went pretty deep. Juanita watched him intently. Suddenly she screamed:

"Tiburon, Tiburon!"

Yasha followed her gaze and noticed something like a log under the water. The log moved quickly towards Gianni. Without hesitation, Yasha jumped into the water, pushed the child away, and bravely covered him with his body.

"Shark, shark!"

A cry of horror swept the beach. But the shark, having made a clever maneuver, went back into its ocean. Juanita was in shock and cried sobbing. She got scared for the life of the child. Yasha tried to calm the girl down, but nothing helped. Then he hugged and kissed her gently. Juanita immediately stopped crying. Her eyes opened wide and Yasha read in them:

"You saved Gianni! You're a real man! I love you!"

Then Yasha took the girl by the hand and in his eyes, she read:

"You are a very beautiful girl! I have not seen anyone better! I love you too!" And the waves, realizing that this was true love at first sight, danced around them some kind of wedding ocean waltz.

Gianni interrupted the budding romance:

"Juanita," he cried. "I'm hungry. I want to go home. I'm scared of sharks."

Juanita packed up their belongings, then took a piece of paper and wrote something on it.

"Yasha, come in the evening when I finish the work," she whispered. "Let's go somewhere."

She handed him a piece of paper with the address of the house.

In the evening, Yasha searched for the address indicated by Juanita for a long time. The house turned out to be very similar to the palace that Mr. Critini offered him. Juanita lived in a small room next to Gianni's bedroom. As soon as she opened the door, some unknown force pushed them into a hug with each other. How long did this kiss last? Five minutes? Ten? They did not know. As always, they were interrupted by Gianni.

"Juanita, I want to sleep," he squealed in his room.

"I'll lay him down and return. His parents left; they will be back tomorrow."

Gianni quickly fell asleep and they went out to the swimming pool. The lovers sat on a bench and returned to the occupation that Gianni interrupted. And in between kisses, they told each other about themselves. Yasha told the girl about something, which he did not admit to anyone in the world. He spoke English poorly, Juanita spoke even worse, but they understood every word. Yasha said that he came to America to receive the deceased aunt's inheritance. And if he wins the case, then this inheritance will immediately be taken from him by the Soviet state. And that special KGB agents are watching him.

"They will kill you anyway," the girl said decisively. "I know them, they are like cocaine barons. You have to run away."

"Where to run!? You know, they will find me anywhere."

"They would never find you in Horcon!" said the girl with conviction.

"Where is this Horcon?"

"In my country, in Chile. Not far from Valparaiso. This is a fishing village on the very shore of the Pacific Ocean. There are a wonderful beautiful horseshoe-shaped harbor and eternal spring. There come actors, poets, and musicians from all over Chile."

Only a few hours passed from the moment they met, and the ardent Chilean no longer separated her plans from Yasha's. After checking whether Gianni was sleeping, Juanita took Yasha's hands in her own and looked directly at him in the eye.

"I have to show you something very important," she said and took him to the back of the house.

Juanita opened the door of a walk-in-closet and let Yasha inside. On the shelves were plastic bags with white powder. And then Juanita entrusted Yasha with a secret that he was better off not knowing.

"This is cocaine. Here are three million worth of goods. My master is a cocaine baron," she said, turning off the light.

Cocaine made no impression on Yasha. For him, at that moment there were only Juanita's lips, which he immediately spotted in the dark and kissed. Suddenly he remembered something.

"They seem to have a surveillance camera that recorded us," he said anxiously and turned on the light.

Indeed, the eye of the camcorder between the cocaine bags was aimed directly at them.

"Tomorrow evening the owner will return and look at the tape. He forbade me from opening this closet," Juanita said with undisguised fear. "They can kill us."

"I see. All that remains is Horcon," Yasha concluded. "But I don't even have a Chilean visa."

"A visa is not a problem. I have a friend at the consulate. Everything will work out in one day."

"And the money?"

"No problem, I saved my salary for six months!" Juanita resolutely said.

The next day, the cocaine baron returned home and watched the videotape. Then he put a gun in his pocket and headed for the servant's room, but she had already disappeared.

Chapter 26

THE FIRST AMERICAN COMMUNAL APARTMENT

The most remarkable inventor was Willis Carrier. Yasha realized this on his first day in sultry Miami. Willis Carrier was an engineer. He was probably also in Miami during summer, thought Yasha, and suffered from the heat, and because he was a genius, Willis invented an air-cooling device, which he named the air conditioner.

The hotel where Yasha checked in had plenty of the Willis Carrier devices, so it was cool inside even on the hottest days. Unfortunately, Dr. Carrier's invention did not work for the outside. Having learned that, Yasha would not walk more than a few hundred yards away from the hotel during the first few days. Prompted by unbearable swelter, he would hurry back immediately for a whiff of cool air.

It was during one of those short jaunts that Yasha met Mrs. Kulmacher. Mrs. Kulmacher was a retired teacher and lived at the hotel next door. Every morning, at 10 a. m. sharp, she fed a fifteen-head colony of stray cats, spending the rest of her time criticizing the American government.

That day, Yasha went a little farther from his hotel than usual and got lost. He approached an old woman feeding stray cats and, making the best of his English, asked her for directions.

"Where are you from?" the old lady asked in turn. "Russia?" she cheered up. "That's a wonderful country! They have recently launched a man into space! And healthcare is free. What's your name? Yasha? So you'd be Jacob! Jacob, why did you come here!?" she exclaimed in a tragic voice.

Yasha hesitated, his lawyer had advised him to keep silent about the purpose of his visit.

"America is dying, dear Jacob," Mrs. Kulmacher continued. "Dying by the minute. Have you noticed?"

"No, I haven't," Yasha confessed.

"Jacob! Open your eyes. Gas is forty-five cents for a gallon. Who can afford it at this price? And the real estate costs? A one-bedroom apartment rent has grown to one hundred dollars a month."

Unfamiliar with the concept of a "one-bedroom," Yasha embarked on a mental calculation of how many *rooms* it would have.

"And don't you feel the dollar is falling?"

"I don't," Jacob admitted.

"You're so lucky, Jacob, to live in the Soviet Union, unaware of all this evil. I'll introduce you to Mr. Crabson. He'll be happy to meet you. He's in love with the Soviet Union."

It turned out Mr. Nat Crabson resided at the same hotel as Yasha. Mr. Crabson was sixty-five. He had been a member of the American Communist Party since the Great Depression. His Hollywood actor-style head of grey hair was attracting quite a few elderly female communists, who whirled constantly around him. The two things he detested most were the Republicans and soft-boiled eggs. He also hated a new singing band from Great Britain, the one that called themselves The Beatles.

"You see what the Republicans have done to our country? President Eisenhower doesn't understand a thing. How can an ex-general rule a whole country?" Mr. Crabson stormed at Yasha. The little old party ladies were standing close to Crabson, nodding their grey heads in accord. They all hated the Republican Eisenhower. "A postal stamp now costs as much as five cents. A bus ticket, ten cents. Where are we going to next?"

Yasha did not know the answer, so he kept courteous silence.

"The cost of living is getting ridiculously high! The new Mustang is eighteen hundred dollars."

"Mustang is a wild horse, isn't it?" Yasha decided to show his expertise.

"The Mustang is a new car made by Ford," Mr. Crabson explained. "And take art and music. Have you seen those longhaired

Beatles boys? They don't know how to sing. They're as pointless as soft-boiled eggs!"

One of the little old ladies, Fruma Gerstein, stopped nodding and asked, "Jacob, I hear the USSR has solved the longevity problem, what do you know about it?"

Yasha had no idea. Mr. Crabson, on the other hand, knew everything about his beloved Soviet Union.

"Of course it has, Fruma. The elderly in Abkhazia now live a hundred and twenty years because they eat that special yogurt designed by Soviet scientists."

Yasha had never heard of the yogurt but shyly refrained from asking. Mr. Crabson spent another ten minutes or so talking to Yasha, then jotted down a few words in his little notepad and concluded, "Jacob, why don't you come to our gathering on Thursday? It'll be fun. A bunch of people will be happy to meet you."

The gathering was held in Miami Beach, in Flamingo Park at the corner of 11th Street and Jefferson Avenue. The activists pulled a few benches together. One bench was facing the others in imitation of the Presidium. It was occupied by Nat Crabson and his inner circle.

"Please welcome our guest, Jacob Abramovich," Mr. Crabson opened the meeting. "He comes from the Soviet Union, the country where socialism triumphs! The country where the government protects the old age. As a Soviet song goes, 'where the old are honored everywhere!'"

The activists applauded.

"Jacob! You told me, didn't you, that you have a brother, Mikhail Abramovich, a famous pediatrician?"

"Yes," Yasha confirmed. "Ph.D. in Medicine, author of many books."

"How much did he pay for his medical education?"

"It was free," said Yasha.

"IT WAS FREE!" Nat Crabson echoed thunderously. The activists cheerfully applauded. "IT WAS FREE! What's more, the state was paying him a monthly scholarship."

The activists clapped again. Each of them would love to wind up in the wonderful Soviet Union and get a scholarship.

"By the way, Jacob lives in a commune," Nat continued. "They call it a communal apartment. Eight families live together. So they decided. People help each other. That's very good. They've been even awarded a Prize for Exemplary Communist Lifestyle."

"What's so good about that?" an activist inquired gloomily. "One stove for eight families, not to mention the toilet."

"What is it that you cook all day long?" the chairman lashed out. "Once you're done, make way for others! And how many toilets do you need if you only have only one ass, I beg your pardon?"

The activists laughed and clapped in unison. Everyone had grown fond of the prize-winning communal apartment of an exemplary communist lifestyle.

Mrs. Kulmacher stood up.

"I have a great idea," she said. "Let's address the Soviet government asking them for a communal apartment in Abkhazia. We'll eat yogurt and live to be one hundred and twenty."

An ovation drowned her last words. Some Party members jumped on the benches, despite their arthritis and other ailments, and applauded vigorously. A team of the first American communal apartment residents was elected at once. Nat Crabson was appointed head representative of the apartment. Fruma Gerstein and Mrs. Kulmacher became his deputies.

From then on, everything went smoothly. The retired petitioners, led by Mr. Crabson, were greeted most favorably at the Soviet embassy. The plan of the first American communal apartment in Abkhazia took just one month to be endorsed. A communal apartment in Sukhumi, the capital of Abkhazia, was made vacant for them, its occupants temporarily sent to cultivate the virgin and abandoned land territories in Kazakhstan.

The ideology department of the Soviet Communist Party Central Committee established a division to deal with communal apartments for American workers. Mr. Crabson was allocated a special substantial pension totaling 62 rubles 50 kopecks per month. The little US Communist Party oldies were allocated pensions of 27 rubles each. Their US pensions in hard currency were placed at the

Soviet state's disposal. The Americans were granted free public transport services. They were also granted unlimited free entrances to the local Lenin museum.

At last, the happy day arrived for the American occupants to leave for their communal apartment in the Soviet Union. A Soviet embassy representative, a press photographer for the newspaper *Pravda* and a few prominent members of the American Communist Party came to see them at the hotel.

The prospective Soviet residents and their friends posed joyfully for the photojournalist. Two of the future residents, however, were noticeably nervous. Those were Mrs. Gerstein and her husband Saul. They surrounded the elected apartment head, Mr. Crabson.

"We need two rooms!" Fruma Gerstein implored. "Saul is a terrible snorer! I can't sleep."

"Each family gets one room, and you're no exception," the head repeated firmly.

"But I won't make it in one room!"

"You will! Plug your ears with cotton wool!"

"Plug yours!" Fruma wept and darted from the hotel lobby. At the doorway, she bumped into Mary Kulmacher. The latter was carrying two cat cages.

"My little pussies are going with me," she announced happily. "I was going to take all the fifteen of them, but thought better of it."

"Mary! You're out of your mind. They'll stink up the entire apartment!" Crabson reproved.

"Well, they're not as stinky as your cheap cigars," retorted Mary.

Weirdly enough, the vibes of a constant brawl typical of a Soviet communal apartment had somehow crossed the ocean and reached a Miami Beach hotel lobby. Before long, all the residents of the future communal apartment were squabbling with gusto, ignoring both the *Pravda* photographer and the Communist Party bosses. When the bus finally arrived, the only ones who climbed aboard were the Soviet comrades, the American communists, and Mr. Crabson. The Soviet embassy man was glaring at him with hate.

"No problem! We'll find new residents, better than the old ones!" the elected head of the apartment stated energetically. Suddenly, slapping on his pocket, he turned pale and announced mournfully that he had left behind his passport. He got off the bus and walked towards the hotel.

He never came back. The holder of the special substantial Soviet pension, the elected head of the apartment had disgracefully fled. The cherished communal American dream was shattered.

Chapter 27
THE KGB REVENGE

Juanita saved a mindboggling $3,000. After buying Miami-Santiago tickets, they still had more than two thousand dollars. For the first time in his life, Yasha saw such an unbelievable amount of money. In the Soviet Army, he received only three rubles a month. At that rate, he may receive such a great amount of money after a hundred years of service. This money, according to Yasha, could be enough for the rest of his life. However, he did not consider the abilities of Juanita. In just twenty minutes at the airport shop, she managed to spend half a soldier's lifetime salary. She bought Yasha an Omega watch for a fabulous sum of three hundred dollars, as well as fashionable Bali low shoes.

"Why do I need such an expensive watch? Why do I need Bali?!" Yasha was horrified.

"A real man must have good watches and shoes," Juanita explained and complemented the explanation with a strong kiss. Meanwhile, the flight was postponed for two hours. In order not to toil in anticipation of take-off, Juanita again went shopping and the next ten years of the salary of corporal Abramovich disappeared in the cash registers of the airport. These were gifts to relatives and friends. The first family scandal was brewing. Yasha began to frown and thought for the first time about whether he should go to a distant country, where his earnings would disappear at such lightning speed. Juanita interpreted his frowns in her own way.

"Do you have a girlfriend in Miami?" she turned pale and became jealous right away.

"No girl!" swore Yasha.

"Then what is the matter?"

"I don't speak Spanish. What will I do in Chile? How will they treat me?"

"Very good. You have blue eyes. Chile loves gringos with blue eyes."

"Who are the gringos"?

"That's how we call North Americans."

"I'm not American, I'm from Russia and also I am a Jew."

"You are a Jew?" Juanita exclaimed joyfully. "That is wonderful!"

"What is so wonderful?"

"We have very few Jews in Chile, but they are all rich. And you too will become rich."

"I'm afraid I will be the first poor Jew in Chile."

"You will be rich with me," Juanita said decisively and again ended the discussion with a long kiss. When entering the plane, the couple was stopped by the pilot.

"Senorita Juana?" he asked. Juanita did not like it when she was called Juana.

"I am Juanita," she corrected.

"A present for you, Senorita Juanita. It was taken aboard at the last moment." The pilot pulled out a small box decorated with a red bow. Inside were two tiny dolls depicting a man and a woman.

"Dolls?" Yasha wondered. "Is that from the children's store?"

Juanita turned over the tiny figures. A long sewing needle stuck in the back of each head.

"Very strange toys. Why torture the dolls?" Yasha did not understand.

"These are not toys! This is the threat of a cocaine baron! I understood right away. The man is you, and the woman is me. Needles in the heads mean they are going to kill us!" said Juanita and became very pale.

"To kill?" repeated Yasha. He did not believe in these puppet messages. Juanita did not say anything. She sat silently, not uttering a word. So depressed Yasha did not see her. Obviously, she perceived threats too seriously. Yasha decided to calm her down.

"I know how to avert the danger." he whispered mysteriously.

"How?" Juanita winced.

"I read in an old book. It is necessary to break these needles, take burnt chicken feathers, grind a little bit of pepper."

"Red or green?"

"Red, certainly red. Mix everything together and at midnight throw it into the ocean from a high cliff."

"And this will remove the danger?" the girl asked hopefully.

"Very easy!" Confidently said Yasha.

"How smart you are! I love you!" she cried, throwing her arms around his neck.

"Yasha, are you a Communist?" she asked after some thought. Yasha was already used to the fact that she suddenly changed the topic of conversation in the most unexpected direction.

"I'm a Komsomoles, a member of the Komsomol."

"And I'm a real Communist!"

"You are?"

"That's what my relatives say, because I give everything to the people and I hate oppressors like the cocaine baron. Yasha, what does Komsomoles mean?" she suddenly remembered. Juanita could not pronounce Russian 'ts'.

"It is a young communist. Everybody who serves in the army has to be a Komsomolets."

"Then I am a Komsomoles." Juanita rejoiced.

"I am a Komsomoles!" she said to a flight attendant who was passing by.

"Com-so-mo-les," the flight attendant carefully repeated and smiled.

Suddenly the plane rocked. "Fasten your seat belts, we are approaching Santiago," the pilot announced on the radio.

Yasha looked out the window. Mountains parted. The city of Santiago was supposed to be at their foot, but it was not visible. Instead, a huge cloud of an unpleasant bluish color spread between the mountains.

"Smog," explained Juanita. "This is a terrible disaster. It is impossible to breathe on such days. People wear respiratory masks. Children do not go to school. Plants, factories do not work. The airport does not accept flights."

Having made a useless circle over the city, the pilot announced that landing was impossible, and the plane will fly to the Argentinian city of Mendoza.

"Fine," Juanita rejoiced. "I have a friend in Mendoza, whom I must meet."

Yasha noticed that wherever they were going, Juanita had man friends. Chile was separated from Argentina by a mountain fence three miles high. Having jumped over this three-mile barrier, the plane began to land. Mendoza, which looked like a huge garden, was very close to the border.

After leaving the plane and entering the transit lounge, Juanita found a payphone and called somebody. Soon a guy with a dark-haired beard and a beret came to visit Juanita. They kissed each other and then whispered for a long time about something. Then it was Yasha's turn to become jealous of Juanita.

"Who are you kissing with?" he asked when the beret left.

"Don't be jealous, this is Ernesto Che Guevara. Soon the whole world will know about him. He is preparing a proletarian revolution."

"In Argentina?"

"No, he says Argentina is not ripe. He is trying to choose between Paraguay and Bolivia."

"But there is no proletariat there," said Yasha. From school textbooks, he understood that a proletariat is needed for a proletarian socialist revolution.

"Therefore, he seeks advice from the great Pablo Neruda. He gave me a letter for the poet. The greatest poet of Chile lived in solitude on the island of Isla Negra. He was the most famous Communist in Chile and the world's only poet who was awarded the Stalin and the Nobel Prize simultaneously."

Juanita and Yasha went directly to the poet from the airport. Juanita first wanted to see her parents who lived in the mountains, but the meeting had to be postponed since the fate of Bolivia and Paraguay was more important than personal plans.

Until the very last moment, Yasha doubted that the great poet would accept them. But he was wrong. Pablo warmly greeted them at his huge house facing the Pacific Ocean and filled with overflowing bookshelves and cabinets. While waiting for the poet, Yasha noticed a volume of the Great Russian poet Pushkin in Russian. He opened and began to read: "In the depths of the Siberian ores, keep proud patience..."

"It's very good" The poet himself appeared. Pablo Neruda, winner of the International Stalin Prize for the Peace between Peoples. It turned out he spoke a little Russian. The poet treated them to coffee and then invited them to take a walk in a private park full of centuries-old trees.

Juanita outlined the request of Che Guevara. When they returned to the house, Pablo wrote something on a piece of paper and handed it to her.

"Pass it on to Che," he asked.

Juanita took the sheet and read aloud, "Give me silence, guitar, and ocean waves. And the nights will fall like dark wings. Homeland, I call you the names of gold and mountain eagles. I am a drop of dew and a cornflower on your way! I am a ring in the harbor of Horcon! Maestro! What a coincidence!" exclaimed Juanita. "We are going to live in Horcon, but what about Bolivia, what about Paraguay?"

"Pass it to Che," grimaced great poet. "He will understand."

At this, their audience with the great writer ended. Upon arrival in Horcon, Juanita handed over the sheet of poetry to party couriers. They immediately transported it to Argentina. Ernesto Che Guevara read the message and understood everything. After some time, he began revolutionary actions in Bolivia.

The Harbor of Horcon turned out to be the most beautiful place in the world. Nature created it in the form of a horseshoe, one end of which was crowned by a rock in the form of a huge ring described by the great maestro Neruda. At the other end of the horseshoe was a flea market. They sold souvenirs, paintings by artists, as well as items necessary to combat corruption and the evil eye. Juanita bought burnt feathers and a couple of clumps of dried red pepper. Exactly at midnight, according to Yasha's recipe, they broke the needles of the cocaine baron, mixed with pepper and burnt feathers, and threw them into the ocean from a high cliff. The full moon approvingly watched their actions.

"The cocaine baron problem is over, "Yasha summed up. "But what to do about the KGB, which is chasing me?"

"Are there Communists are working in the KGB?" asked Juanita.

"Of course."

"Then do not be afraid. The Communists do not harm anyone."

Yasha shook his head but did not argue. The next day they began their new life. A tiny apartment was rented for the remaining money, and Yasha went to learn the trade of the local fishermen. He was the only gringo in the whole fishing village of Horcon and he was treated very well.

A week later, Yasha finished his fishing classes and bought a used longboat. For this, they sold the Omega watch, the gift of Juanita. Now the well-being of their small family depended on the successes of the novice fisherman. But Juanita said that Yasha will catch a lot of fish, enough to buy 10 watches.

Yasha liked to sail on his longboat and read poetry aloud. The ocean, Pushkin's poems, and the bright sun, could there be a better combination? But few fish were caught. Fish were not attracted to his poems. Maybe they did not understand the Russian language?

One day the back of a huge fish appeared next to the tiny longboat. After a second, Yasha realized that this was not a fish, but a submarine.

"There must be the military exercises of the Chilean Navy," thought the novice fisherman.

Suddenly the cabin door of the submarine opened, and there appeared none other than Major Yanchuk. After half an hour, ocean waves pushed the overturned longboat, and Yasha was lying down with his hands tied in the hull of the submarine.

Chapter 28
BUREAUCRACY THE AMERICAN WAY

The disappearance of Yasha caused a real commotion in the KGB. The fate of the ten-million-dollar inheritance hung in the balance. Yasha's chief, Major Yanchuk was accused of neglecting his subordinates, lack of vigilance, and was urgently recalled from Miami to Moscow.

Unfortunately, this was also the time that the hearing of the inheritance case was scheduled in court. The judge was furious because of the failure of plaintiff Abramovich to appear, whom he loudly accused of contempt of court. The hearing was postponed for a month, and the judge threatened to award money to the other side in the event of a repeated failure to appear by Mr. Abramovich.

The news of a possible loss of ten million in convertible currency reached the Central Committee of the Communist Party. The Secretary of the Central Committee, comrade Suslov, summoned the chairman of the KGB, made a commotion, and ordered them to find Corporal Abramovich at all costs.

However, not trusting in the KGB agents, Secretary Suslov also turned to friendly Communist parties with a request to help in the search for the missing heir. And the Communists did not disappoint. Soon Luis Corvalan, the chief of the Chilean Communist Party, reported to Moscow that a new fisherman, very similar to the man wanted by a comrade Suslov, appeared in the small Chilean city of Horcon.

A correspondent of newspaper Pravda, the official organ of the Soviet Government, quickly arrived in Horcon. He also was the main resident of Soviet Intelligence Services in Latin America. Losing no time, the correspondent wrote an article about the capitalistic oppression of poor fishermen, and at the same time established surveillance of the apartment which Juanita and Yasha rented. Soon, the pictures of the young couple, as well as of Yasha's fishing longboat, went with a diplomatic courier to Moscow.

The question arose of how to remove the defiant Abramovich from Horcon without causing friction with the Chilean Government. Not so long ago, the whole world heard the news about how the Israeli Intelligence Service successfully abducted Nazi criminal Eichmann from Argentina and took him by submarine to Israel for trial. Suslov's technical assistant, professor Kusakin, decided to imitate the Israeli experience and suggested sending a submarine to capture the fugitive. Suslov agreed with the assistant. Closest to Chile at that time was a Komsomolets type submarine based in Cuba. The assistant called Yanchuk and ordered him to fly from Moscow to Havana to join the Komsomolets, which was supposed to track down Abramovich while fishing and arrest him right in the open ocean.

The mission was top secret and therefore it was forbidden to use the Panama Canal. The Komsomolets went around the tip of South America, passed through the Straits of Magellan, and around Tierra del Fuego. The passage to Horcon took a whole week. Early in the morning, the Komsomolets crept up in the harbor of Horcon and put up its periscopes.

However, because of the high sides of the longboats, it was impossible to see the faces of the fishermen. Yasha, like others, was fishing within the 12-mile border zone. The submarine could not surface in this zone for political reasons, so as not to violate the sovereignty of Chile the submarine was forced to look for Yasha blindly. Listening devices were added to the periscopes.

According to intelligence, Yasha loved to read aloud poetry of Pushkin and Shakespeare while fishing. There were about twenty longboats in the harbor. The Komsomolets needed to travel from one boat to another, listening for any conversations, until the Radioman heard the words of Prince Hamlet, "To be or not to be." The radio operator immediately called Yanchuk. Among the half-literate fishermen, only Yasha could quote William Shakespeare.

"Yes, Yasha, to be, to be," rejoiced Yanchuk. He pressed a button and a special gripping device emerged from the torpedo compartment, which resembled a huge metal arm. This arm grabbed the longboat underneath and pulled it into the open ocean. Yasha, preoccupied with his future role of Prince Hamlet, did not notice as he quickly drifted far away from the coast.

As soon as the longboat was outside the 12-mile zone, everything happened like in a science fiction movie. The ocean parted and the Komsomolets submarine surfaced right in front of Yasha's longboat. After that, the waterproof doors of the wheelhouse opened, and Major Yanchuk himself appeared. He had a gun in his hands.

The place of Yasha's detention was a small and cramped hold. At first, he was kept with tied hand and foot, but then the ropes were removed. The personnel of submarine were told that this was a spy and a traitor to the motherland, and sailors shoved the spy whenever they could.

Yasha's fairy-tale life was over. Surprising and unbelievable for an ordinary Soviet soldier, the trip to the USA and Chile suddenly came to an end. For Yasha, now came days of Soviet prison. From the first day, the prisoner was fed bread and water. The daily diet consisted of a mug of water and a half-pound of bread. Yasha remembered the stories of his elder brother Zakhar, who survived the Leningrad blockade during World War II.

Then, they were given only a quarter pound of stale bread per person. To survive, Zakhar divided his microscopic ration into four parts, one quarter for breakfast, one quarter for afternoon tea, a quarter for lunch, and the remainder for dinner. When they brought his ration, Yasha also rationally divided it into four parts, as Brother Zakhar once did, but then he could not stand it and ate it all at once. In addition to hunger, Yasha suffered from the cold. The temperature in the submarine was only 55 degrees. Therefore, while the whole crew wore warm sweaters, but Yasha only had the light shirt in which he was fishing in the Horcon harbor.

After several days of hunger and cold, the prisoner was greatly weakened. He was in bad condition, exactly as Yanchuk needed.

By the time they went ashore, Yasha looked like he was suffering from a serious illness.

After returning to Cuba, without losing time, Yanchuk took Yasha and headed to the American Interests Section, which was the name of the American Embassy in Cuba. Yanchuk was in a hurry. There were only three days left before the final hearing in Miami. The embassy employee, Mr. Miller, greeted them rather cordially.

"How can I help? You look so pale!" he turned to Yasha.

"His boat was carried off to open sea, he almost died," Yanchuk explained.

"Where? In the Florida area?" asked Mr. Miller.

"In Miami. He went fishing. Suddenly the boat was dragged into the open ocean."

"Yes, there are very insidious currents." the American agreed.

"He drifted for five days. He was picked up by a Cuban cargo ship. It's good that he had some bread with him, about half a pound per day."

"But he's not sunburned at all!" The adviser was surprised.

"It was raining most of the time," the Major said after some thought. "Now, he urgently needs to return to Miami. He has an inheritance case there." The Major handed the court papers to Mr. Miller. "He needs an American visa."

"Give me your passport!" said Mr. Miller.

"All the documents were lost, sir, I don't have a passport!"

"Shipwreck, you see, sir," Yanchuk insisted.

"I understand, but he still needs a passport."

"It is clear that these American bureaucrats are worse than ours," thought Yanchuk. He rushed to the Soviet embassy to report the situation to Professor Kusakin by phone and ask for advice. The situation seemed hopeless. But for the professor, there were no hopeless situations.

"We can make a passport within an hour," he thought aloud. "But how to get it to Cuba?"

"Maybe by scheduled flight?" advised Yanchuk.

"The plane took off yesterday, the next flight is in 3 days."

"In three days, the money will be gone," Yanchuk sighed.

"Not gone. A mighty Soviet rocket will help us!" the Professor found a unique solution.

"What rocket?" the Major did not understand.

"Read the newspapers! Tomorrow they will close the ocean to the north of Cuba. A new Soviet ballistic missile will be tested."

"They don't deliver newspapers to the submarine," Yanchuk wanted to say, but said nothing, he was happy that the problem will be resolved.

"In the head compartment of the rocket," Kusakin continued, "my assistants will put a fireproof metal box with the passport. You will receive it tomorrow morning! Like airmail!"

The next morning, the scientific vessel Academician Vavilov approached the ballistic missile test area. Two American destroyers were already there. The visibility was poor. It was raining. The burnt missile warhead flopped into the water somewhere in the middle, between the Soviet and American ships. Academician Vavilov and the destroyers rushed to the warhead.

The Academician was the first to release the trawl device and pulled the smoking head compartment onto the deck. The destroyers were left with nothing. The sailors cut the rocket casing with a welding torch and took out the fireproof box with Yasha's passport. Five minutes later, a helicopter took off from the deck and headed for Havana.

Soon the passport from the rocket reached the addressee, and Yanchuk and Yasha again went to the Section of American Interests. Mr. Miller met them even more cordially than the first time.

"How can I help you, gentlemen?" he smiled.

"Here is his passport, sir." the Major said.

"Excellent, excellent." Mr. Miller rejoiced. "And where is the second document?"

"The second!? You never said anything about a second document yesterday!" cried the Major.

"We need a second document. That is the law, sorry."

"The shipwreck, sir, everything perished, you know?"

"I understand, but a second document is needed."

Yasha did not have a second document. Mr. Miller politely said goodbye to them. The hopes for an American visa and ten-million-dollar inheritance finally collapsed. The Major distinctly imagined his follow-up demotion, and the sergeant shoulder straps on his shoulders to replace his Major's star. This will be his punishment for the failure of the operation. They went outside. Yanchuk got into the car and drove nowhere from frustration. He took Yasha with him. They stopped at a deserted beach.

"It is only a stone's throw from here to Florida, only ninety miles," thought Yanchuk.

He could almost see Key West through his military binoculars. Not far away, he noticed a group of Cubans. They were assembling some strange device. There were old boards, inflatable chambers from Soviet-made tractor wheels, and a lot of ropes.

"A raft," Yanchuk realized.

He saw such rafts on Miami television. Illegal Cuban immigrants used such shaky handmade vessels to cross the strait and reach the desirable American coast. One of the Cubans went up to them. He interpreted their interest in his own way.

"Just five hundred dollars, and you are in Miami, señors!" he winked conspiratorially.

The Major did not immediately realize that fate gave him one last chance.

"And how many days does your raft express take to reach America soil?"

"Three or four, depending on the wind, señor."

"We need to be there the next day."

"That is impossible, señor!"

"Maybe!" suddenly thought Yanchuk. He had a brilliant idea. He went to the car and returned with a Soviet-made Zenit E camera, which had a high value in Cuba.

"I have no dollars. Here is a camera. Take it."

"I'll take it!" the Cuban agreed. "Don't be late. Departure is exactly at midnight."

Immediately after meeting with the Cubans, Yanchuk called Moscow and reported on his initiative to professor Kusakin. Kusakin immediately understood and approved. Exactly at midnight, Yanchuk drove Yasha to the place of the secret departure. The Cubans sailed away quietly without much talk. They did not smoke, so as not to attract the attention of border guards.

The passengers did not know that in the open sea, deep underwater, the mighty Komsomolets was waiting for them. At the place of their encounter, the Captain pressed a button and the powerful steel arm grabbed the clumsy raft and carefully carried it forward. In the morning, the passengers were greatly surprised to see Miami skyscrapers on the horizon. They had no doubt that this was the work of Saint Caridat, the patroness of Cuba.

Having completed the mission, the Komsomolets carefully pulled the metal hand back and headed again to Havana. Now it was time for the cat-and-mouse game, which was played by Cuban immigrants and the Coast Guard. The game had a name: wet foot—dry foot. If the Cubans managed to reach solid ground, they were saved and could apply for asylum in the USA. But if the Border Patrol caught them in the water, with wet feet, then by law they were subject of deportation back to Cuba.

Noticing the patrol, the passengers jumped and swam to the shore. Yasha did not know the rules of the game and hesitated. Therefore, border guards rushed to him first and it cost the Soviet state the tidy sum of ten million dollars. He was detained and sent to a patrol ship.

Chapter 29
FREEDOM FOR JACOB A!

Major Yanchuk patiently waited until the raft with the Cubans and Yasha disappeared over the horizon. The raft was hastily made up of chambers from Soviet tractor wheels, construction waste, and clotheslines. This ridiculous craftwork was destined to deliver Yasha to the American coast. A huge tropical moon illuminated the entire Cuban harbor. The Major saw the periscopes of the Komsomolets submarine, which moved close behind the awkward Cuban ark.

The Major was afraid that local border guards would intercept the slow-moving raft while leaving the harbor. But his fears were in vain. The guards of the Cuban maritime borders decided that the raft would sink by itself, without their intervention. That would probably be what happened, but upon reaching the open ocean, the raft was grabbed the giant hydraulic arm of the Komsomolets submarine and carefully carried it towards Florida.

Having slept for a few short hours, the Major flew to the Bahamas, and from there by scheduled flight to Miami. Upon arrival at Miami Airport, he called a secret phone and was told that "his nephew had arrived at the resort." Translated, this meant that the raft was safely delivered to the Florida shores and that the mission was accomplished.

At half-past nine in the morning, Sergey Andreevich Yanchuk was already in the courtroom. The lawyer soon appeared, but Yasha was not with him. Then the back doors swung open and the judge in a black robe entered in. Exactly at ten a. m., he struck with his wooden hammer, declared the meeting open, and called Mr. Abramovich. But Yasha was absent.

"Where is that SOB?" the Major was perplexed.

He found out the inconvenient truth later, when he listened to a news report on the local radio station. It was about a group of illegal Cuban immigrants who just reached American soil on a makeshift raft. They all successfully ran away from border patrol, except for one, who was immediately detained. And this one was not a Cuban, but a Soviet soldier. It was not clear how he managed to get onto the Cuban raft.

After waiting a few seconds, the judge announced that Mr. Abramovich's repeated failure to appear demonstrated a blatant disrespect for the court. After that, the judge hit the gavel again and announced that the inheritance will be awarded to the other side. To the Major, it seemed that the judicial gavel was the size of a huge sledgehammer that hit him right in the back of the head. The mission of the Central Committee, which was entrusted to him, was shamefully failed. He closed his eyes and the sergeant epaulets were attached to his shoulders.

Meanwhile, an international scandal was brewing. One of the passengers of the raft had reported that a submarine from an unknown country had relentlessly followed them. He saw its periscopes well. The escort began right off the coast of Cuba and ended at the American coast. The immigrant also claimed that the submarine, using some device, helped them reach the shore in six short hours, instead of three days.

The Miami Herald immediately reported a violation of American territory by an unknown submarine. Comparing the facts told by Cuban immigrants, as well as interviewing Pentagon employees, the newspaper concluded that the offender was a Soviet submarine of the Komsomolets type, the only one in the world equipped with special hydraulic grip for landing an amphibious assault.

Pravda immediately rebuffed the presumptuous newspaper. They published an editorial entitled 'Freedom for the Soviet Soldier!' According to Pravda, a group of Cuban counterrevolutionaries on a makeshift raft fled from Liberty Island to America. To appease the Americans, they kidnapped a Soviet soldier and took him to the USA. However, the courageous warrior, Corporal Jacob A. refused to provide secret information, so he was imprisoned in an American jail. The whole false story with Soviet submarines, according to Pravda, was fabricated to distract the attention of the world community from the illegal detention of serviceman Jacob A. and the difficult life of the American working class.

The day after the publication of the article, workers of Moscow plants and factories rushed to a demonstration. Special buses hired by the KGB took them directly to the American embassy where they expressed their anger, which knew no bounds. They demanded freedom for the Soviet soldier Jacob A. The whole country joined the Muscovites protests.

The case has taken on an international dimension. Progressive Dutch singer Paul Lars wrote the song "Freedom for Jacob A." In France, communal workers refused to clean streets until the Yankees released the Russian soldier. All French people supported their President, who called an American colleague and asked to release Jacob A.

Under the pressure of progressive mankind and at the request of the French president, Jacob A. was released and flown to Moscow. Medical nurses and school children wanted to greet him with flowers. Everything was ready for his triumphant return, but according to the Soviet TASS news agency, Jacob A. got ill and went directly to the hospital from the airport.

The next day, Soviet newspapers suddenly stopped writing about the hero. The workers returned to the factories, and the school children went back to school. Jacob A, instead of the hospital, went directly to Lefortovo prison. The Secretary of the Central Committee, Comrade Suslov, held a meeting with a short agenda; What to do with Jacob A.

"To the firing squad," the Secretary suggested. "For disrupting the work of the Central Committee."

"The correct solution!" supported members of the Central Committee.

"Nikita Sergeyevich recommended not to use cruel Stalinist methods. He recommended a lenient sentence, ten years of hard labor," said Alexei Adjubey, a member of the Central Committee and Khrushchev's son-in-law, "one year for each lost million!"

"Good," Suslov grimaced. "Ten years of hard labor, without permission of correspondence, instead of being shot."

"The correct solution!" supported members of the Central Committee.

Several months had passed. The Congress of Soviet Journalists was held in Moscow. The famous journalist Simon Abramovich sat in the hall and absentmindedly listened to the orators. The fate of his younger brother, a serviceman in the Soviet army, did not give him any rest. Over the past twelve months, there has not been a single letter from him. All attempts to clarify the circumstances with military authorities led to nothing. Simon hoped to meet his old university friend Alexei Adjubey at the Congress and ask him for his help.

Suddenly, a note was brought to him. He was asked to go to the lounge of the members of the presidium of the Congress. Simon immediately recognized the handwriting of Adjubey.

The lounge of the presidium members was reminiscent of a cross between an elegant restaurant and a study. On the tables were vases with fruits, black caviar, and other various dishes. Alexei Adjubey sat in a corner at his desk and read something. There was no one else in the hall. Simon stood up like a soldier at attention, put his hand to his head, and jokingly reported,

"Comrade General! Journalist Abramovich has arrived at your order!"

"They don't put a hand to an empty head!" Adjubey, who was a reserve general, recalled an old military joke. According to the Soviet military code, a soldier who greets a superior has to be fully dressed and have a military hat on. Without a hat, the greeting is invalid. He stopped reading, went up to his guest, and gave him a warm hug.

"I wanted to ask about my brother Yasha," Simon asked right off the bat.

"Do you remember the hype associated with the private Jacob A?"

"Of course!" Simon confirmed, not understanding where Adjubey was going.

"Jacob A. and your brother Yasha Abramovich are the same person!"

It seemed to Simon that his heart sank in his chest like a heavy ball. He involuntarily crouched.

"I will write a note to the director of the Uhta Labor camp. Your brother is there," Adjubey took a sheet of paper and began to write.

"How did he get to this camp?" Simon asked with horror.

"Yasha will tell you himself."

"Comrade Adjubey, you are late for a meeting of the Central Committee," his secretary appeared at the door.

"I'm coming!" Adjubey thrust a sheet of paper to Simon and disappeared at the door. Three days later, three men sat in the office of the director of the Uhta Labor camp. They were brothers Abramovich, Simon, Zakhar, and Mikhail. They came a long way to the heart of the Komi ASSR in hopes of seeing their younger brother. According to the verdict, Yasha was deprived of the right to correspondence and visits. But Adjubey's note did its job. The head of the camp, Major Podnyukov, looked at the portrait of Nikita Sergeyevich Khrushchev and permitted a visit.

Through the window, the brothers saw prisoners returning under escort from logging work in the forest. They were tired and barely on their feet. A Sergeant, the chief of the convoy, appeared at the door of the office. He prepared to report something, but the Major was ahead of him.

"Deliver prisoner Abramovich!" he ordered.

"He disappeared, Comrade Major!" answered the Sergeant.

"Disappeared?" exhaled unanimously the brothers Abramovich.

"Either a bear got him, or he froze," the Sergeant spread his hands. "Tomorrow we'll figure it out once its daylight again."

Obviously, the life of the prisoner had no value in the camp.

"Tomorrow? That is not acceptable! We need to search immediately!" cried the brothers.

The Major obeyed the brothers. Adjubey's note was doing its job.

"Come on, Sergeant, get my jeep ready, let's go to the forest!" he ordered. The five of them could hardly fit in the small jeep. The work field was not far, three miles away. The brothers jumped out of the truck and immediately got bogged down in the deep snow.

"Yasha!" they shouted. "Yasha!"

There was no response.

Chapter 30
WHO WILL SAVE YASHA?

Zakhar had a basket in his hands. From time to time, he lifted the lid and corrected something. Inside the basket was the most precious gift for Yasha, his dog Daisy. Daisy was very smart. If pets could have their own country, Daisy would be the President. Zakhar gave this dog to his brother about ten years ago. Over the years, Daisy grew old, but she had stayed almost the same size since she was a tiny dachshund.

She perfectly understood that she was brought on a visit with Yasha, whom she had not seen in a long time, and whom she missed. The tired Daisy dozed all the time and only occasionally opened her tired eyes to check if Yasha had appeared. Next to her was her favorite toy, Yasha's old hat. Upon arriving at the forest, to the place where Yasha had previously disappeared, Daisy opened her eyes wide and became alert.

When the brothers shouted "Yasha, Ya-ya-sha!" into the dense forest, hoping that he would hear them, the basket lid flew open and Daisy quickly jumped out of it. She instantly turned from a sluggish retiree into an extremely powerful force of energy. Despite the deep snow and her little legs, Daisy skillfully rushed between the trees.

"Where did this mutt come from?" asked the head of the convoy.

"This is Yasha's dog," the brothers explained to him. After ten minutes of painful waiting, Daisy did not return.

"Well, first the owner disappeared, and now the poor mutt is gone," the guard concluded. "Why rush? Tomorrow we'll easily find the body in the daylight."

He did not understand why such a fuss had flared up because of such a useless person as a prisoner. However, the Sergeant was mistaken. Daisy was not lost. She returned excitedly, rushed to the basket, took out Yasha's hat, and hurried away.

"It seems that she brought the hat for the owner," Zakhar realized.

Everyone rushed after the dog. Yasha was found about a hundred yards away. He lay face down in the snow. It looked like a tree fell on Yasha and left him unconscious. He was wearing a prisoner's wadded jacket and trousers, but was without a hat. His head was covered in snow. It became clear why Daisy returned for the hat.

The brothers carefully lifted Yasha and carried him to the jeep. Doctor Mikhail took Yasha by the hand and felt for a pulse.

"He's alive," he said with relief. "Daisy found him in time!"

On the road, they tried not to disturb Yasha, but it was difficult because the jeep jumped over each pothole. It was like riding a wild horse. Once the passengers landed on the seats, the car flew up again, and again they found themselves in the air.

When they finally got to the camp, Yasha was put in the Lenin Room, which was used as a place to meet with the relatives of prisoners. Yasha was laid on a wide wooden bench. Daisy, the hero of the day, was resting next to him in the basket.

Yasha received medical assistance of the highest level. His brother, professor Mikhail Abramovich, was the author of more than a hundred scientific works and an excellent doctor. As expected, Mikhail had a suitcase with medical supplies. As a young doctor, he was worked in an emergency department and saved hundreds of lives. Simon and Zakhar excitedly watched the actions of the brother-doctor. Daisy quietly snored in her basket; she did not doubt Mikhail's talent. And for sure, after an hour of persistent efforts, Yasha opened his eyes.

"Mikhail!" he said in surprise when he saw his brothers. "Simon! Zakhar!"

At that moment, the lid of the basket again flew open and a happy dachshund landed next to Yasha.

"Daisy!" he shouted and hugged his darling. The happy moment was interrupted by the anxious Mikhail.

"Tell us, Yasha," he asked. "What the hell we are doing in this terrible camp? And most importantly, why the hell are you here, why did you get a ten-year sentence?"

"Take it easy," Simon pleaded. "This is difficult for him, and you are pouring salt on his wounds. And the kid is hungry."

Simon, who had the soul of an angel, could not get used to the fact that Yasha was not a baby anymore, but a twenty-year-old man. He took out some chocolate covered raisins, Yasha's favorite treat, and handed the box to his brother.

"Yasha, tell us quickly, because the visit will soon be over," the elder brother Zakhar asked.

Yasha happily set to work on the chocolate raisins, then he took Daisy in his arms and, stroking his savior, began his extraordinary story.

"Did you know that we have, or rather, there was an aunt in America who recently died?"

"Aunt Feiga," confirmed Zakhar, who in his spare time wrote the story of the Abramovich family, "is the sister of our mother. When she was a girl, before the revolution, she immigrated to the United States and married the future millionaire Mr. Pechuk."

"So," Yasha continued. "The Soviet Department of the International Affairs of received information that Aunt Feiga died and left all her inheritance to me, Yakov Abramovich, as much as ten million dollars."

"What about the other brothers?" asked brothers in one voice.

"That's the mystery. She left almost nothing even to her daughter."

"As far as I know," said Simon. "Inheritance cases which involve more than a hundred thousand dollars go directly to the KGB, and they 'work' with the heirs. And here is ten million!"

"So the KGB immediately found you?" guessed Zakhar.

"This is the hitch that the KGB could not find me."

"The omnipotent KGB could not find you?" Zakhar was surprised.

"An error has occurred. A soldier, a former stove-maker, served with me. His name was also Yakov, and his last name was Abramov. Our clerk, Ensign Dubina, mixed up the documents. Thus, I became Russian, Jan Abramov, and the stove-maker became Abramovich, a Jew. The KGB agents went on the trail of the stove-maker, who was a false Abramovich, and the case stalled. In addition, the Soviet Department of International Affairs received a new message that Gail, the daughter of Aunt Feiga, found a second testament, where she is the heiress, and filed a lawsuit in the city of Miami."

"Ten million were at risk!" commented Mikhail. "Not a joke."

"The matter went to the Central Committee of the Soviet Communist party, everything was turned upside down and finally, they found me. The KGB organized a special group for a trip to the United States consisting of Major Yanchuk, Lieutenant Pyreeva, and me, Corporal Abramovich, the heir to ten million. By the way, the error was clarified and my real name, Abramovich, was returned to me."

"So you managed to visit America?" the brothers were amazed. It was easier for regular Soviet citizen to get to Mars, then to America. Yasha did not have time to answer.

The door of the room opened, a Sergeant appeared on the threshold and announced, "The meeting with prisoner Abramovich is over!"

The brothers did not even notice that the morning came. But they could not leave. They have to hear the end of the story. The quick-witted Zakhar pulled out a pack of American Marlboro cigarettes and handed it to the guard.

"Give us another half hour, Sergeant!" he asked.

But the Sergeant was not in a hurry. He was definitely expecting another bribe.

"Take the chocolate raisins." Simon handed out the box.

"Okay, another twenty minutes," the Sergeant agreed, throwing a handful of chocolates in his mouth.

It was not easy to meet the twenty-minute time frame, but Yasha tried to do it. He told the brothers about his arrival in Miami. About how he met a Chilean girl named Juanita, how they fell in love. And then they decided to flee to Chile because Juanita was pursued by the Colombian cocaine mafia. To escape from the KGB and the cocaine mafia, the lovers bought plane tickets and flew to Santiago, the capital of Chile. However, due to bad weather, the plane landed in the Argentine city of Mendoza.

There, Juanita met with the famous revolutionary Ernesto Che Guevara. He gave her a letter for the Chilean poet Communist Pablo Neruda. So, they managed to meet with the great poet, who received the lovers in his mansion and even read them Pushkin's poems. He also promised to help them, if needed. They settled not far from Pablo, in a fishing town of Horcon on the Pacific Ocean, where after a couple of weeks Yasha became a real fisherman.

But as it turned out, the KGB did not forget about the ten million. Early one morning, while fishing, while Yasha hummed the songs of Soviet composers and quoted Shakespeare, he was kidnapped by a Soviet submarine of the Komsomolets type.

"Get out!" the enraged Sergeant appeared. "They will tear off my head because of you!"

Zakhar quickly pacified him with another pack of cigarettes, then said loudly, "I know who will save Yasha!"

"Who?" breathed out Mikhail and Simon.

"Laureate of the Nobel and Stalin Prize for the Consolidation of Peace between the People. The great Chilean poet Pablo Neruda!" punctuated Zakhar.

The brothers looked at Zakhar in surprise. Even Daisy stopped snoring and stared at him in amazement.

Chapter 31
YASHA-JOSE

Yasha's elder brother Zakhar was considered a genius in the family. Mathematical abilities came to him at a young age. All family festivities in the house of Abramovich usually ended with mathematical shows, which were arranged by the five-year-old kid. To do this, he crawled under a huge dining table, the guests called aloud any two digits numbers, and the young Einstein under the table multiplied them in his small head, and immediately gave out the result to the friendly delight of those present.

At the age of six, Zakhar made his first invention. Mom had a friend, Aunt Fruma. Zakhar suspected that Aunt Fruma was completely bald and was wearing a wig. To test his hypothesis, the boy climbed onto a huge monumental sideboard with two carved out lions and waited for the guests to arrive. In his hands was a fishing rod with a fishing line and a hook. When everyone enthusiastically started to snack, the young naturalist deftly picked up the wig with a fishing rod, which hung over the bald head of unsuspecting Aunt Fruma.

Aunt Fruma was his father's boss's wife. Thus, the first invention of the eldest son almost resulted in the loss of employment for the father. This deserved severe punishment. But the good-natured Israel Zalkovich only laughed and said:

"Oh son, try to invent something better next time."

And Zakhar tried. Then one invention was followed by another, and he became a well-known engineer, author of more than a hundred patents, and head of the design bureau. Like a good chess player, he always knew how to find the correct and often unexpected solution. And now, in the labor camp, he came up with a unique solution to release his younger brother from prison with the help of famous poet-laureate Pablo Neruda.

The heavy prison gates clanged behind them. There were miles of barbed wire fences with huge dogs patrolling along them. Menacing guard towers were on every corner. The brothers sighed heavily, looking at this sad dwelling of their brother.

"So, what we are going to do now?" asked Zakhar.

"Now we are going to Moscow," said Simon, "I know a man in Moscow, who will help to connect us with Pablo."

"Great idea, Simon, who is it?" praised Zakhar.

"Kirill Prosadin, poet and interpreter. He dedicated many years to the poetry of Neruda."

"Where does he live?"

"In a village of poets and writers by name Peredelkino, close to Moscow."

"So, next stop is Peredelkino!" Zakhar resolutely announced. "The Vorkuta-Moscow train stops at the Uhta railroad station in three hours, we have to catch it!"

Mikhail had a scientific conference to attend, but looking at the determination of his elder brother, he said nothing. Two days later, the three brothers arrived at the village of Peredelkino, at the house where the poet-translator Kirill Prosadin lived. The huge two-story cottage was one of the largest in Peredelkino.

Ten years ago, Prosadin was known as a poet-loser, he was rarely published, and was forced to make a living by teaching lower grades. But then some of his relatives with good connections had him become an official translator of Pablo Neruda and other Communist poets. It was a life-changer. He bought a Volga car, quit teaching, and recently he was awarded with a large cottage in Peredelkino. The poet-translator recognized Simon right away.

"Simon," he shouted, "do you remember that blonde in Kislovodsk? Who is this with you?"

"Kirill," Simon was embarrassed. "Now not the time for blondes. We have a very serious problem. My younger brother is in jail. One time he met Pablo, who promised to help him in difficult times. Maybe you'll talk to Neruda?"

"In jail? Talk to Neruda?" asked Kirill. The good mood of the poet instantly disappeared. He became gloomy. "Simon, dear, do you see this huge country house?" he asked.

"I see a wonderful cottage," Simon confirmed.

"You see this beautiful Volga car?"

"I'm not blind, I see." Simon nodded.

"I can lose everything. I record all my conversations with Pablo in detail and pass them on to the KGB. A misstep and my successful career will end. Do you understand?"

However, their failure with Prosadin did not discourage the brothers. "Forget this Prosadin," said Mikhail, when they went away from the poet's summer house, "I know a wonderful person who will give a letter to Pablo!"

"Who is it?" aroused Zakhar.

"Professor Lavatour, from Chile. He really likes my book, Restoring Motor Reflexes After Poliomyelitis. He believes that it is a revolution in physical therapy and rehabilitation."

"He is correct," Zakhar agreed, "I also read an enthusiastic review of your book. Where is the professor now?"

"He should be in Leningrad, at my university, if he hasn't returned to Chile yet."

"It is clear," said Zakhar. "Our next stop is the city of Leningrad."

Unfortunately, at the railroad station, the cashier informed them that there were no more tickets for today, only for tomorrow. Zakhar got upset, but Mikhail saved the situation by using his favorite trick.

"Don't you recognize me?" he asked the cashier with a charming smile. Tall and smart, with delicate facial features, Mikhail looked like the famous movie star Tikhonov.

"Of course, I do, Comrade Tikhonov!" the cashier gasped. Three tickets to Leningrad appeared.

"Comrade Tikhonov, why do you have the name Abramovich here?" the girl asked in bewilderment, returning Mikhail his passport.

"Transformation for a new movie role," Simon explained shortly.

"I understand! I understand!" The girl looked with lust at her hero. "What is the name of your new movie?"

"The title is pending approval from the Ministry of Culture," Simon explained again.

"I can't wait!" promised the happy admirer of the artist.

The Red Arrow express train was the fastest one in the Soviet Union. It took only eight hours to race from Moscow to Leningrad. From the railroad station, the three musketeers went directly to the Pediatric University, where Mikhail worked. Unfortunately, Professor Lavatour already was gone.

"He left for the airport an hour ago," said his secretary.

This did not stop the pursuers. They grabbed a taxi and rushed to Pulkovo International Airport. Fortunately, the flight was postponed, and they found Professor Lavatour at the restaurant, where he was sitting with a glass of his beloved Soviet champagne. Without looking up from his glass, the professor listened to Mikhail's ardent request to convey a letter to Pablo Neruda. The sharp professor did not mind, he realized that it was time to fulfill his dream and earn a lot of money.

"Professor," he turned to Mikhail. "I would like the rights to publish the Spanish translation of your famous book on motor reflexes."

"Yes, you also can even have right for Portuguese," Mikhail agreed with joy. "Just pass the letter."

The Chilean took the letter and hid it in his jacket pocket.

Six months had passed. In the forest, where the convicts worked on cutting down trees to meet unbearable daily production rates, a jeep rolled in with the security chief on board. Prisoner Yakov Abramovich was ordered to sit in the cabin.

"It's probably time for your execution," an elderly prisoner advised. He spent ten years in the camp and was very knowledgeable about everything. "The bosses don't just drive to the forest for no reason."

"They will shoot me?" asked Yasha, bewildered.

"Don't worry," the prisoner reassured. "They now shoot at the back of the head. You won't even feel it."

"My brothers, mother, Juanita will endure," Yasha thought. "No one will even know where they threw my body into the ground."

He heard that the shot ones were buried without any monuments or even markers. After a couple of hours, the security chief's jeep brought him to a military airfield. There, next to a long transport plane, a tall man in a black coat and hat was waiting for them.

"Major Mostov." he advised.

The Major released the security chief and ordered Yasha to go inside the plane. Yasha sat on the hard seat and fastened his seatbelt. The Major was silent throughout the flight. The transport plane had no windows, and Yasha had no idea where they were flying. After landing, they put him in a Black Crow, a closed police car, and again he saw nothing. The Major sat beside him and remained silent and gloomy.

"Will he shoot me himself, or will someone else?" thought Yasha sluggishly. To his surprise, he was not afraid.

The Major stopped at a large house.

"Probably the KGB administration," Yasha thought. "Some say that they shoot people right there in the basement."

However, the Major did not lead him to the basement, but the second floor. Then he left Yasha in a large room and ordered him to wait.

"It will happen now," Yasha realized.

Suddenly, the door at the other end of the room opened, and an elderly bald man entered.

"I have seen him before," Yasha thought.

The man took out a volume of Pushkin and began to read with a strong accent, "In the depths of the Siberian ores, keep your patience."

"Pablo!" screamed Yasha. "Pablo, is that you?"

Then Major Mostov returned to the room and solemnly said, "Due to the request of the great friend of the Soviet Union, the poet Pablo Neruda, you, prisoner Yakov Izrailevich Abramovich, are being released ahead of schedule. You will receive documents at your place of residence."

Pablo listened carefully to the words of the Major, relaxed, and nodded his head.

"But that's not all." the Major declared with a smile and opened the door.

Juanita appeared on the threshold. Wearing high-heeled shoes and a tight-fitting dress, she was fabulously beautiful. Together with her, a wonderful fat-cheeked kid with curly hair rolled into the room.

"Oh, sailor, you sailed for too long, so I managed to forget you," the words of the popular song flashed through Yasha's head. He rushed to Juanita and hugged her.

"Congratulations, Juanita, you got married, and you already gave birth to a son." Yasha said, looking at the boy.

Juanita snuggled up to him and cried.

"This is your son, Yasha," she whispered through tears. "His name is Yasha-Jose!"

Chapter 32
JUANITA MIGUELEVNA

"**M**y son, my son!" Yasha grabbed the curly Yasha-Jose in his arms and threw him high into the air. He was interested in everything about his son. Juanita barely had time to answer.

"What was his birth weight?"

"Ten pounds!"

"Athlete, real athlete, well done, and his height?"

"One foot and nine inches."

"Wow! And when did he start walking?"

"At ten months!"

"Well done! And his first words?"

"First words?" Juanita thought about it. "The newspaper!"

"News-pay-per!" repeated Yasha in syllables. "Well done. Everyone says mom, dad, and his is newspaper. Wow. He will be a writer!"

Yasha carefully lowered the future writer to the floor. It was a mistake. Feeling freedom, Yasha-Jose rushed to the desk in the room and with extraordinary speed opened the drawers and emptied the contents on the floor. Even the vigilant KGB Major did not have time to respond. Papers and envelopes scattered on the floor. Yasha-Jose shone with his mischievous eyes and a happy smile. The Major clearly did not share his joy. If Yasha-Jose was a prisoner, the Major would know what to do, but there were no instructions on how to deal with the children of foreigners. The young parents looked at their child in bewilderment. Juanita rushed to pick up the papers, and Yasha hardly restrained his son, who could not wait to invent something else.

Suddenly the door opened, and a crowd of people appeared, led by a very large woman. It was Riva Israelevna, she was Yasha's paternal aunt. She lived in the Ural city of Sverdlovsk. She was the head of the Jewish community and was able to get the permission of the party bosses to allow them to bake matzo during Passover.

"Who are you?" the Major was indignant and tried to stop aunt Riva.

"We are the Abramoviches!" snapped Aunt Riva and pushed the Major aside. "We were informed that Yasha was released, so we have come."

Aunt Riva had remarkable strength. The family remembered an incident that happened with Aunt Riva many years ago. Two thieves entered her wooden house on the outskirts of the city of Sverdlovsk. As it turned out they did not know anything about Riva, otherwise they would not have dared. Aunt Riva met the uninvited guests with a rake and other gardening tools. When the police arrived, the unlucky robbers lying on the floor, tied with a clothesline, while Aunt Riva sat at the table and calmly sipped tea.

Juanita smiled faintly. It was she, who through an interpreter, informed the family about the release of Yasha. But she did not expect that all members of the huge Abramovich family would come.

"Yasha!" Aunt Riva was delighted to see her nephew. "You're alive. They did not torture you!?"

She picked up Yasha and slightly tossed him into the air, how he did with Yasha-Jose. Feeling that no one was watching him, Yasha-Jose rushed again to the desk, but Aunt Riva deftly intercepted him.

"This is my son!" proudly said Yasha.

"Beautiful boy!" The aunt took the boy in her arms and kissed him with her huge lips. Yasha-Jose, a charming minx who was not afraid of anyone, suddenly burst into tears.

"Don't worry, Grandma Riva will do you well, she will circumcise you." the aunt calmed the crying child.

Pablo, who smiled at the reunion of the Abramovich family, glanced at the Major and pointed at the clock.

The Major, who had recovered from the shock caused by the collision with Aunt Riva, announced loudly, "Comrade Pablo Neruda has to go. I'll ask you to clean the room. Wait for me."

Soon he came back.

"I have pretty annoying news." the Major said.

"What?" asked the wary Galina Solomonovna, mother of Yasha.

"Pablo invited Juanita to visit your apartment!"

"Our terrible communal apartment?" gasped Galina Solomonovna.

"How does she know about communal apartments?" said Aunt Riva judiciously. "Then I will make such stuffed gefilte fish that she licks her fingers and will not notice anything else."

"And if Uncle Misha gets drunk and starts throwing things out the window?"

"I'll throw him out," Aunt Riva promised.

The Abramoviches went straight from the hotel to the railroad station, and from there, to Leningrad, to Yasha's apartment. Fortunately, everything was quiet. Uncle Misha was drunk but slept soundly on the landing right in front of the apartment. There was no light in the corridor. Residents were unable to agree on payment and the lights were cut off by the utility company, so no one noticed how Juanita cried.

"Such good people live so terribly," she repeated again and again.

Not drunk uncle Misha, not even the absence of electrical lights scared her as much as visiting the common bathroom. There were 22 people and only one toilet. Juanita went inside to the smelly lavatory with fear. One minute later uncle Misha knocked on the door. He woke up and now needed a toilet urgently.

Juanita stormed out crying and told Yasha with tears, "Our child will not be able to live like this."

Yasha agreed.

Leaving Yasha-Jose with his grandmother and aunt Riva, the next day the young parents went to the Chilean embassy in Moscow to apply for a visa for Yasha. The embassy quickly found out that they were not legal spouses and refused a visa. They had to return to Leningrad and apply to the ZAGS, Civil Registry office.

At the registry office, they were treated very warmly, but at first, they refused to issue a certificate. The hitch was that Juanita did not have a middle name, and it was forbidden to omit the space for the middle name, according to the law. The bride had two first names, Juanita and Luisa, and two last names, Araya and Valdes, and at the same time not a single middle name. Juanita's father was called Jose Miguel. In the end, the bride was recorded in books as Juanita Miguelevna Araya Valdes Abramovich and issued a marriage certificate.

Having received the coveted visa at the Chilean embassy, Yasha went to the OVIR to ask for permission to leave the USSR. After two hours of waiting, he was invited to the office of the principal. The conversation was short.

"You are lucky," the principal told him. "Two years ago, you would have been sent to Siberia for such a request, or maybe they would have shot you, but now we are still talking."

"But what about my visa?" asked Yasha.

"It was refused," the principal joked. "Invent the reason yourself."

Juanita called Pablo Neruda in Moscow, announced her decision to return to Chile and the refusal of the OVIR.

"You are making a big mistake," the Communist poet began to instruct her. "The Soviet Union is a country of victorious socialism and Chile is ruled by a corrupt junta."

"I think Aunt Riva is much smarter than our great poet," Juanita thought, but did not say anything to the famous poet.

Pablo reluctantly helped the young couple. His request worked. They received a call from the OVIR and were told that Yasha should immediately go there. Not believing his luck, the bridegroom, accompanied by the entire family, rushed to the Visa Office where Yasha, indeed, received a visa from the same strict principal.

"Well, now the path to Chile is open," concluded Aunt Riva.

"No, we must first stop in Miami," Juanita objected.

"Wouldn't that be more expensive?" Yasha asked.

"I think the stop in Miami will pay off," mysteriously said Juanita.

At Pulkovo International Airport, people looked with surprise at the huge crowd of Abramoviches, who came to see Yasha, Junita Miguelevna, and their son Yasha-Jose.

"Yasha, you are leaving first," Aunt Riva prophetically remarked. "Someday we'll all leave. It's a pity that I didn't have time to circumcise Yasha-Jose."

She remarked, and for some reason cried. Looking at her, other women also cried.

"Yasha! Tell your mom, brothers, and all relatives that we will return soon, so that they would not cry," Juanita asked.

"And your Juanita, not a Jew, but a good girl," Aunt Riva praised through tears.

Soon, the airplane with the Jewish-Chilean couple took off and headed for Paris, and from there, after an hour-long stopover, to Florida. Yasha-Jose twice tried to get into the pilot's cabin, but when his attempts failed, he calmed down and slept until Miami.

From the airport, Juanita went to see Yasha's lawyer. It was about the inheritance of the ten million, which was willed to Yasha by his American aunt. Since he failed to appear in court, his cousin contested and finally won the judgment. The lawyer explained to Juanita that in order to appeal and start a new case, Yasha would need a huge sum of two hundred thousand dollars. On the other hand, Golda will never live in peace, since Yasha can always file the case against her. Therefore, the lawyer advised to compromise.

After several days of negotiations with Golda and her lawyer, a compromise was reached. The papers were signed at the office of Golda's lawyer. After signing, Yasha received a red envelope with a check inside.

In the waiting room, Juanita was waiting for him, along with the restless Yasha-Jose. With trembling hands, she pulled out the check and announced, "One million!"

Yasha-Jose rushed and tried to tear the million-dollar check. Juanita barely had time to move her hand.

"Well," she said with satisfaction. "This money should be enough to get Yasha-Jose an education at the famous Harvard University."

And she hid the check in her handbag.